MIDNIGHT

MIDNIGHT

A Folly Beach Mystery

BILL NOEL

Front cover photo and design by Bill Noel

Author photo and original map painting by Susan Noel

ISBN: 978-1-958414-33-0

Enigma House Press

www.enigmahousepress.com

Goshen, Kentucky 40026

Also by Bill Noel

Folly

The Pier

Washout

The Edge

The Marsh

Ghosts

Missing

Final Cut

First Light

Boneyard Beach

Silent Night

Dead Center

Discord

A Folly Beach Mystery COLLECTION

Dark Horse

Joy

A Folly Beach Mystery COLLECTION II

No Joke

Relic

A Folly Beach Mystery COLLECTION III

Faith

A Folly Beach Christmas Mystery COLLECTION

Tipping Point

Sea Fog with coauthor Angelica Cruz

Mosquito Beach

Pretty Paper with coauthor Angelica Cruz

Adrift

A Folly Beach Mystery COLLECTION IV

Overkill with coauthor Angelica Cruz

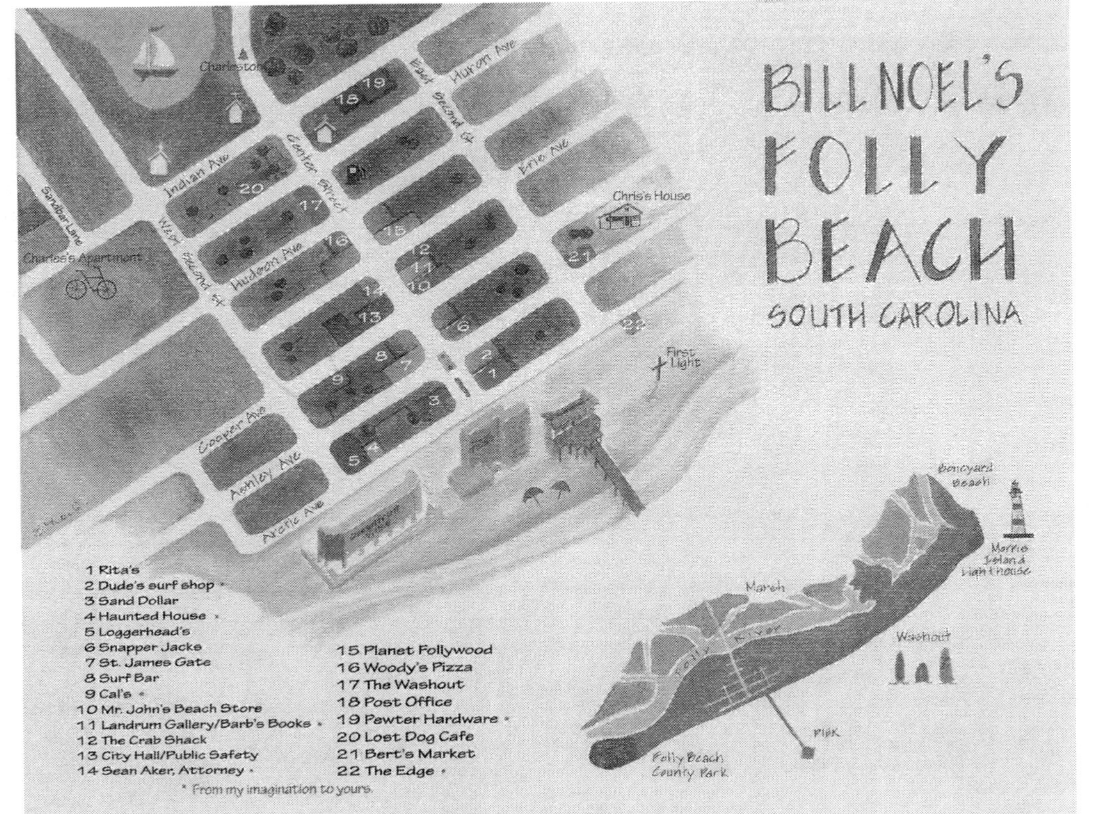

BILL NOEL'S
FOLLY
BEACH
SOUTH CAROLINA
Charleston
Sandbar Lane
Charlee's Apartment
Indian Ave
West Island St
Hudson Ave
Cooper Ave
Ashley Ave
Arctic Ave
Center Street
East Second Ct
Huron Ave
Erie Ave
Chris's House
First Light
Boneyard Beach
Morris Island Lighthouse
Marsh
Washout
Pier
Folly Beach County Park
1 Rita's
2 Dude's surf shop *
3 Sand Dollar
4 Haunted House *
5 Loggerhead's
6 Snapper Jacks
7 St. James Gate
8 Surf Bar
9 Cal's *
10 Mr. John's Beach Store
11 Landrum Gallery/Barb's Books *
12 The Crab Shack
13 City Hall/Public Safety
14 Sean Aker, Attorney *
15 Planet Follywood
16 Woody's Pizza
17 The Washout
18 Post Office
19 Pewter Hardware *
20 Lost Dog Cafe
21 Bert's Market
22 The Edge *
* From my imagination to yours.

Chapter One

"Few things can beat a peaceful walk on the beach," Charles Fowler said as we traipsed though soft, warm sand away from where we entered the shoreline at the Folly Beach Fishing Pier.

I'd met Charles more than a dozen years ago during my first week on the small South Carolina barrier island. We'd quickly become friends although we had as much in common as a walnut to a walrus. One thing that did draw us together was an interest in photography.

"True," I said.

"You could've picked a cooler day, though."

It was mid-August, and the humidity level was as high as the current upper-eighties temperature.

"Charles, you forget this walk was your idea?"

"There you go, splitting hairs. Let's walk closer to the dunes. I want to photograph some of those itty-bitty pink flowers."

The farther we got from the Pier, the nine-story, beach-front Tides Hotel, and the area where most vacationers on Folly first stick their toes in the Atlantic, the quieter, and according to Charles, the more peaceful our walk was becoming. I followed him as he angled closer to the dunes and the pink blooms on railroad vines snaking over the barrier separating the beach from private residences. It was refreshing seeing him bend to photograph blooms since his primary area of focus is normally discarded candy wrappers and vehicle-flattened drink cans.

My friend's photo shoot was interrupted by a dozen college-age young people illegally trampling over the dunes on their way to the wide expanse of sand while carrying coolers, a pop-up tent, folding chairs, and a volleyball set. I'm no psychic but would wager from the sounds of the exuberant guys the coolers weren't holding soft drinks and water.

Charles glared at the loud crowd like they'd disrupted him photographing the cover for *National Geographic.* He pointed his ever-present, homemade cane at them and said, "Did you invite the circus?"

That didn't deserve an answer, so I suggested we head farther away from the group that was now planting their tent in the sand for anything but a peaceful day at the beach. The guys who had carried the coolers distributed cans of beer to the others, despite the often-ignored law prohibiting alcoholic beverages on the beach, while two of the females were yelling for someone to get the tent finished while they opened the chairs and arranged them in a semi-circle. A hundred yards past the group, we reached a spot occupied by only the two of us, and Charles once again headed closer to the dunes to continue photographing native wildflowers.

A scream grabbed our attention. This time it wasn't coming from the beach, but from a large three-story house under construction near where Charles was photographing flowers. We turned toward the house but didn't see anything. Seconds later, three men wearing hardhats exited the door at the top of the stairs leading down to a concrete patio.

That's all it took for Charles to grab my arm, point to the men, and say, "What are we waiting for?"

He didn't wait for my answer. He was already at the newly constructed stairs leading from the beach to the house's yard. Taking two steps at a time, he was near the top of the stairs before I'd managed to cover three steps.

Before I reached the top of the stairs, two other construction workers exited the house and the five of them were staring at something on the patio. A sour taste grew in my stomach when I saw that the something was a woman; a woman face down, her arms twisted behind her, her head twisted in an unnatural position. I had no doubt she was dead.

Charles inched his way between two of the workers like he was one of the crew. I stood behind him but turned my head away from the gruesome sight. Two more workers emerged from the house and stood beside me.

"Anyone call 911?" I asked the man closest to me.

He looked at me like I didn't belong with the group. No surprise since I didn't. He pointed to the man probably in his sixties standing on the other side of the group. "Randy done called."

If I'd waited a few more seconds, I wouldn't have asked. The distinct sound of a Folly Beach fire engine came from the center of the small island about six blocks from where we were standing. The high-pitched siren from one of the city's patrol cars approached from the other direction on West Ashley Avenue, the island's longest street.

Charles nudged me with his elbow and pointed at a man in his thirties wearing a white T-shirt with Donnelly Plumbing in large red letters on the back. He said, "I'll ask Kyle what happened."

Before I could say okay or ask who Kyle was, Charles made a beeline to the plumber, leaving me beside the older gentleman who'd removed his hard hat and was holding it over his heart. He shook his head and mumbled, "Tragic, so tragic." He then put his hard hat back on, turned to me, and said, "I'm Lucius. You live in one of those houses?" He nodded toward the house on each side of the construction site.

I reached to shake his hand and said, "No, I'm Chris Landrum. My friend and I were walking up the beach and heard a scream. Came to see if there was anything we could do to help. What happened?"

He looked at the body on the concrete patio, sighed, and said, "Don't know. I'm an electrician and was inside working on the electrical panel. Heard people out here yelling and came to see what was going on. You know as much as I do."

A member of the Folly Beach Department of Public Safety came around the side of the house, saw the woman on the deck, waved for us to move back, and knelt beside the lifeless body. Public Safety Officers double as firefighters and many are certified EMTs. I didn't know the officer. Two firefighters arrived next. I also didn't know them but did know the next person who appeared. I'd known Officer Rodney New since he'd joined the force three years ago. He took a quick look at the body, did a police gaze at the group standing around the patio, stopped when he saw me, rolled his eyes, pointed to the far corner of the house, and said, "Gentlemen, please move over there in the shade. I'll be with you in a minute."

The way he said it left no doubt it wasn't a suggestion.

Charles joined me as we headed to the shade and said, "Her name's Shelly Whitley, a carpenter. Husband's named Raymond. No kids, no pets. Hubby's a bartender in Charleston."

"Charles, you got all that from, umm, what's his name?"

"Kyle, yeah."

"He know what happened?"

"Not really. Said it looks like she lost her footing and fell off the roof." Charles looked toward the top of the house. "Got a peaked roof up there. Kyle said it was a bear building it. Sees how she could've fallen."

"Did he know if anyone saw her fall?"

"Nope."

"Nope he didn't know or nope to anyone seeing her fall?"

"He didn't know if anyone saw it."

Two more Public Safety Officers arrived while we were gathering beside the house. Officer New waved for Charles and me to follow him to the street where he slowly shook his head and said, "Chris, Charles, I know you're too lazy, and I might add, too old, to be working on this house, so what in blue blazes are you doing here?"

I'd finally reached the age of seventy, way too quickly, I might add. Charles was two years younger.

He said, "You know us well, Rodney. We were walking down the beach. I was taking photos of—"

Rodney interrupted with, "Unless you photographed the lady tumbling off the roof, skip the history lesson and tell me what happened."

I smiled and answered before he could go into a lengthy monologue about no telling what. "Rodney, we heard a scream then saw guys coming out of the house and staring at the patio. We came to see what the commotion was about. You know as much about what happened as we do. All I can add is her name's Shelly Whitley."

"Did you know her?"

"No, one of the workers told Charles who she was."

"Charles, I know I may regret it, but is there anything you can add? Anything relevant?"

Yes, he did know my trivia-collecting, irrelevant information-accumulating friend well.

"Umm, she was a carpenter, married to Raymond, no kids, no pets. Guess that's it."

"Thank you," the officer said, bordering on sarcasm. I don't see any reason to keep you two around. We'll be spending time with the workers; besides, I know where to find you if we need more."

I knew Charles wouldn't be happy being dismissed without learning more about what happened.

"Officer New," he said, "sure you don't need us to stay?"

I rest my case.

"Goodbye, Charles, you too, Chris."

I took Charles by the elbow and pivoted him toward the steps leading to the beach. He followed my lead, but not without a huff, a mumble, and possibly a muted profanity.

Chapter Two

I'd be lying if I said sleep came quickly. My mental image of the woman on the concrete pad floated in and out of my consciousness. Thinking about her young life ending while she was simply earning a living left me saddened. Her dreams about the future, her life with her husband, the possible addition of children to her family, vacations, gatherings with friends and relatives, all wiped out by one wrong step on the vaulted roof. As the construction worker had said, "Tragic, so tragic."

The summer sun peeking through the slats in my window blinds woke me at least an hour later than my normal seven o'clock awakening. Other than the memory of staring at the lifeless woman on the new house's patio, I remembered Charles saying I should call Cindy LaMond, Folly's Director of Public Safety, aka Police Chief, to find out more about the incident. Granted, Charles knows the Chief as well as I do and has her phone number, so he could've made the call. I reminded him of that yesterday before we went our separate ways. He reminded me that the Chief thinks he is, in his words, an idiot, a pain in her posterior, and not someone she'd confide in. He's partially correct.

"Morning, Cindy."

"Let me put on my fortune-teller hat," she said after an audible sigh. "You called so I could tell you everything, everything in exhaustive detail about what happened yesterday at the construction site, the construction site where you and your shadow happened to be nosing in business that's none of your business. How am I doing so far?"

I was hoping for a response more along the lines of, *Good morning, Chris. How are you this fine morning?* While that was my hope, I'd learned years ago that a civil comment was seldom the beginning of many calls on Folly, especially on calls with Cindy. I'd known her since she'd moved here eleven years ago. I also counted her and her husband Larry good friends.

"You're right."

"Of course, I am." I heard paper rustling in the background. "The late Shelly Whitley turned thirty-two in July. She won't be turning thirty-three. She was married to Raymond Whitley, age thirty-five, who, with luck, will turn thirty-six in January. No children, and you can tell Charles, you know, the guy who cares more about people's pets than he does about people, that the Whitleys didn't have any critters in the house."

She hesitated so I figured it was time to say something. I didn't want to tell her Charles had already learned that much about the Whitleys, all but their ages. "And?"

"Gee, you want their Social Security numbers, blood types, and shoe sizes?"

I held back a chuckle. "I was more interested in what happened."

"Me too, but there's not much more. According to Randy Lee, the foremen, Shelly was working on the bonus room, at least that's what he called it. It's at the top of the house and has a vaulted roof. Apparently, she was on the slant, lost her footing, and fell to her death. Cause of death, most likely a broken neck. End of story, and sadly, end of Shelly."

"Anyone see her fall?"

"No one said they did. Each guy claimed to be in the house working on, well, whatever he was supposed to be working on."

"There's nothing to suspect it was anything but an accident?"

"I know you think you're a private detective and like to stick your nose in every death that happens here, but there's nothing to indicate it was anything but a terrible accident."

"Charles is the one who claims to be a detective."

Since retiring to Folly from a boring, mind-numbing career in the human resources department of a large health-care company in Kentucky, I'd stumbled across a few murder situations. Through fate and good, or many would say, bad luck, I and a few of my friends had managed to solve crimes that'd stumped the police. Charles, whose imagination knew no bounds had proclaimed he was a private detective. No, he has neither formal training nor a license to back up his claim, but those minor stumbling blocks were no barrier for my friend.

"If you say so."

There was no need to respond. She'd hung up.

One of Charles's quirks, one of many, was if I learned something he felt he needed to know and didn't tell him within seconds, if that long, I was violating one of the Amendments to the Constitution and probably one of the Ten Commandments. With that in mind, I knew it'd be a matter of minutes before Charles would be calling to hear what I'd learned from Cindy, that is, after asking why it'd taken me so long to tell him.

He always wanted to know what I'd learned, but often made it difficult. I called three times to no avail. He has a cell phone but leaving it in his apartment was something he managed to do more often than taking it whenever he ventured out.

My growling stomach reminded me I hadn't eaten. For most people, that was easily remedied by a trip to the kitchen. In my small cottage, a trip to the bedroom housing my computer would be as fruitful as walking to the kitchen for finding food. Fortunately, my abode was next door to Bert's Market, Folly's iconic grocery that's open twenty-four hours a day, three-hundred-sixty-five days a year and sells everything from beer to bananas.

I don't drink beer or like bananas, so a prepackaged sandwich was my focus as I took the short walk where I was greeted by Denise, one of the store's friendly and helpful employees. We spent a couple of minutes sharing the obligatory comments about the weather and the many vacationers invading the island before Denise said she had to get something out of the storeroom and left me searching for lunch.

I was deciding between a ham on rye sandwich or turkey on whole wheat when I saw Brad Burton heading my way. Brad retired from the Charleston County Sheriff's Office a few years ago and moved to a house on the far side of mine. When he was still working, we'd had several run-ins. He accused me of murder the first month I was on Folly; hardly the welcome I'd hoped for. I helped the police catch the killer, but it didn't affect how Detective Burton viewed me.

When his daughter was killed three years ago, Brad spiraled into deep depression. What bought him out isn't recommended by mental health professionals. His daughter's killer planted a bomb in Brad and his wife Hazel's house. Through divine intervention and his nosy neighbor, aka me, I saw the killer leaving the house and went to check on the Burtons. I managed to drag Brad out of the house seconds before it exploded. Fortunately, Hazel wasn't home at the time. Saving Brad didn't turn him into a member of my fan club, but he began tolerating me without sneering. His house was rebuilt last year, and I'd regularly run into him, mainly here in Bert's and occasionally talked with him when he crossed through my yard to get to and from the grocery.

"See you're shopping for lunch," he said as he pointed to the sandwich in my hand.

I guess his detective instincts hadn't evaporated when he retired.

"Yes, my chef has the day off."

"Cute." He nodded in the direction of the sandwich. "If it wasn't for Hazel, I'd be getting all my meals prepackaged from here."

"How's Hazed liking the new house?" I asked, not knowing what else to say.

He smiled. "She loves the house. It's me being there all the time that's driving her crazy."

I returned his smile. "I thought she would've adjusted to you being there by now. You retired, what, four years ago?"

"Five years next month." He shook his head. "She put up with me being in her space the first few years. After the house, umm, was destroyed, we were too busy with every-thing, busy enough it didn't bother her having me around. She keeps telling me I need to get a hobby." He smiled again. "Get a hobby, anything as long as it's out of the house."

"Having any luck?"

"I tried golf. Hated it. Can you see me surfing out there?" He nodded in the direction of the Atlantic.

"Umm, no."

"Right. Fishing is more boring than watching grass grow."

"Sorry. I know it's hard. If I didn't have photography to fall back on when I retired, I'd have gone bonkers."

When I moved to Folly, I'd opened a photo gallery on Center Street, Folly's figurative center of the island and its literal center of commerce. Unfortunately, my dream became a nightmare when I realized locals and vacationers would rather spend their money on necessities like food, lodging, and lottery tickets rather than photos. The gallery closed five years ago but my interest in photography hasn't lessened.

Brad rubbed his chin. "If memory serves me correct, catching killers and interfering in police investigations is another of your hobbies."

"Not really. I've occasionally been lucky to have been in the right place at the right time."

"Most of the time your, umm, hobby pissed me off." He hesitated then smiled. "I still owe you for my life and catching my daughter's killer, so I won't complain about one of the times you nosed in where you shouldn't have."

No comment struck me as the best response.

"Well," he said, "don't want to hold you up. Nice talking to you."

He pivoted and headed to the coolers on the side of the store.

That was the first time he'd ever acknowledged it was nice talking to me.

Chapter Three

My ringing phone showed that Charles was calling. It'd "only" been nine hours since I tried to get him to answer this morning.

In the spirit of surrendering to non-normal phone etiquette, I answered with, "About time you called."

"Yeah, whatever. You on your way?"

Okay, I deserved that.

"Might I ask where and why?"

"Yes. Loggerhead's."

That answered where but still left why a mystery. I also knew the best, and possibly only, way to find out the reason I was summoned was to say, "On my way."

The early evening temperature was comfortable, so I walked three blocks to one of the beach's more popular dining spots. I reached the top of the stairs to the elevated deck and entrance to the colorful restaurant where I saw

Charles on the packed deck at a table near the bandstand. He would've been hard to miss in his crimson University of Alabama long-sleeve T-shirt. Now that I knew where he was, the next unanswered question was who were the two people with him?

I weaved around several tables packed with loud groups enjoying the weather, the food, and from what I could tell from the number of glasses and bottles, the drinks.

Charles saw me approach, glanced at his empty wrist where most people wore a watch, his way of saying I was late, which, of course, I wasn't.

Instead of standing, Charles pointed to the man I would guess to be in his late-thirties, and said, "Chris, meet Kyle Manger and," as he nodded to the other person at the table, "Pat, umm—"

"Zellner. She's my girlfriend," Kyle said as he stood to shake my hand.

Kyle wore jeans, a black T-shirt with CREED on the front, and well-worn work boots. He was roughly five-foot-eight, thin, with black hair, and a short beard. It finally struck me that he was the man Charles had talked with at the site of yesterday's incident.

We shook as I said I was glad to meet him. I nodded toward Pat who remained seated, and added I was glad to meet her as well. She also wore jeans and a white T-shirt and was even thinner than Kyle. She nodded my direction but didn't say anything. Kyle returned to his seat and I took the chair beside Charles.

Becca, one of Loggerhead's servers, was quick to the

table to ask what I wanted to drink. The other three were drinking beer but I opted for white wine. Kyle said they hadn't ordered, so I wasn't far behind.

Becca left for the bar and Charles said, "Chris, remember when we were at the house under construction, and I went to talk to Kyle? This is him. He's a plumber working where Shelly slipped off the roof."

It was beginning to make sense why Charles had two people at the table with him.

Kyle said, "We saw Charles over at the bar where he told us he was meeting you for supper. He invited us to join you. I didn't want to, but he insisted. Hope you don't mind."

"Of course not," I said as if I had a choice.

Kyle said, "I didn't remember seeing you there with Charles, but I was traumatized seeing Shelly lying there."

"Isn't that an amazing coincidence, Chris? Us being there and me running into Kyle tonight."

It would've been amazing if I believed it was a coincidence that Charles, the alleged private detective, had run into Kyle.

I didn't have time to tell him how amazing it was. Pat leaned toward Charles and said, "That's all he's talked about since he got home yesterday." She rolled her eyes. "Like I want to hear about some dead person."

I had no idea what Charles would say, but the odds were it would probably irritate Pat more than she already appeared to be.

I said, "I was shaken seeing her on the patio, and I didn't know her. I imagine it was traumatic for Kyle since they worked together. Sometimes talking about the experience can help."

"Whatever. Are we going to order or what? I'm starving."

Becca returned with my drink and asked if we were ready to order, hopefully in time to prevent Pat from starving. We each nodded.

Kyle and Pat ordered fish tacos, Charles a cheeseburger, and I chose a fried flounder sandwich. After we ordered, Pat tapped Becca on the arm and said she needed another beer. The rest of us said we were okay with our drinks.

"Chris, Kyle's a plumber," Charles said like it was the most logical thing to say after declining more drinks. Besides, I knew that from seeing him in the Donnelly Plumbing shirt at the job site.

"Me and Joshua are doing most of the plumbing on the project for Custom Builders Group. That's the company building the house."

"When you got here, Chris, I was asking Kyle how well he knew Shelly." Charles turned to Kyle. "You were saying?"

"Didn't know her well. She was usually working on a different floor from where I was."

That wasn't enough for Charles. "What'd you know about her?"

"He thought she was a looker," Pat said then glared at Kyle.

"Charles," Kyle said, ignoring Pat's comment, "she was the only gal on the crew. Couple of the guys thought she got off easy because she was female."

Charles said, "Did she?"

Becca set Pat's beer in front of her.

"I'll take another one," Kyle said.

Pat put her arm on Kyle's shoulder. "Maybe you ought to slow down. That's what, four?"

"Another beer," he said to Becca, as if she hadn't heard him the first time.

Pat removed her hand from his shoulder and grabbed her drink.

"Did she get off easier than the guys?" Charles said ignoring Kyle and Pat's tense exchange.

"Best I can tell there were five carpenters; six when it started, one got fired. I wasn't around them most of the time, so I didn't see any difference, but they did a lot of bitching about her slowing them down. Joshua and me had enough work to keep us more than busy. No time to see what was going on with the hammer swingers."

Pat said, "What about the guy you said was always hitting on her?"

"What about him?"

"Bet he didn't think she was goofing off."

Kyle's beer arrived.

"Don't know what he was thinking." He took a long draw on his drink then continued, "All I know is he has a reputation as a lady's man and I know from hearing him a couple of times he was doing his best to get her to have a drink or grabbing a meal with him." In a lower voice, he added, "and more." He slowly shook his head. "I heard her tell him she was married. He said, no big deal, her husband would never know."

Charles said, "What'd she say to that?"

Our food arrived before Kyle answered. Kyle took a bite of his taco, a sip of beer, and said something about the nice weather.

As I could've predicted, it took Charles fewer than ten seconds before he repeated his question.

Kyle took another bite, swallowed, and said, "Know the old saying *if looks could kill?*"

Charles nodded.

Kyle took a large draw on his drink, then smiled. "If that was true, Mason would be dead instead of Shelly."

Charles said, "Mason?"

"Mason Playboy Ryle."

"Where was he when Shelly fell?"

"Don't know," Kyle said as he brought his beer to his lips. "Know what's got me a little confused?"

"Probably the number of beers you've had," Pat said before taking another bite.

Kyle ignored her. "Know what Shelly told me a couple of weeks ago?"

Of course, none of us did, but it was Charles who said, "What?"

"It's so sad. Said she was terrified of heights. And look what killed her. Poor thing."

"Crap, Kyle," Pat said, "if it'd been any of the guys who fell off the roof, you'd said *oh well, shit happens*. It's a cute chick, so you go all mushy. Oh, so sad. Poor thing. Boo-hoo."

Charles pointed his fork at Kyle. "You thinking someone may have pushed her off?"

"Not really. I know how hard it was to work on that roof. Accidents happen. I think it's sad, no matter who it was." He turned to Pat. "Doesn't matter if it was a gal or guy."

Charles said, "So, you think it was an accident?"

Isn't that what Kyle said?

"Seems like it. But I'll tell you one thing, if someone pushed her, I'd put Mason at the top of the list."

Charles leaned closer to Kyle. "Why?"

"He's a hothead. He don't like being rejected."

"And you don't know where he was working the day of the, umm, accident?"

"Could've been anywhere. He's a carpenter. If I had to guess, I'd say on the top floor."

"Why's that?"

"A lot of the work's been finished on the other floors, but again, it's only a guess."

"Who do you think knew Shelly best?"

"You mean besides Mason?"

Charles nodded.

"Probably the boss man."

"Randy something?" I added, to rejoin the two-way conversation between Charles and Kyle.

Charles gave me the look that probably meant how did I know the name of the boss, or foreman.

"Randy Lee, old guy, he's foreman. I don't know for sure but suspect he knew her better than the others since he hired her."

Pat grabbed Kyle's arm. "Enough about what's her face."

Kyle reached for his beer. Charles and I didn't reach for

anything but took the far from subtle hint. Shelly wasn't mentioned the rest of the evening.

Chapter Four

The phone jarred me awake. A glance at the out-of-focus clock told me it was midnight. The equally out-of-focus screen on my phone read *Charles*.

I managed to hit the button to answer and said, "You better be dialing in your sleep or calling to tell me I won the lottery."

"Nope, but the call's your fault."

"Why are you calling?"

"I was peacefully sleeping when the sleep fairy whispered in my ear that you forgot to tell me at Loggerhead's how you knew the name of the foreman. See, it's your fault."

"And you couldn't wait until a decent hour in the morning to ask?"

"Of course not. So, are you going to tell me? You're keeping me awake."

My eyes were focusing better, so maybe I could

remember and share the highlights of my talk with Chief LaMond. As I went through the story sharing what little she knew or felt comfortable telling me, I knew Charles wasn't fully awake since he didn't interrupt with a thousand questions. His only question was if I was sure Shelly didn't have any pets. I reminded him he'd said the same thing at the construction site the day of her death. He confessed he may not be thinking clearly. I told him I was certain he wasn't since he called at a time he knew I'd be asleep.

"Good point," he mumbled. "Meet me at the Dog at seven-thirty to tell me the rest."

There was no rest to tell, but it sounded like the best way to get him off the phone.

I said I'd see him there and tapped *end call*.

THE LOST DOG CAFE, called the Dog by most locals and many vacationers, was Folly's go-to spot for outstanding breakfasts, lunches, socializing, fact collecting, and gossip. Since I used my kitchen about as often as an albino rhinoceros knocked on my front door, the Dog was my informal dining room and had been for years. It was roughly five blocks from the house and less than a block off Center Street. It may be called Lost Dog, but there was seldom a shortage of canines on its two outdoor patios, none appearing lost and were hanging out with their owners. Charles didn't own a dog but considered every canine he encountered his.

My friend was sitting on the front patio petting a collie

and telling it something in collie-speak. The dog's owner did what many people do when near Charles and their pets. The man in his seventies continued eating while ignoring Charles conversing with the canine.

I walked to the side entrance to the patio and pulled out the chair opposite Charles.

"Hey, Chris, meet Libby," he said as he nuzzled the friendly collie.

I rubbed Libby's head while Charles told her he'd talk to her again before leaving. If Libby was excited about it, she didn't let it show. Charles returned to the table and his bacon and eggs.

Kathy, one of the servers, arrived with a mug of coffee without me having to say anything. I thanked her and said I'd like an order of French toast, the item I ordered most every time I'd been here.

Charles watched Kathy head inside then said, "So, what'd you forget to tell me last night?"

"You mean when you called in the middle of the night?"

He smiled. "That'd be the call."

"I think I told you everything Cindy said."

"You dragged me over here this early after keeping me up most of the night to tell me nothing?"

Revising history is one of Charles's numerous quirks.

"You know that's not what happened, don't you?"

"Whatever. So, what'd you think of Kyle and cranky Pat?"

"Seems like a nice guy. Other than that, I don't think much either way. As for Pat, I agree with you. Disagreeable would be putting it kindly."

Charles reached over to the next table and gave the collie another pat on the head as her master paid and headed to the exit. He then turned to me. "Guess she's not disagreeable to Kyle. What about the guy hitting on her?"

"Hitting on Pat?"

"Get with the program, the guy Kyle said had been hitting on Shelly."

"Mason Ryle."

"That's the one."

"Why do I get the impression you think Shelly's death wasn't an accident?"

He shrugged. "Seems suspicious."

"Why?"

Kathy returned with my French toast, refills on our coffee, and asked if we needed anything else. We said no and she moved to bus the table that'd been occupied by the collie's owner.

Charles said, "Why what?"

"Why do you think the death was suspicious?"

"Duh. She had a conflict with at least one person on the crew. She was afraid of heights and was working on the top of the house. Umm, there was one more reason I thought of in the middle of the night, but it escapes me."

So does common sense, I thought.

"I don't think telling a co-worker you don't want to have a drink, a meal, or whatever with him is much of a conflict. And what does being afraid of heights have to do with someone killing her? It was her job to be there, and from what we've heard, there wasn't anyone near her when she fell."

"Wouldn't you avoid the edge of a roof if you were afraid of heights?"

"Yes, unless my job required me to be there. Besides, the roof was slanted so we don't know how close she was to the edge when she slipped."

"Okay, Mr. Pessimist, as Harry Truman said, 'A pessimist is one who makes difficulties of his opportunities and an optimist is one who makes opportunities of his difficulties.' I still think it's fishy."

Charles looked over my shoulder. "Hey, Marc. How's my city today?"

I turned to see Marc Salmon, one of Folly's City Council members, approaching the entrance. He walked to the railing separating the patio from the entry.

"Charles, Chris, good to see you. Charles, to answer your question, something I pride myself doing for my constituents, the city's doing fine, just fine."

Marc is a daily regular at the Dog. He usually meets Houston Bass, another member of the Council, to allegedly discuss city business. I say allegedly, because regulars know the two politicians are collecting and spreading gossip far more than city business.

"Now a question for you guys. Did you hear about the lady who died in a construction accident at a house in the six-hundred block of West Ashley?"

City business or gossip, you decide.

"Sure did," Charles said. "We got there right after it happened. Sad."

I said, "Why'd you ask?"

"I'm a member of the Council, have been for years,

know a lot about what's going on around here, but whenever there's a death on the island, you and Charles know more about it than I ever do. Figured this time wouldn't be the exception." He chuckled. "From what Charles said, it wasn't. I hear it was an accident. That your take?"

"Yes," I said.

Charles said, "Not sure. What do you think?"

"No idea."

"Bet there is something you do know," Charles said.

"What's that?"

"Who's owns the house?"

Marc smiled. "Oliver Trescott, mid-sixties. Moved to our neck of the woods a while back. Came from Maryland, I hear. Got a building permit seven months ago. That lot's been vacant for years. It had an old concrete block house on it back in the dark ages. Construction on Trescott's mansion began in April. That's all I know."

"What about the company building it?"

"Custom Builders Group owned by Joe Argyle. He's built several of the larger homes over here, some on Kiawah too. Why?"

"Curious, that's all."

"If you say so. Gotta get in there. Don't want to keep Houston waiting. City business can't wait." He saluted in our direction and headed inside.

I said, "What was that about?"

"What?"

"Asking about the house's owner, the construction company."

"I'm simply collecting information. That's what detectives do, you know."

"In case you haven't been listening, there's nothing to detect."

"We won't know that until all the questions have been answered."

"To quote you, 'Whatever.'"

Chapter Five

I finally got a peaceful night's sleep. No phone calls from my faux-detective friend, no dreams about someone falling off a roof. With sleep under my belt, or under my top sheet, I was up at six-thirty, in time to see the sun rising over the house across the street and the first few early workers driving past the cottage on the way to their jobs. I enjoyed watching vehicles pass the house while knowing I had nowhere I had to be. Cruel, I suppose, but wouldn't be surprised if some retired person took pleasure in me driving by his or her house during the forty-plus years I was a member of the workforce.

Two cups of coffee later, I realized the morning rush-hour was over and a cottage in dire need of a good cleaning was waiting for me. Before I lugged the vacuum cleaner from the closet, I saw Charles peddling his classic 1961 Schwinn bicycle up the road and turning into my front yard. He owned a motorized vehicle but preferred using his bike around the island and also used it to deliver packages for our friend Dude Sloan, owner of the surf shop.

Charles was wearing his black, long-sleeve, NYPD T-shirt he often wore when he was focused on performing what he called *private detecting*. I had no doubt his arrival wasn't a social call. He leaned the bike against the screened-in porch, took a cardboard tray out of the basket on the front of the bike, and said, "See you're waiting for me. Sorry I'm a little late. Had to stop at Bert's for this." He held up the container as if I wouldn't have known why he stopped at Bert's.

"How would I be waiting for you if I didn't know you were coming, late or not?"

"Excellent question. Glad you're in a mood to question things. I brought a bunch of them."

I opened the door, glanced in the carton, then told him to take it to the kitchen. I followed and grabbed two paper plates so we could divide the cinnamon-covered packaged donuts. He handed me one of the cups of coffee from the container, and no, I didn't tell him I'd already had two cups and wasn't ready for more.

While I was using all my culinary skills separating the donuts from their packaging, he said, "Knew you wouldn't have anything to eat, and I got these so we could have a breakfast meeting."

"Thoughtful. Would it be too much to ask the agenda for this, umm, meeting?"

"Shall we retire to the living room? The meeting will commence in there."

We did. Charles wolfed down two donuts, took a couple

of sips of coffee, before removing a folded sheet of lined paper from his pocket, and spreading it out on his knee.

"Know what this is?"

"A written apology for disturbing my peaceful morning."

"Horrible guess. You have no idea, do you?"

"How would I?"

"Our suspect list," he said, leaned back in the chair, and nodded his head like that said it all.

"Gosh, how did I not know that?"

"Suppose you're not as good a detective as yours truly. I'll give you a hint. They're suspects in the killing of some young lady we happened to sort of became acquainted with on a walk the other day."

"I knew what you meant. What I didn't know was how or why you think she was murdered, thus the need for a list of suspects."

"Allow me to enlighten you," he said and took a bite of his third donut.

"Please do."

"Last night while you were, umm, heck if I know, but am certain it was nothing worthwhile, I was at Cal's having a beer."

Cal's was a country music bar owned by Cal Ballew, a friend who'd ended up on Folly after traveling the south for forty years singing his brand of classic country music at any venue that'd have him.

"How's having a beer at Cal's more worthwhile than me doing nothing?"

"Glad you asked. I was talking to Cal when he pointed to a guy sitting at the bar and asked if I knew him. He looked familiar but I couldn't place him until Cal said he worked for a construction company building a house out West Ashley. Then it clicked. It was Randy Lee. Since I'm such a friendly guy who likes to make everyone feel welcome on my island, I took my beer and sidled up to Randy who was looking bored and needed someone to talk to."

"Let's see if I have this right. You saw a bored guy and wanted to make him feel welcome. Nothing more?"

"Sure, but since he was there, I didn't see harm in learning what he knew about Shelly's death. Anyway, he seems like a nice guy. He let me buy him a couple of beers and is a talker. Did you know he lives in a thirty-three-foot-long travel trailer? Got it parked at the Oak Plantation Campground off Savannah Highway."

I told him I didn't know any of that while not wasting any time or words asking how he thought I would have.

"He told me he hangs out at Cal's almost every night; something about loving his travel trailer, but it gets cramped being stuck in it too long. Anyway, he's been with Custom Builders Group nine years, but only got promoted to foreman for the job over here."

"What'd he do before that?"

"Said he was a jack of all trades. Did electrical work, carpentry, and occasional drywalling. Little of everything, I suppose."

I nodded to the sheet of paper balanced on Charles leg. "And that list has something to do with Randy?"

"You're catching on." He tapped his forefinger on the sheet of paper. "These are the guys working in the house when Shelly fell, umm, was pushed."

"Your suspect list is everyone who was at the house?"

"Some higher up on the list than others, but yes."

I motioned for him to continue. After another bite of donut, he picked up the list, studied it like he was prepping for an exam, then said, "Let's see, we've already talked to Kyle Manger, remember the guy from Loggerhead's?"

"That was two days ago. My memory's not that bad."

"Just checking. Okay, then there's Mason Ryle, remember, Kyle told us about how he'd harassed Shelly?"

I nodded.

"Scott Rawlins, another carpenter according to Randy. He's one of the ringleaders who said Shelly got by easy because she was a she. Randy thinks Scott may have a drinking problem, but it never bothers him at work. Add Timothy Hale to the group. Another carpenter. He was hired at the beginning of the project. No issues that Randy mentioned. Let's see, Lucius Walker, a black guy who's an electrician with Bolt Electric. Randy said his first name is Latin and means luminous in a biblical reference."

"I met Lucius the day we were on the building site."

"See, you already know two of the suspects: Lucius and Kyle. That's progress."

"That's not—"

"Hang on, let me get through the list. Mitchell Baldwin, one more carpenter. Big surfer according to Randy. Then there's Luis Ortez, another electrician. Born in Puerto Rico but has lived in Charleston since he was six. Only been with Bolt Electric three months; guy before him quit. Finally, we have Joshua Bennett. Randy said he had several run-ins with Joshua."

"Kyle mentioned Joshua," I said.

"There you go, Chris. The odds are good one of them killed Shelly."

"Didn't you forget someone?"

Charles looked at the list and ran his finger down the names. "Don't think so."

"Randy? Wasn't he there?"

"Yes, but … but he—" He looked back at the list. "Okay, you're right. See, you're a better detective than you think."

I shook my head. "I admit, that would be an appropriate list of suspects if there had been a crime. But, as I've tried to get through your thick skull, no one says Shelly's death was anything but a tragic accident."

"You're wrong, aspiring detective. One person has said it was murder."

"Who?"

"*Moi.*"

Chapter Six

In addition to Charles finishing the donuts, before leaving, he'd talked me into meeting him tonight at Cal's. So, here we are.

Cal's, formally named Cal's Country Bar and Burgers, is located on West Cooper Avenue across the street from and a little past the city's Department of Public Safety. It's the perfect example of a quintessential country music bar. Entering the door feels like you're walking in a tavern from the 1940s or '50s. The walls are dark green, a beat-up dark wood bar is on the right side of the room with a tiny kitchen behind it. The dozen tables along with their chairs look like they're on their last legs. Occasionally, one of the chairs can no longer support an overweight or overenthusiastic patron and collapses. So far, only the customers' pride has been hurt, quickly soothed by a complementary beer or two from the owner. The smell of stale beer and greasy burgers permeates the air as does the country classics from days gone by emoting from the Wurlitzer jukebox located on the small stage where Cal entertains his customers with sets on weekends.

Cal was behind the bar when Charles and I entered the near-empty venue. The seventy-six-year-old owner is six-foot-three, looking taller in his sweat-stained Stetson that'd travelled with him most of his life. Adding to the country-crooner look, he wore a white rhinestone trimmed coat that also had accompanied him throughout the south. In a break from tradition and a concession to his life on Folly, a red Folly Beach T-shirt peeked out from under the jacket.

Cal saw us, gave a quick, stage-perfected smile, and waved us over.

"Beer and white wine?" he said as way of a greeting.

"You bet, partner," Charles said and tipped his Tilley at the owner.

Cal grabbed a beer out of the cooler behind him, handed it to Charles, then poured a glass of Chardonnay for me, before saying, "What brings you two vagrants out? It sure wasn't to mingle with the crowd." He waved his hand around the room that held exactly three customers at a table by the twelve-by-twenty-foot laminate dance floor hugging the front of the stage.

Charles said, "We came to see you. What more reason would we need?"

Cal rolled his eyes. "Pard, you can't out-crap this old crap spewer."

The country crooner was from Texas, so I assumed—hoped—that was a Lone Star State saying.

Without tipping my Tilley, I said, "You're always the

main reason we stop by. We're also looking for Randy Lee. He been in tonight?"

Cal looked at his watch. "Came in thirty minutes ago, started to mosey over to the table by the wall, snapped his fingers, shared a profanity, didn't clean it up by saying crap, told me he had to grab something at Bert's, but for me to keep a beer cold, he'd be back."

That was more than we needed to know, but bottom line, he'd probably make another appearance. A customer I didn't know came in and headed to the bar. I told Cal we'd be at a table in the middle of the room. Cal focused on the new arrival as Johnny Cash shared his thoughts from the jukebox on blues in Folsom Prison. Charles and I settled at the table in hopes Randy would return soon.

The next person through the door wasn't Randy. Brad Burton looked around, then surprised me when he headed our way. In his detective days, he often had a slovenly appearance with his wrinkled suit, white shirt pulling out from his dress slacks, and a tie that was seldom centered on his torso. Since retiring, his casual wear maintained the unkept look. His green polo shirt was a size too small for his expanding stomach and his casual slacks were too long. Unlike every time I saw him at work, he was smiling.

He reached the table then looked around like he didn't know how he got here. He finally said, "Hi, Chris, Mr. Fowler."

I said, "Care to join us?"

"Umm, I don't want to interrupt anything."

"You're not," Charles said, "We were having a drink and killing time. Take a load off."

Charles had heard my stories about conflicts with Brad but had few contacts with the retired detective.

"If you don't mind."

"Not at all," I said, hoping I sounded sincere.

"Hey Brad, want a beer?" Cal yelled from behind the bar.

"Yes."

I'd only seen Brad in here one other time and said, "Come here often?"

"Two, three times a week. Hazel tries to kick me out of the house more, but I don't get much satisfaction hanging out in bars. At least in here there's good music, beats the stuff played in some of the other places."

Brad liking country music surprised me as much as knowing he was here that often. "It's a special place," I said as Conway Twitty sang "You've Never Been This Far Before."

Cal set a beer in front of Brad and said, "First time I've seen you three together: a retired detective and two private dicks. Who would've thought?"

That proved Cal didn't know about the bad blood between Brad and me, or if he did, he was trying to get an argument started.

I said, "Brad's the only one who's been a detective, a good one at that."

"I'll be back," Charles said as he pushed his chair back and headed toward the entry.

I turned and saw Randy Lee at the door. He looked around and headed to the bar. My friend followed. I thought, *Charles, please don't bring Randy over*. That would be just what I needed, him meeting Brad as Charles interrogated the foreman about Shelly's death.

I dodged a bullet, figurative speaking, when Randy took a seat at the bar, Charles took the stool beside him, and Cal headed behind the bar to see what Randy wanted. Problem averted, for now.

Brad watched Charles put his arm around Randy's shoulder. "I've heard Mr. Fowler knows everybody over here. That true?"

I smiled. "Everybody with pets." I said, slightly exaggerating. "He knows many who don't have pets, but I suspect a few fly under his radar."

"Also hear he, and you, I might add, still stick your noses in every murder on the island, and now have expanded your interference to deaths over on Mosquito Beach. Suppose that's what Cal was talking about when he called you two private detectives."

That was one topic I didn't want to get into with Brad. It dredges up too many memories, some a mere few feet away related to how hostile Brad had been with my involvement. That was even after Charles, and I'd learned the identity of the person who killed Brad's daughter and I'd saved Brad's life.

"Brad, we were lucky a couple of times, nothing more." Time to change the subject. "Have you figured out a hobby to get you out of the house?"

Brad showed an emotion I'd never seen from him. He chuckled. "Know what one of the tells is in an interrogation when a suspect is lying or feeling trapped?"

"Can't say I do."

"He changes the subject."

Perhaps Brad was a better detective than I'd given him credit for. "Like I did when I asked if you'd figured out a hobby?"

"Exactly."

"You're right, of course. I was serious when I said that I've been lucky a few times when—"

"Hey guys," Charles said as he appeared behind me, "look who I found at the bar?"

I knew who he'd found. There may be examples of worse timing, but I couldn't think of one.

"Hi, Randy," I said. "Meet Brad Burton. Brad, this is Randy Lee. He's foreman on a new house being built out West Ashley Avenue."

Brad stood and shook Randy's hand while adding the obligatory *nice to meet you* regardless if he meant it or not.

Charles said, "Randy said he wouldn't mind having a drink with us. I told him you'd pick up his tab, Chris. That okay?"

"Sure," I said, knowing Brad would detect the lack of sincerity, although he wouldn't know the reason.

After everyone was seated, Charles said, "Randy, tell them what you were telling me over there." He nodded toward the bar.

"Umm, I don't know. It wasn't anything more than a reaction I had."

"That's okay," Charles said and patted Randy's arm. "Go ahead."

"Well, umm, I was telling Charles I'd been thinking a lot about Shelly's death." He took a sip of beer, hesitated, then said, "I think I told you before, this was my first job as fore-men. I knew when I took the promotion, I'd have to keep up with everything happening on the job, knowing not only what the crew's doing, but what needs to be done next to make sure materials were delivered and the right number of employees were where they need to be. Logistics is what the company's owner calls it. A pain in the ass is what I call it." He hesitated.

Charles, being as patient as a hungry newborn, said, "And?"

Randy looked at Charles. "And what?"

"What you were telling me about Mason."

"I was getting there."

Not quick enough for Charles.

Randy frowned at Charles, turned to me, and said, "I'm learning that in addition to the building things I have to keep up with, knowing how the crew relates to the other members is almost as important. I think I already told you that Mason had been giving Shelly a hard time. Truth be told, hitting on her would be more accurate. Anyway, since her death he's been acting strange."

Charles said, "Strange?"

If Brad still carried a badge, he'd probably be pulling it out about now while he figured out how to arrest Charles, and yes, me, for interfering in police business.

"Umm, before it happened, he struck me as even-tempered, calmer than most of the guys. He went about his business without making a fuss. Since her death, he's flown off the handle two times I know of. Blew his top over a minor delay in the truck getting drywall to the job site. Then this morning he jumped all over one of the electricians claiming the guy was slowing him down by not getting the room wired in time. Stuff like that." He snapped his fingers. "Almost forgot, there've been two times when I was talking to him about things that needed changing and he acted like he didn't hear me. I was looking him right in the eyes, not three feet away, and he ignored what I was saying."

I said, "Think he was distracted?"

Randy finished his beer before answering. "If he was, it was something in his head. We were in an empty room, nothing going on except me and him talking."

I was surprised when Brad said, "Where was Mason when Shelly fell?"

"Don't know. He was supposed to be in the owners' suite on the second floor." He sighed. "Company's owner said we couldn't call it the master suite anymore. Sexist, I suppose. Anyway, Scott, he's another carpenter, told me Mason wasn't there. He'd told Scott it was his break time."

Brad said, "Was it?"

"Could be. I'm generous with breaks. I've been on too many jobs where the foreman is so anal that he, on one job, she, wouldn't let us take a piss unless it was at an assigned time. I didn't want to be that way once I got in charge." He looked at his watch. "Guys, I've got an early morning. Thanks for the beer, Chris."

"It's not that late," Charles said. "Sure you have to go?"

Charles wasn't done fishing.

"Afraid so," he said as he glanced at his watch a second time. "Have to stop at the construction site to make sure everything's okay." He chuckled. "Seems like one of my guys make a habit of leaving some equipment on nearly every day. Don't want to have the house burn down on my first job as foreman."

"That's too bad," Charles said. "Which guy leaves stuff on?"

"No one in particular. Someday this one; someday that one. They're always in a hurry to get out of there when their shift ends. I often wake up in the middle of the night worrying and have to get dressed and check it out. Course I could do a better job checking all the stuff before I leave after work. It's hard breaking my habit of clocking-out and getting as far from work as I could back before I was promoted. Guess that's why I get the big bucks now. Thanks for the conversation and drink."

He started for the exit, stopped, turned back to the table. "Nearly forgot. One more thing about Shelly. Guy named Raymond, said he was her husband, stormed into the house this morning demanding to talk to the person in charge. My guys were quick to point their fingers my way. None of them wanted to deal with the guy." He shook his head.

Charles said, "What'd he want?"

"Wanted to know who he needed to see about life insurance the company had on his wife. I told him I had no idea, that he could talk to the owner of the company and gave him the phone number for Custom Builders Group."

I said, "How'd he take not learning more than that?"

"The boy was pissed. Before he stormed out, he said something about suing me, the company, the homeowner, and hell, probably God for creating gravity that yanked

Shelly off the roof headfirst onto the concrete patio." He looked at his watch once more. "See you guys later."

Freddy Hart was singing "Easy Loving" when Cal returned and asked if we needed anything else. Brad said he could handle a second beer, Charles did the same, and I said I was okay. Cal looked around the near-empty room, said he figured he'd have time to get the drinks.

Charles said, "Looks like we have ourselves a good suspect, possibly two."

Brad glanced at me. "Tell me again how you and your friend aren't playing cop."

I didn't waste my breath repeating what I'd told him earlier. I shrugged.

Charles appeared oblivious to what Brad and I were talking about and said, "Brad, you were a detective, what do you think?"

I was surprised when he didn't shower Charles with a profanity-infused tirade about it not being any of my friend's business.

He said, "First, I didn't hear anything remotely indicating that Whitley's death was anything but an accident."

"But," Charles interrupted.

Brad stuck his right hand in Charles's face. "And, even if it was something more sinister, nothing he said about, umm, the carpenter, or the husband indicated they were responsible."

"Of course, you're right. That shows how great a detective you were back in the day," Charles said, nodding the entire time. "Let me ask you this, if you were the detective on this case, what would be your next step?"

"Mr. Fowler, if I were still with the police and investigating, I'd probably write up the death as an accident and close the file. Now if my boss, who happens to be a police officer, told me I had to pursue it, I'd look to see who, if anyone, had something to gain from her death."

Charles said, "How would you—"

Brad used his hand in the face motion once again. "Mr. Fowler—"

Charles interrupted. "Call me Charles."

Brad sighed then continued, "Charles, I wouldn't do anything. I'm a civilian. I'm no longer a member of a law-enforcement organization. I have no authority to do anything. And, in case you haven't noticed, neither does anyone else at this table. Now I've got to get home. Wouldn't want Hazed to think I've run away." He smiled. "On the other hand, she probably would be thrilled if I had." He stood, went to the bar to pay Cal, then headed home, or to run away.

Chapter Seven

The sun had set long before I walked home from Cal's. I approached Bert's Market where I saw Dude Sloan staring at the large mural painted on the side of the building featuring Bert, the market's namesake, shown dressed as a pirate with a devilish smile plastered, more accurately, painted on his face, and a hook replacing his hand.

I moved beside Dude and said, "Talking to Bert?"

My friend of more than a decade glanced at me. "No be silly. He faux. Admirin' hook."

Dude was in his late sixties, thin, five-foot-seven, with long hair, and wearing one of his ever-present tie dye T-shirts. He also has a speaking style slightly more articulate than a chimpanzee but was much smarter than many people assumed based on his verbal quirks.

"Contemplating getting a mural painted on your building?"

He's owned the surf shop for more than thirty years and is one of the island's most successful business owners.

"Contemplated it two revolutions around sun ago. Called drawer of this. He be Douglas Panzone. Pondered it. Poultry out."

Charles had known Dude way longer than I had and often served as a translator of Dudespeak. While I wasn't nearly as articulate, I figured he called the artist a couple of years ago since Dude's hobby, other than confusing listeners, was astronomy and the earth circles the sun once a year. The rest was merely guessing that he chickened out. It didn't matter, so I wasn't hung up on an accurate translation.

"I see," I said, although far from it.

"Talking about seeing, see about dead chick at house out W. Ashley?"

"Unfortunately, yes. Charles and I were nearby when it happened."

Dude nodded twice. "Figures."

"Why?"

"You plus Chuckster be private detectives. Always around bad stuff happening." He nodded again, like it was obvious.

"How'd you hear about it?"

"Mitchell," he said and nodded again.

"Who's Mitchell?"

Dude rubbed his chin. "Umm, piano, young dude."

"Mitchell Piano?"

He shook his head. "Mitchell Baldwin, like piano."

The name sounded familiar but took me a few seconds

to remember why. It could have come to me quicker if I hadn't had to work my way through the piano reference.

"Is he a surfer who works on the construction project where the woman died?"

"Proof you be detective."

I translated that as a yes. "What'd he tell you?"

"Said one tick of watch she be on roof. Next tick she be on patio. Tim agreed."

I followed all of that except the part about Tim agreeing. "Tim?"

"Mitchell's bud. He be hodad."

It'd taken me nearly a decade but learned a hodad was someone pretending to be a surfer but isn't. I also vaguely remembered someone else on the crew at the house was named Timothy, or Tim.

"Does Tim work with Mitchell?"

Dude nodded. "Both be woodcutters."

"Carpenters?"

"Yep."

"When were they telling you about it?"

"Day this side of fall. Chick fall, not season."

"Did they say anything else?"

"Yep, Tim couldn't come up with lucre to get wetsuit."

"Anything more about what happened with the woman?"

"They be sorry she dead but not for good reason."

"What's that mean?" I asked, an often-used phrase when talking with Dude.

"Sorry because they had to do their work plus her work. Sorry, but wrong reason."

"Anything else?"

"Nope." He snapped his fingers. "Yep, told Pluto be at *casa* now. Gotta go."

Pluto was Dude's Australian terrier. I didn't ask how Pluto could tell time but simply told him it was nice talking with him.

Dude wasn't going to be the last person I talked to this evening. Charles called as soon as I got home.

"Okay, I'm convinced," he said as a greeting.

"Convinced of what?"

"Shelly was pushed off the roof."

"What convinced you?"

"Not what, who. Weren't you paying attention to Randy? Not only did he tell us about one guy who had reason to do her in, he gave us two."

I tried to remember back to what'd been said in Cal's. Nothing came to mind implicating one, much less two people as having reason for killing her.

"Okay, help me understand, who are the two and what was said to convince you?"

"Fantastic suspect number one, Mason Ryle. He'd been hitting on Shelly, harassing her. That could get Mason in big trouble, right? Then after he killed her he was feeling guilty, letting his temper get the best of him; being distracted, not listening to Randy giving him instructions. Mason is torn up with guilt. Yes, he killed her."

"If he killed her, what about the second person you mentioned?"

"Raymond, her husband. It's obvious. He killed her for money. She hadn't been dead long enough to be buried and he's asking about life insurance the construction company had, then if that isn't enough, he's hinting he'll sue the company. Cindy tells us the spouse is the first suspect, always. She's got it right this time."

"If Raymond killed her, what about Mason? You know, your *fantastic suspect number one*."

"You caught that. To be honest, I'm a little confused. Both couldn't have killed her, could they? Like been in cahoots."

"I suppose they could've been, as you said, in cahoots, or either one of them could have killed her. I only see one small problem with your theory."

"See, that's why we work so well together as detectives. What's the small problem?"

"There's no evidence her death was anything other than an accident."

"My friend, how many times have you and I stumbled on a situation, a situation where someone was dead, and the police were convinced the death was an accident or suicide or some space creature did the person in?"

"Space creature?"

"Okay, that was an exaggeration, but the point is, how many times?"

I got the point that occasionally Charles's imagination bordered on lunacy, but that wasn't what he wanted to hear.

"I suppose it's happened more than once."

"Way more than once. This is another one of those times. She was killed and we, okay, I know the killer."

"And you know it's Mason, oh wait, no, you know it's Raymond?"

"Did you miss the part where I said I was a little confused?"

"I get that you're confused."

"You making fun of me?"

"A little."

"Fair enough. Anyway, the point is I need your help. I'll let you think it over and we can get together tomorrow, figure it out, and then you can let Cindy know who killed Shelly."

He didn't give me a chance to say how absurd his plan was. He'd already hung up.

Chapter Eight

Rain filled the morning air as I sat on my porch sipping coffee and watching a steady stream of cars passing the house carrying sleepy commuters to work. I was again thinking how good it felt not being among that group when the phone rang. I figured it had to be Charles since he'd said we needed to get together today to *figure it out*. I still wasn't sure what *it* was other than an alleged murder fomenting in Charles's vivid imagination.

Instead of looking at the phone's screen to see who was calling, I answered with, "Good morning, Charles."

"That's by far the most insulting thing you've ever said to me," Bob Howard bellowed.

That'll teach me not to look at the name of the caller. Bob was the realtor who helped me find the cottage I was talking to him from. I met him when I first arrived on Folly and quickly learned he was loud, boorish, gruff, opinionated, and profane. Those were some of his better qualities. For reasons I can't explain, even though many people have asked me why over the years, we became friends.

"Sorry, thought you were Charles."

"No kidding. I figured that out after you said three words."

"Okay, let me start over. Good morning, Bob."

"Better, but it'll take me decades to get over being called your quarter-wit friend."

Like with many of my friends, it's best to ignore many of his comments. "Bob, why'd you call?"

"Crap, couldn't it be because I wanted to see how my friend's doing?"

I smiled. "No."

"You're damned right. So, here's the question. Are you and your eighth-wit friend sticking you noses in the untimely death of some carpenter-chick on a building site on your quirky island?"

"Bob, why would you ask that?"

"Hell's bells, how about because you two meddle in every death that happens over there. Why would this time be different?"

"I don't know what you've heard, but the carpenter-chick, as you call her, is Shelly Whitley. The police and those who were working there when it happened believe she accidentally slipped and fell off the roof. A tragic accident, nothing more."

"Remember, you're talking to your buddy Bob. I heard you say the police believe and the folks who were working there believe she slipped and fell. You're too old to be a cop and I know you and definitely Charles are too lazy to work anywhere. What do you think happened?"

"I have no reason to believe it was anything other than an accident. Charles and I were there seconds after she fell."

"If that's not the chocolate icing on the cake, I don't know what is. You simply happened to be there. I bet Charles interrogated everyone who was around. Am I right?"

"No interrogation, Bob. Everyone was shocked. We waited until the police arrived then left."

He chuckled and said, "So, the cops ran you off."

I sighed. "They asked us if we knew anything about what happened. We didn't and left—left without a police escort."

"Who's the builder?" Bob asked like it was a logical question after me telling him we left the site.

"Custom Builders Group."

"Joe's outfit."

"You know him?"

"Did you forget you're talking to one of the Lowcountry's most successful realtors? That is until I retired and bought one of the Lowcountry's most famous bars."

The first half of that was true. Bob had been a successful realtor in both commercial and residential real estate until he retired a few years ago and bought an aging, rundown bar in Charleston from his long-time friend Al Washington. Bob wouldn't admit it, but he bought the bar that was in debt more than it was worth to help his friend who had suffered serious health issues. If Al had remained owner much longer, he wouldn't have survived.

"Does that mean you know Joe Argyle?"

"Do I have to spell out damn near everything? Yes, I know him. He's one of the best in this market. He's built houses on Kiawah, Mt. Pleasant, and a few on your island."

"Have you heard rumors or anything negative about him or his company?"

Bob laughed. "Let's see if I have this right, you and your sixty-fourth-wit friend aren't sticking your nose into what happened?"

"Curious, that's all."

"You know the word curious comes from the Latin word *nosy*?"

"You made that up."

"Yep, like you made up not nosing in police business."

"So, you don't know anything negative about Joe or his company?"

"Like he kills one of his employees at every house he builds?"

"That would qualify."

"I don't know him well. He's got a good reputation and I sold one of his houses a while back in Mt. Pleasant. The owner ran out of money before he ran out of people he owed it to and had to sell. From my times in the house, it appeared well-built and passed the inspection with flying colors."

"That's it?"

"I'm a lowly bar owner. I don't think Joe Argyle has ever been in Al's. He's never called me to say he was planning to kill one of his employees. Tell you what, though, if he does, you'll be the first to know."

"Thanks."

"Do you think he had something to do with the, umm, accident?"

"Not really."

"Was he at the house when the woman fell?"

"I don't think so. No one there mentioned him. How's Al?"

"Sassy, obstinate, getting lazier each day. Why?"

"I was wondering more about his health."

"I know. Don't want to talk about it. I worry about him. He's old you know, not young or in good shape like me."

Al was eighty-three, only five years older than Bob. And Bob was in as good shape as many people in the ICU at Roper Hospital, plus he carries roughly a ton more pounds than recommended for someone with his six-foot-tall frame.

"Tell him I said hi."

"Hell, tell him yourself when you come over to get a cheeseburger at my world-famous restaurant and bar."

"I will."

"Good, and I'll check around to see if there're any rumors about Joe Argyle, not that it matters to you since you're not nosing in police business."

He hung up before I thanked him and denied I was anything but curious.

Chapter Nine

There was a break in the rain, so I walked to Bert's to grab breakfast. Before I reached the double-door entry, I received my second phone call of the day. This time I looked at the screen.

"Morning, Charles."

"Looks like I'm going to have to cancel our appointment."

"Appointment?" I said, although I suspected I knew what he was talking about.

"Duh. To figure out the killer."

"And you're canceling?"

"Aloysius called."

"Aloysius?"

"Remodeler. I've helped him before on a couple of projects. You remember?"

I didn't remember. "Okay, he called, and?"

"Needs help with the sunroom addition he's sticking on

a house out East Cooper."

Charles hasn't been burdened with a real job since he was in his mid-thirties but picks up enough "off the books" income to meet his modest expenses by making deliveries for Dude, helping a couple of restaurants with clean-up during busy season, and lending a hand to contractors. By lending a hand, that's about all he can offer since he's shared he has difficulty pounding a nail or sawing wood. His talent is in hauling lumber and holding wood or drywall in place while someone who can drive a nail does his thing. Apparently, Aloysius is one of those contractors.

"Shall we reschedule our appointment for tomorrow?" The one I didn't know had been scheduled for today.

"I'll call you."

"Okay," I said to a phone that'd already ended the call.

With the appointment I didn't know I had canceled, my agenda for the day was blank, but I still needed something healthy and nourishing for breakfast. What better place to find something than the pastry cabinet, I rationalized?

I grabbed a cinnamon roll from the display, took a step back, and nearly stepped on Randy Lee's foot.

"Morning, Randy. Sorry for almost stomping you."

"That's okay, Chris, right?"

I nodded.

"I spend my day running into my workers or them running into me. Feet are often trampled. Nearly a dozen workers spending the day working in a house gets crowded. That's one reason I wear steel toe shoes. Add a bunch of power tools and it can get quite harried."

"I imagine so," I said, not knowing what else to say

about his observation. I noticed two boxes of donuts in his hands. "You must be hungry?"

He smiled, the goal of my comment. "We're running behind finishing the house. We were scheduled to do some work on the exterior today and this rain screwed up those plans. And don't even mention cops. They stole a day and a half from us. Each of us had to answer question after question from the local cops and then some detective from Charleston had us tell him the same thing. Add to that, we couldn't work on the upper level for four hours while guys in white suits looking like astronauts were doing no telling what up there."

I was glad to hear the police had taken the death seriously and didn't automatically buy the explanation about the carpenter slipping and falling. Of course, I didn't share that with the frustrated foremen.

"That's too bad."

"Sorry for bitching. I'm pissed we're behind. The owner expects, no, demands, that we have his house ready for him to move in next month. He bought the property a decade ago, and now he wants us to have the place ready for His Highness to occupy." He hesitated, looked around the store, then back at me before saying, "You don't know the owner, do you?"

"Don't think so."

"I shouldn't have said that about him. After all, he's paying my salary. The guys have been working extra hours to get us back on schedule. That's why I'm getting these. Donuts are great for bribing construction workers. Not quite food for the soul, but they cheer up a bunch of workers. I know they did when I was in their shoes."

"They're fortunate to have a concerned foreman."

"I guess. It's my first gig with that title, so I want to do everything I can to keep them happy while bringing the job in on schedule. Speaking of on schedule, I better get back before they start a revolt."

"Good talking to you, Randy. One more quick question. Have you heard anything else from Shelly's husband?"

"Not directly, but Joe, my boss, was on-site late yesterday and told me Raymond came to his office yesterday morning demanding to know about insurance. Joe told him the company didn't carry life insurance on its employees. If they wanted any it was their responsibility to buy it through the company benefits plan."

"How'd Raymond react to that?"

"Joe said an exploding stick of dynamite wasn't as loud as Raymond's eruption. Joe thought he was going to have to call the cops."

"Did he calm down?"

"Yeah, enough to tell Joe he'd be hearing from Raymond's lawyer."

"How did Joe react?"

"Said he didn't. By then one of the other guys in the office, a big bruiser, used to be a wrestler from what I understand, heard the commotion, and came in the office to see what was going on. He and Joe escorted the irrational guy out of the building."

"Sounds like that may not be the end of it."

"You've got that right. I told my guys to keep an eye out

and let me know if they hear or see Raymond around our project. Gotta go."

I watched him head to the register and wondered what would happen next. The sound of thunder reminded me I'd better get home before the rain returned. A day puttering around the house without any appointments had a lot of appeal.

Chapter Ten

The next morning, I awakened to the sound of silence. Most of yesterday and a couple of times during the night, rain pelting my metal roof and periods of rolling thunder disturbed my peaceful day and night of rest. Having lived in the Lowcountry more than a dozen years, I knew flooding would be an issue for houses on several streets as well as in the low-lying areas in nearby Charleston. Fortunately, my cottage was on high enough ground to avoid most of those problems.

The morning silence was interrupted by the phone. It was better than even odds that Charles was the person on the other end, after all, he wanted to reschedule our getting together to figure out something. I'd learned my lesson yesterday and glanced at the screen on the phone before answering. Virgil appeared rather than Charles.

I'd met Virgil Debonnet about a year and a half ago.

He'd been a stock market analyst until bad investments, bad habits including gambling and drugs, and bad luck cost him his marriage, his magnificent house on Charleston's Battery, the city's premiere residential location, and his wealth. Despite losing more than most people ever had, he's one of the most optimistic people I've known.

"Morning, Virgil."

"Have you heard?"

"I need a hint. Heard what?"

"The electrocution."

I waited for him to elaborate. The wait was futile. "Virgil, what electrocution?"

"Some guy at a house under construction out West Ashley Avenue."

"Where are you?"

"The Dog."

If Virgil knew more, getting it out of him on the phone appeared remote.

"I'll be there in fifteen minutes."

"Good, you can buy breakfast."

Ten minutes later, I was parking at a space at the far end of the restaurant's gravel parking area. Virgil was sitting at a small table on the front patio. He waved when he saw me heading his way. I entered the side entrance to the patio and joined him at the table.

Virgil was in his early forties, my height at five-foot-ten, thin, with black hair. He wore sunglasses that seldom left his face, a long-sleeve, button-down light-blue shirt untucked over navy-blue chinos. He also had on his pride and joy, resoled Guccis.

Before I had a chance to say anything, Amber Lewis set a mug of coffee in front of me.

"Virgil said you'd be joining him. French toast?"

"Why not."

Amber smiled. "I can give you several reasons, beginning with the big one, eventually, clogging your arteries and then a heart attack."

I'd met Amber my first week on Folly. She was my favorite server on the island; always in the know about gossip, and unlike many servers, listens to her customers. We'd dated for a while and after deciding to go a different direction, we'd remained close friends.

"I appreciate your concern. I'll risk it today."

"It's your heart," she said, pivoted and headed inside to place my deadly order.

I turned to Virgil. "Okay, spill it."

He raised his glass. "Don't suppose you mean my orange juice."

I sighed. "Virgil."

"Okay. I got here a half-hour ago and heard two guys talking. They were standing by the entrance. Each had a to-go cup of coffee so I figured they'd already eaten and were heading, well, heading somewhere. Anyway, I heard them saying something about a construction worker getting himself electrocuted overnight. Said he was working on a house under construction. Now, don't ask me what the guy was doing working overnight."

That wasn't much more than Virgil had shared over the phone. "Did they say anything else?"

"They did, but they were walking to their truck and I

couldn't hear anything else. I thought about following them to their vehicle but figured that since I'd never seen them before that'd be rude."

"On the phone you said the house was out West Ashley Avenue. Did they say that?"

"Hmm, if that's what I told you, they must have. I haven't heard anyone else saying anything about it. Why, you know the house?"

"I've only noticed one being built out that way. If it's the same house, it's where the woman fell to her death from the roof the other day."

"Wow, that's one whale of a coincidence."

"Yes, it is. You sure they didn't mention the person's name?"

"Not that I heard. They may've said it after they left the entry over there, but I didn't hear it if they did."

Amber arrived with my heart-unhealthy breakfast and a refill on my coffee. She headed to the far end of the patio where the only other two patrons were seated.

A Folly Beach Department of Public Safety cruiser pulled into a spot in front of the restaurant where a minivan had departed. Trula Bishop stepped out, yawned, then headed to the door.

Trula had joined the police force about seven years ago. She was in her forties, five-foot-five, and African American.

I said, "Good morning, Officer Bishop."

"Oh, hey, Mr. Chris, umm, you too, Mr. Virgil. Didn't see you there. My eyes are a bit fogged after being up all night."

Trula stepped away from the door to let two customers

get in, then moved to the railing separating the patio from the entry.

"Officer Bishop," Virgil said, "since you were up all night, were you out there where some guy got electrocuted?"

"Afraid so. Tough scene."

I said, "What happened?"

"Hard to tell. The guy was working near the electrical panel. The floor was wet because of all the rain, water seeped under some of the equipment. Looks like a wire was hot and he didn't know it. You can guess the rest."

"Any way to tell when it happened?" I asked.

"Midnight."

Virgil said, "How do you know?"

"There was a clock radio plugged in a socket beside the panel. Was one of those old-fashioned ones, real clock hands, not digital. Don't remember when I saw one of those last. Anyway, the workers listened to it while they were working. The power to that area got blown when the man was killed."

Virgil said, "What was the guy doing working out there at midnight?"

"No idea, and he's in no condition to tell us."

"Was anyone else there when it happened?"

"If there was, he or she didn't hang around."

I said, "Who found him?"

"Two guys on the crew. Apparently, they were behind schedule and came in early to catch up. Got there a little before sunrise. It wasn't the way they wanted to start their day."

I said, "Who were they?"

Bishop took a small notebook from her pocket, flipped through a few pages, and said, "Mason Ryle and Scott Rawlins. Why?"

I told her I'd been at the site when the woman fell off the roof and had met a few of the workers. I was afraid I knew the answer to my next question, but asked anyway, "Who was the man?"

"Name's Lee, Randolph Lee. He was the foreman."

I told her I knew Randy; that I'd talked to him a couple of times.

"Why was the guy out there at midnight?" Virgil asked for a second time. "Seems weird."

I shared what Randy had told me about having to occasionally check to make sure all the equipment was turned off since some of the workers failed to.

"That's strange," Trula said and jotted a note in her small notebook. "When I asked Ryle and Rawlins if they had an idea why he was there, they said no. I would assume if the foreman had to visit the site after hours, he would've made a big stink with the crew about taking care of their equipment. I know I would've."

"Me too," added Virgil.

I agreed with both of them but didn't say it.

Bishop looked at her watch. "Guys, I've got to pick up a to-go order for two guys at the fire station. Good talking to you."

She headed inside and Virgil turned to me. "Chris, if you ask me, that sounds mighty suspicious."

I knew what he meant, but instead of agreeing, I said, "Why? People pick up to-go orders all the time."

Virgil's sunglasses prevented me from seeing it, but from the wrinkles on his face, I'd put money on him rolling his eyes at me. I wouldn't have blamed him.

Chapter Eleven

The first thing I had to do after getting home was call Charles and tell him about Randy's death. Yes, I could've made the call from the Dog, but figured doing it in private might avoid having to debate my friend in front of others.

"Figured out who killed Shelly?" Charles said instead of hello or any of the other civil responses to a phone call.

"No, haven't thought about it this morning."

"You're failing to meet the minimum requirements of a private detective. Do I have to give you a refresher course?"

"I've been busy."

"What could be more important than catching a killer?"

Instead of leading him further down the yellow brick road, it was time to share what was more important, knowing once he heard, he'd agree.

"Learning about an electrocution."

"How's that more—whoa, electrocution?"

"Randy Lee was electrocuted at the job site around midnight."

"Oh crap, he seemed like a nice guy. Did you say midnight?"

That's what Trula Bishop said."

"Where'd you see Trula?"

This is a textbook example of where a partial answer is better than a complete one. "Ran into her this morning."

"What else did she say? How did it happen? Why was Randy out there at midnight? Who found him?"

All excellent questions, I thought. Answering them would allow me to slip past telling him I'd been at the Dog with Virgil.

"Trula didn't know much. Mason Ryle and Scott Rawlins found Randy this morning. They didn't know—"

Charles interrupted, "Mason the harasser, the guy who'd hit on Shelly?"

"Yes. May I continue?"

"Was clarifying."

I didn't ask how many guys named Mason he knew working at the construction site.

"According to Trula, the floor was wet and Randy either stepped on or grabbed a hot wire. And remember, Randy told us he often went to the site at all hours of the night to make sure the equipment was turned off and stored safely. I suspect that's why he was there that late."

I waited for Charles's response. None was forthcoming.

"Charles, you still there?"

"You know what this means, don't you?"

I was certain I knew what Charles thought it meant but asked anyway.

"Means there's a murderer on the loose. Done killed Shelly, now Randy."

"We don't know that. Construction site accidents happen all the time."

"Chris, oh Chris, since you don't read anything more complicated than road signs, let me tell you what I read a couple of weeks ago. Did you know five construction workers died during the building of the Empire State Building?"

"Were they murdered?"

"Let me finish."

I mentioned for him to continue.

"That's five accidental deaths out of, umm, guess how many construction workers built it."

"A bunch."

"A big bunch, 3,400."

"And how does that archaic fact relate to a house on West Ashley Avenue?"

"There are, what, maybe ten people working on the Ashley Avenue house? Now, two of them are dead. I suppose one of them could've been an accident. But two, get real. Shelly and now Randy were murdered. Period. No, make that an exclamation point."

"You could be right, but I still don't see anything other than the odds on it being more than two unfortunate accidents."

"Did Trula tell you anything else?"

"No."

"I'll call Kyle Manger to see what he knows. Before I go, put these words in that brain under your Tilley, *they were murdered.*"

I didn't have time to tell him where I'd have liked to put the words. He'd hung up.

I didn't want to give Charles the satisfaction of knowing I wasn't far behind him thinking two deaths at the site appeared extraordinarily high for such a small project. Perhaps Cindy could shed light on what was going on. Before I could punch in her number, the phone rang, and the Chief's name appeared on the screen.

"Morning, Cindy. What did I do to deserve a call?"

"Absolutely nothing. But seeing that it's noon and you haven't pestered me about what happened overnight out West Ashley Avenue, I was afraid something terrible happened to you."

"It's nice you care about my health."

"Hell yes, who'd buy me meals if you kicked the proverbial bucket?"

"You're all heart."

"Enough foolishness. First, did you hear about this morning's death?"

"Yes, Vigil told me he'd heard about it at the Dog, and then I ran into Officer Bishop and asked about it."

"Figured you'd heard."

"Think it was an accident?"

"Looks like it. Seems the deceased often went out there after hours to make sure everything was okay. It'd been raining and for some reason he grabbed a hot wire, and you know the rest."

"Anything suspicious about it?"

"Okay, Mr. Charles in training, other than it being the second death at the house in less than a week, I didn't see anything that set off alarm bells."

To share the Empire State Building statistics or not, that is the question. Knowing I'd have to reveal how I knew its history, I chose not.

"So, that's the end of it?"

"Almost, the Sheriff sent over one of his detectives to take a gander, but I'd be shocked, pun intended, if he finds anything. The guy couldn't be old enough to have graduated from middle school. I could be wrong, but if he's been a detective longer than it takes your buddy Dude to say a three-word sentence, I'll be surprised."

"I appreciate you letting me know."

"Hell, I only called so you wouldn't be calling during my exciting luncheon meeting with our mayor."

"I still appreciate it. Enjoy your exciting meeting."

Chapter Twelve

Early-morning walks are one of the pleasures of my retirement, probably because I had little time to take them during decades in the workforce. Today would be one of those times. I grabbed a cup of coffee from Bert's before making my way a block to Center Street.

With the sun casting its glow along the upper levels of stores and businesses along the west side of the street, the temperature in the upper seventies, and the sidewalk occupied by a mere handful of people on their way to a couple of restaurants open for breakfast, I told myself I'd made the right choice on how to spend part of the day.

While I had control over how I spent the morning, I couldn't help but think about the tragic events over the last few days. Shelly Whitley went to work the other morning thinking it was simply another day of work. I didn't know how much she loved her job or if she only endured it to earn a paycheck to afford her lifestyle. If, like most people, she had thoughts of what she would do after work, or on the weekend, or on the vacation for which she may have been saving part of her earnings. I doubt it entered her mind that it would be the last day of her life, the last day she'd see her husband, the last day her dreams of the future would exist. When Randy Lee left his travel trailer to return to the job site to make sure the equipment was turned off and stored properly, I imagine his thoughts were on how irritating it was he had to make the long drive back at midnight rather than thinking it would be his last night going there.

These weren't the thoughts I wanted to have as I approached the spot where Center Street dead-ended at the entrance to the Tides Hotel. Rather than pushing them out of my mind, they were intensified when I saw Lucius Walker, reminding me he was the first person I'd met at the construction site the day Shelly fell to her death. He was headed my way carrying two boxes of donuts.

"Good morning, Lucius?" I said as he got closer.

"Oh, hi, umm, sorry, I forgot your name. That was a terrible day when we met."

"Chris Landrum, and I agree."

"Chris, got it."

I pointed to the boxes in his hands. "You hungry?"

He started to respond, hesitated, then smiled. "Funny. No, they're for the guys at the job site. Boss man used to get them for us. Made the workday a little more pleasant." He looked at the sidewalk and slowly shook his head. "Now he's gone. Figured I could pick up where he left off."

"That's kind of you. I hated to hear about Randy's accident."

He stared at me, his gaze narrowed, then he said, "Yeah, right."

"What's that mean?"

"Nobody's asked me, but if they did, I'd tell them I didn't think it was an accident."

"Why not?"

"I'm an electrician, have been going on twenty-five years. I know my way around everything electrical. Know what's safe, what ain't. Randy knew what he was doing. He was foremen on this job, but he was also a certified electrician. Unlike me, he could also do carpentry work with the best of them, even did some plumbing in a pinch. He shook his head. "There's no way in hell he would've stepped in a puddle and grabbed a wire that had a chance of being hot. No way."

"It was late, and he was probably tired. He may not have noticed the water or picked up the wire without thinking."

Lucius sighed. "Randy was in his sixties. Know how electricians live that long? They don't make that mistake."

"You say you haven't told anyone your theory?"

"May've mentioned my suspicions to a guy or two on the job, but like I said, no cop asked me. Since it was after hours when it happened, none of us were there, so we couldn't have seen anything. Seems to me, the cops figured it was an accident and closed the books on it."

"Let's say you're right and it wasn't an accident. Any thoughts on who may've been there and, umm, caused him to be electrocuted?"

"Not really. From what I could tell, he got along with

everybody out there. Sure, there were minor blowups. Always are on a job with a group of workers sharing the same space, but nothing stands out. Don't know diddly-squat about his life outside work."

"Let me ask something else. Do you think there's any connection between Shelly Whitley's death and Randy Lee's?"

"Don't see how there could be. Looks to me like she simply slipped on the roof and fell."

I didn't remind him that most people thought Randy's death was an accident, the same as Shelly's.

"You're probably right. Did any of the others out there have a problem with Shelly and Randy?"

"It don't sound like you think her death was accidental."

"It strikes me highly unlikely that there could be two accidental deaths at one construction site in that short period of time."

"That's because Randy's wasn't accidental."

"Lucius, I'm good friends with Folly's Police Chief. If I asked her, would you be willing to tell her what you told me about your theory about Randy?"

"I have to get along with the other guys. I've already had to put up with some comments and snubs because I'm black. I can't afford to get anyone else down on me, so no. Sorry." He looked at the boxes in his hands. "I got to get these out there. Good talking to you."

He didn't wait for me to respond before heading in the direction of the new house.

He said he didn't want to talk to Cindy about Randy's death. I didn't say I wouldn't.

"Morning, Cindy," I said as she answered her phone on the second ring.

"Where are you?"

"In front of the Tides."

"I'll be there in thirty seconds."

She wasn't far off. Her city owned Ford pickup truck pulled in the hotel's lot in less than a minute.

She smiled and said, "Thanks for offering to buy me coffee in Roasted."

Roasted is the coffeeshop located in the oceanfront hotel.

"My pleasure," I said even though I knew I hadn't made the offer.

We entered the hotel through the door closest to Roasted and were greeted by Penny, the shop's personable manager. We each ordered coffee and moved to one of the two small tables in the center of the room.

Cindy took a sip, glanced around the room, then said, "So what did I do to deserve a phone call and cup of coffee?"

I was tempted to say she hadn't done anything for the coffee but knew nothing positive would come from it. Instead, I said, "I was curious if you'd learned anything more about Randy Lee's death."

She tilted her head. "You were curious about that rather than being curious about how I was doing, what I fixed Larry for supper last night, how my meeting went with the mayor, how my aching feet feel after walking a thousand miles around town yesterday, how——"

"Cindy," I interrupted, "of course I was curious about

all those things. So, learn anything more about Randy Lee's death?"

"Good, pizza, bad as usual, sore, no," she said, stared in her cup, then took another sip.

"Taking talking lessons from Dude?"

"He be my idol," she said and smiled.

I returned the smile before saying, "So, nothing new about the death?"

"Last night the baby detective called and said it's clear as day, no question about it, an accident. Case closed."

"What's Cindy LaMond say?"

"I would agree with him if there weren't two alleged accidental deaths there in less than a week."

"Before I called you, I ran into Lucius Walker, he's an electrician on the project. He thinks it's highly unlikely that a trained electrician would've been killed by that kind of accident."

"I thought Randy Lee was foremen on the job."

"He was, but according to Lucius he was also a licensed electrician."

"Good to know. Other than *highly unlikely*, did he have any proof or idea who may've wanted Lee dead?"

"No."

"That figures. The problem with highly unlikely is that it doesn't eliminate likely."

"You're right. I assume by the detective saying case closed, the Sheriff's Office won't be doing any follow-up."

"You assume correctly."

I smiled at the Chief. "I also assume the highly skilled,

competent, and lovely, I might add, Folly Beach Director of Public Safety isn't closing the case."

"You're a highly perceptive, intelligent citizen. A total suck-up at times, but still all those other things. I can't do much but will keep my eyes and ears open and have already told my guys to do the same."

"Good."

"This is where I tell you not to butt in; to leave it to the police."

"You know—"

She pointed her coffee cup at me. "But I know I'd be wasting my words and energy telling you, so let's leave it at be careful."

"Always, Chief."

Chapter Thirteen

When Charles answered the phone, I tried the same line on him that Cindy had used on me. "Where are you?"

"At the spa getting a facial and pedicure."

There was a better chance my friend would be skinny-dipping at the North Pole than being at a spa. I tried again.

"Where are you?"

"Okay, you caught me. I'm delivering sandals to a couple staying at a house out East Cooper. Dude said they absolutely had to have them in the next fifteen minutes or, well, he didn't say or what. You calling each of your friends to see where they are?"

"Good guess but wrong. I'm only calling you. I just met with Lucius Walker and figured you'd want to know what he said."

"Lucius, the guy from the deadly house?"

"How many guys named Lucius do you know?"

"Got it. What'd he say?"

"Head to the end of the Pier after you finish the emergency sandal delivery."

Fifteen minutes later, I saw Dude's local-delivery person. He was wearing a crimson and blue University of Kansas, long-sleeve, T-shirt, tan shorts, his summer Tilley, and tapping his cane on the wooden deck as he approached me on a bench at the Atlantic end of the thousand-plus-foot-long structure. He stopped twice to talk to dogs that were accompanying their masters on a walk along the Pier.

"Sorry I'm late. Had to wait for the couple, who happened to be from Chicago, try on the sandals. It's their first trip to the ocean and wanted to make sure the sandals fit so they could walk for 'hours and hours' on the beach. I was beginning to think I'd have to wait *hours and hours* for them to unpack the shoes, try them on, and model them for each other. The best news is the sandals fit, and here I am."

"Fascinating," I said, not disguising my sarcasm.

"Well, what'd he say?"

I gave Charles a blow-by-blow description of my conversation with Lucius. I was surprised when he only interrupted twice with questions. First was when he wanted to know where Randy received his apprentice training to become a certified electrician. He huffed and puffed when I told him I didn't know. His second question was no-doubt critical to the conversation. He asked what kind of donuts Lucius was taking to the crew. That I could answer.

After I managed to get through my description of the conversation with Lucius, I shared what Cindy and I'd talked about. He was either totally engrossed in my description or fell asleep early in it because he didn't ask anything.

He finally said, "See, told you so."

I suspected I knew what he meant. "You did say you thought the two deaths were suspicious."

"Not suspicious, murder. Clear as day."

"For what it's worth, I'm beginning to agree with you."

"You are?"

"Yes."

"You never agree when I say we need to help the police."

"Can't say that again, can you?"

"Trying to confuse me?"

I didn't think that would be too difficult but didn't say it. "No, I agree with you that we need to get involved."

"With me and the Chief, you mean."

"She's not certain. For that matter, neither am I."

"I am, and the best thing in all of it is Folly's top cop wants us to find out who killed them."

"That's not exactly my interpretation of what she said. She did say she knew we'd have a hard time not sticking our noses where they didn't belong."

"My friend, that's police-speak for the Chief asking, correction, begging us to catch the killer. Us as in you and me. Plain as day."

"How do you, umm, we plan to do that, Mr. Private Detective?"

"Excellent question, Assistant Detective." Charles turned and watched three surfers sitting on their boards waiting for a wave large enough to get excited over.

"You have an excellent answer to go with that excellent question?"

He stopped watching the surfers, turned to me, and said, "Nope."

"That helps."

"Nope."

"Okay, since you're the one with the detective agency, what's your plan?"

"After all the years you've known me, you know coming up with plans ain't my strong suit. You're the college-educated member of the agency. You're the one always making lists, coming up with catching the bad guys strategies, outlining stuff we need to do, all those other textbook learning ways to catch bad guys. I'm the chief stumbler." He patted me on the arm. "So, what's the plan?"

I would've laughed at his analysis, but knew he was serious; off base by a mile, but still serious.

"You have to understand, I haven't given any thought to who might've killed the workers. First, we're not certain their deaths were anything other than accidents. They—"

"I'm certain."

I ignored his comment. "Granted, two deadly accidents in a short span of time on such a small project would appear to defy odds, but still, we have no proof of anything more sinister." I hesitated, then added, "Even if we assume you're right, we know little about the victims. Without knowing more about them, we have no way of knowing who would've wanted them dead. We don't even know if Shelly and Randy had contact with each other outside work. If they didn't, I have a hard time seeing how they could've done something on the job that made someone want to kill them."

Charles smiled. "See, you've already started one of your lists of things we need to do."

I have? "Okay, repeat it for me."

He sighed, held up his forefinger, and said, "Number one, learn everything there is to know about Shelly and Randy." He added his middle finger to the number. "Two, see if Shelly and Randy had a relationship outside work." The ring finger was added to his count. "Three, catch the person who killed them." He closed his hand into a fist and raised it in the air. "*Voila*, another successful crime, umm, crimes solved."

I stared at him and said, "Wow, silly me, I thought it would be difficult."

Charles looked at his watchless wrist and said, "Gotta go. Time for me to start stumbling around. Got a killer to catch."

Chapter Fourteen

I remained on the Pier after Charles left on his quest to stumble into something that would help him, help us, learn who killed the construction workers. What that was, I didn't know. I wouldn't call him the *chief stumbler* in his imaginary detective agency, but he did excel in getting to know strangers. Minutes after meeting them, they were telling him things they wouldn't share with their family or closest friends. Using that innate skill on potential suspects, he could get them saying things that could lead him closer to solving murders. They seldom suspected they were being interrogated, although in a couple of instances, his, umm, nosiness nearly got my friend killed.

He was right about a couple of things. If we had a ghost of a chance at helping the police, we needed to learn more about the victims. Add to that, who are the logical suspects? From everything I've heard, only workers were present when

Shelly met her untimely death. Did any of them see or hear anyone else in the house that morning? Clearly, if no one else entered, and if Shelly was pushed, the killer was one of her fellow workers. Those, of course, were two large ifs.

Then there's Randy Lee. According to Lucius Walker, Randy's death couldn't have been accidental. I didn't rule that out. It had been midnight, dark in the house, he would've been tired, and not paying as much attention to his surroundings as he normally would have been. If Lucius was correct, the suspect pool was unlimited. We had no clue as to who may've wanted to harm Randy. My knowledge of the man was limited to him telling me it was his first job as foreman and that he bought donuts for the employees. Neither reasons for him to be killed nor if he was murdered, a clue as to suspects.

I stared at the group of surfers that'd increased since Charles was here. I appreciated the distraction since I had no idea what to do next and according to Charles, I was charged with developing a plan to catch the killer or killers of two people where no one except Lucius, Charles, possibly Cindy, and in weaker moments, I thought crimes had been committed.

Over the years, some of my best thinking occurred near this spot on the Folly Pier. I couldn't explain why, but regardless, it'd been the case. Today wasn't one of those times, so I headed home.

I was opening my front door when I heard someone behind me say, "Hey, neighbor."

I turned and was surprised to see Brad Burton crossing

his front yard and heading my way. His long-sleeve, white dress shirt looked big on him, mainly because it wasn't tucked in and fell nearly to the bottom of the tan shorts he wore.

"Brad," I said.

"Glad I caught you. Was headed over but didn't know if you were home."

"I am now. Can I interest you in a soft drink?"

"Don't want to put you out."

He wouldn't be if I had any drinks in the refrigerator. With luck, I would, besides, I was curious to know why he was looking for me.

"Don't be silly. Come on in."

He followed me in as I wondered what condition I'd left everything, then stopped wondering about appearances considering how disheveled my neighbor looked. He followed me to the kitchen, the most underused room in my cottage. I opened the refrigerator and was relieved to see four Diet Pepsis and two regular Pepsis.

I gave him the two options and he chose the regular soft drink. I grabbed the diet version and motioned for him to have a seat at the table.

He took a sip, looked around the kitchen like he expected someone to jump out and steal his drink, then said, "Have you heard about what happened to Randy Lee?"

"Yes, so sad."

"What'd you hear?"

To tell or not to tell Lucius Walker's theory of what had happened. Brad had no hesitation to accuse me of nosing in police business, so why not. I told him about meeting Randy's coworker on the street and what he'd theorized about Randy's death not being an accident. I was pleased when Brad didn't berate me for, for what? All I did was repeat what someone had shared.

Not only did he not criticize me, but he also said, "You think he's right?"

"I don't know. In addition to Randy being foremen, he was a certified electrician. That should've made him more careful around electrical equipment, but on the other hand, it was late, dark, and he probably was tired after working all day and then having to return to the job site."

Brad nodded slowly. "Doesn't it strike you strange that there are now two deaths from the small crew on the project?"

"Yes, combine that with some of the crew saying Shelly would've been more careful on the roof. They think it was unlikely she would've put herself in position to slip."

"Does seem unlikely, doesn't it?"

"Yes, but accidents happen."

Instead of focusing on what had happened, I was puzzled about why Brad was sitting in my kitchen talking about the deaths. I didn't have to wait long for an answer.

"Back when I was a detective, this kind of situation would keep me up at night. Each of the deaths can easily be explained. Each could be chalked up to an unfortunate accident. Tell you what, though, I don't like the odds on them being accidents."

"Think your old office is taking it seriously?"

He shrugged. "I don't know much about the young guy

who caught the deaths. I suppose he's good, but he hasn't been a detective long. He has other cases, so it's a lot easier to write these off as accidents than to look for something that might not exist. That's especially true since no one is breathing down his neck about them being murders."

"If you were still on the job, what would you be looking for?"

He took a sip of his drink, grinned, and said, "You're not playing detective by any chance?"

"Interested, that's all."

He slowly nodded. "Let's for a moment assume both people were murdered. The first question would be did the same person kill both of them? Logic would tell me yes. It'd be unlikely that there'd be two murderers killing people who worked at the same small construction site." Brad scratched the side of his face, looked at his drink, and continued, "Then the next question would be why were they killed? If it isn't already confusing, it'd get there fast. For example, were they killed for the same reason? If so, what was the reason and what was the connection between the victims other than being coworkers? Next, did Randy Lee figure out who killed Shelly Whitley and the killer did him in so he couldn't tell the police who it was? Finally, if they weren't killed for the same reason and it wasn't because Randy figured it out and was killed so he couldn't divulge the name of the killer, why were their lives ended?"

"Brad, you're right about it getting complicated."

"That's why I retired." He tapped his finger on the table. "And that's why an amateur has no business meddling in police business."

"I get your point."

"But it's not going to stop you, is it?"

He took another sip, stood, saluted me, said he had to go, and was out the door before I had a chance to lie to him about meddling.

Chapter Fifteen

Brad was right about me wanting to learn what happened to the two workers but wanting to and learning were separated by a gap wider than the Grand Canyon. The next morning, I decided a walk would be the best way to get my brain working, possibly come up with something I could use to get closer to the answer to the question, and if not, the day was pleasant with a temperature in the upper seventies and exercise would do me good.

It was later than my normal early-morning walking time, so foot traffic along Center Street was busier than I would've preferred. I crossed Center Street and headed west on Ashley Avenue. There wasn't a sidewalk but enough space to walk without worrying about being hit. I'd gone a couple of blocks when I noticed Chief LaMond's pickup off to the side of the road with the chief leaning against the fender and talking to two men. The men looked vaguely familiar, but I couldn't recall where or when I'd seen them.

"Morning, Chief," I said as I approached her vehicle.

"You walking to the County Park," Cindy said with a smile, knowing the odds on that were slim since County Park was on the west end of the island nearly two miles from where were standing.

"Nothing that exciting."

"Nothing that strenuous, you mean. I'm aware of your aversion to exercise." She smiled, glanced to the two men she'd been talking to, turned to me, and said, "Chris, you know Tim Hale and Scott Rawlins?"

"Guys, you look familiar, but I don't recall from where."

The younger of the two, probably in his early twenties, stepped forward and held out his hand. He was six-foot-two, thin, with long black hair.

"I'm Tim Hale. Pleased to meet you."

I shared the same sentiment and told him my name.

The other gentleman, probably in his early sixties, was a half foot shorter than Tim, muscular but with much of it turning to fat, with long gray hair pulled into a ponytail, put a large paper bag he'd been carrying on the ground and offered me his hand to shake.

"Scott Rawlins."

He didn't appear pleased to meet me, or if he did, he didn't mention it.

Cindy said, "Tim and Scott work on the construction site where the two deaths occurred. They were walking back to the house. Walking is good, you know." She smiled then looked at her watch. "Have to go. guys, thanks for the information. Umm, Chris, have fun jogging to the County Park."

That's why they looked familiar. They were standing

around Shelly Whitley's body when Charles and I first approached the construction site.

"Nice lady," Scott said as Cindy got in her truck and pulled out on the street.

"I've known her several years and agree. She giving you jaywalking tickets?" I smiled hoping they knew I was teasing.

Tim returned my smile. "Not this time. We were heading back to work with lunch for some of the guys when she stopped to ask if we remembered anything we hadn't told the cops about the deaths."

"What happened to your coworkers was horrible. I've heard both deaths were accidental. You agree?"

"Afraid so," Tim said as he shook his head. "Both seemed like mighty nice folks. Poor Randy hired me the day they started building the house. He didn't know me from Adam but said he needed another carpenter and gave me a chance. He didn't have to. I appreciated it."

"I agree about Randy." Scott said and turned to Tim. "He hired me, what, a week after he hired you?"

"Yes."

"He was always fair with us. That's not something I can say about many of the foremen I've worked for over the years. About the only negative thing I can say about him is he favored Shelly."

"What's that mean?" I said, although I'd heard the same thing about him treating her with kid gloves.

"He took it easy on her. Mind you, it wasn't a big deal, irritating, that's all."

Tim patted Scott's arm. "Randy had a soft spot for

Shelly, but like Scott said, it wasn't a big issue. He made up for it by giving us more freedom when it came to breaks, lunch time, leaving early if we had doctor appointments or other stuff we needed to do. Damn terrible what happened to him."

Scott said, "It was sort of our fault he got electrocuted."

"How?"

"He was so, umm, what's the word, conscientious about everything, he often went out to the site after all of us left to make sure everything was buttoned down like it was supposed to be. If we, especially some of the younger guys, did everything we were supposed to do, he wouldn't have had to go out there in the middle of the night to check our work."

Tim looked at Scott. "Younger guys like me, you mean?"

"Tim, you may be the baby on the job, but I've never seen you do anything wrong. You may've not noticed, but I've seen you straightening up after Mason left a mess and once left the circular saw turned on when he went on a break."

"Guys," I said, "I know it's only a rumor, but I heard someone in town say he heard Shelly was pushed off the roof and it wasn't an accident. Is that possible?"

"Anything's possible," Scott said, "but I wouldn't put credence in it. I ain't heard anyone say there was somebody else up on the roof when she fell. Tim, did you hear of anyone being up there?"

"Not that I heard. I agree with Scott, anything's possible, but I don't see how."

Scott said, "Do the police think something like that happened?"

"If they do, they haven't said anything to me," I said. He didn't ask if Charles or I thought it was possible. "How well did Randy know Shelly?"

Scott said, "He gave her the easier jobs, like I said. Is that what you mean?"

"I meant did they know each other outside work? If there was any truth to someone killing them, it seems there could be some connection between the two."

Tim said, "I don't know about you, Scott, but I never heard anything that made me think they had any contact off the job site. Shelly was married, married to a jerk, but still married. Randy lived by himself in a small RV somewhere off Folly. I never heard him say nothing much about his personal life."

"Chris, I agree with Tim. I never heard either of them mention anything about the other one that wasn't about work."

"That's what I figured. There's probably no truth to the rumor. Tim, what do you mean about Shelly's husband being a jerk?"

"That's my impression. The couple of times I saw him at the job site, he was bossing her around. Stuff like *be home by five,* or *don't forget to pick up bread on the way home.* It wasn't what he was saying but how he said it. He was almost yelling. Who yells about getting bread on the way home?"

"Did either of you see him there the day she died?"

Tim shrugged. "Not me. How about you, Scott?"

"No, but I was stuck in one of the bedrooms most of the

day trying to get the walls finished. Didn't see much of anything so he could've been there. Why?"

"Curious, that's all."

Scott looked at the bag of food on the ground and said, "Would like to talk longer. It's easier than work, but we'd better get back. Nice meeting you."

Chapter Sixteen

I realized the next morning that the only thing in the house I had to eat was a Hershey's Bar with almonds. It covered two food groups, but I suspected it wasn't on the list of breakfast recommendations by the American Heart Association. A walk to the Lost Dog Cafe would achieve two things. It would get me some much-needed exercise and a plate full of calories to negate any advantage from the walk. That equaled out, didn't it?

The temperature had fallen short of the seventy-degree mark, so I chose to sit inside. Amber met me at the door and pointed to a table on the far side of the room and said my coffee would arrive momentarily. Before I reached the table, Marc Salmon motioned me to his usual spot in the center of the room.

He was by himself, so I said, "Where's your table mate?"

Marc looked at his watch. "He should be here in the

next five minutes," the councilmember said and looked toward the entry. "Update, make that the next five seconds."

Houston was making his way around a table of two adults and three kids, patted me on the back, said it was good seeing me, then took the chair opposite Marc.

I started to head to my table, when Marc said, "Hear anything else about the two deaths?"

"Nothing you don't already know, I suspect."

"Give me a call if you do. I'm always interested in knowing what's going on over here. City business, you know."

City gossip, I know, but said he'd be the first to hear if I learned anything. He said he'd look forward to it, then turned to his fellow gossip. Not hearing an invitation to join them, I continued to the table Amber had pointed me toward, the one where she'd already set a mug of coffee.

She was back at the table before I had time to take a sip.

She glanced at Marc and Houston's table and said, "You giving the council members advice on how to run the city?"

"It's my observation they're the ones giving the advice."

She tapped my arm. "You know them well."

Before I agreed, Sean Aker entered the restaurant, looked around, and headed my way.

Sean is a local attorney I'd used when I was starting my photo gallery. When he was accused of killing his law partner nine years ago, Charles and I muddled our way through catching the real killer. Sean said he owed us big time and we'd taken advantage of his legal assistance on several occasions.

"You look like you could use some company," he said as he eyed the other chair at the table.

Sean was approaching fifty, thin, too thin in my opinion, well-toned and athletic; all things I'm not.

I took the hint. "You're always welcome at my table, Counselor."

Amber had drifted to a table on the opposite side of the room to deliver the check to its occupants then returned with coffee for Sean.

Sean looked at me. "You ordered?"

I said no.

"He'll have French toast and bring me a cup of fresh fruit parfait."

It was sad when my attorney knows what I order for breakfast most every time I'm in the Dog. It also goes a long way to explain why Sean's thin and I'm not.

Amber said, "Why am I not surprised?"

She headed to the window opening to the kitchen to place our orders before I could respond to her question that, to be honest, needed no response.

Sean sipped his drink, nodded, and said, "So, what's this I hear about you and Charles sticking your noses in the deaths at a house being built on West Ashley?"

"Where'd you hear that?"

"Let's see, first, Marlene told me she got it from a good source. As you know, Marlene is never wrong."

Marlene is Sean's receptionist and only other employee in his law practice.

"I don't know where—"

"Hang on, she wasn't the only source." He nodded in the direction of the councilmember's table.

"Got it," I said. "Anyone else?"

He chuckled. "Not yet, but if you-know-who over there knows, it'll spread like water at a dam break. Now, if you're done asking about my sources, can I get back to the question?"

I'd already forgotten the question, but suspected it was him nosing into Charles and my nosing.

"Charles and I were at the job site when Shelly fell. We also met Randy Lee, the foremen who was electrocuted. We were curious about what happened."

Sean interrupted, "And you don't buy the deaths were accidents?"

I shrugged and said, "Don't you think it seems like it could be more than a coincidence that there are two deaths in fewer than a handful of days on a construction site with only ten or so workers?"

"Do you have anything more than a hunch?"

"Not really."

"And that's not going to stop you from trying to find out more?"

"I didn't say that."

"Didn't have to. You think I haven't paid attention to what you two have done over and over catching killers? You think I don't owe you my freedom after what you did when I was accused of murder?"

"What happened to those construction workers appears to be tragic accidents. If that's what they were, there's no amount of, umm, curiosity Charles and I exhibit that'll change the facts."

"But if they weren't accidents, do you think you two can do more than law enforcement agencies are able to achieve getting to the bottom of whatever happened?"

"Don't know."

"Well said." He tapped his fingers on the table. "If there's anything you need from me, or anything I can do to help, let me know. I've told you several times, but it bears repeating, I owe you big time."

"I appreciate it."

Amber slipped a plate of French toast in front of me and handed Sean his parfait. "Sorry it took so long, guys. It's been a busy morning."

We thanked her as she left to greet newcomers at the table next to ours.

"Sean, do you know anything about the owner of the house under construction?"

"Who is it?"

"Oliver Trescott, think he's from Maryland or somewhere up that way," I said as I poured syrup on my French toast.

"I don't have any dealings with him, and don't recall hearing his name. Why?"

"I didn't figure you would. I heard he bought the property several years ago and didn't do anything with it until less than a year ago. I'm reaching for anything to help get a handle on why the deaths may be something other than accidents."

"Is this Trescott character over here now?"

"Don't know."

"Have you heard anything about him that would indicate he knew the victims?"

"No."

"Other than working on the house, did the victims have other connections, say outside work, or conflicts with anyone on the job?"

"If they did, no one's mentioned it," I said and took a bite of French toast.

"Who's building the house?"

"Custom Builders Group, owned by Joe Argyle."

Sean ate a spoonful of parfait, then smiled. "I know Joe, helped him with a minor squabble a couple of years ago. Other than that, and even then, it wasn't any fault of his, I got the complaint against him dropped. He's a good guy. From what I've heard, he does a good job for his clients."

"Glad to hear it."

I ran out of things to ask Sean and apparently, he ran out of questions I couldn't answer. The conversation transitioned to some of his hobbies. I couldn't add much to the conversation since I had near zero interest in any of them, including skydiving, surfing, and scuba diving.

He finished breakfast, took a final sip of coffee, and said, "I'd better get to the office before Marlene sends her bloodhound out to round me up."

Marlene's bloodhound is a Shih Tzu that's more at home sitting on her lap at the office, but I took Sean's hint and told him I enjoyed having breakfast with him. I enjoyed it more when he picked up my tab, a rare occurrence from my friends.

Chapter Seventeen

Charles agreed to meet me at Loggerhead's for supper, especially after I said I was buying and that I'd met Tim and Scott, two more of the workers at the ill-fated house. I hung up when he tried to make me feel guilty for not telling him about meeting them immediately after it happened.

Ed, Loggerhead's owner, met us at the top of the stairs on the deck and said there was a fifteen-minute wait for a table. I told him we'd be at the bar and were assured someone would come for us when a table was available. The weather was perfect, and the crowd was two-deep at the bar, so I was surprised the wait was only fifteen minutes. I inched my way through the crowd to get the bartender's attention and ordered a beer for Charles and white wine for me.

Before I managed a sip, Charles started on his lecture about me not calling him the second I left Tim and Scott. I told him I would've if I learned anything worth sharing.

"That doesn't matter, you should've called when—" He

hesitated and looked over my shoulder in the direction of the railing overlooking the parking area on the side of the building. "There's Kyle Manger. Who's that with him?"

I turned to see who he was talking about. Kyle was leaning on the railing and the man facing him was waving his right hand around like he was swatting at a swarm of no-see-ems. He was in his mid-thirties, roughly five-foot-ten, obese, and had a straggly beard that could house a family of field mice. I didn't know who he was but could tell he was irritated about something.

"Don't know."

Charles nodded, glanced back at the men, and said, "Guess we'd better go see."

"They don't look like they're in a mood to meet strangers."

"Kyle's not a stranger."

"Why don't we give them a few minutes to resolve whatever has the other guy so animated?"

Kyle either had to go or had enough of whatever the other man was saying. He pushed away from the railing and headed toward the ramp leading to the parking area. Charles told me he'd be back and followed Kyle down the ramp.

I was beginning to wonder if Charles had deserted me when he reappeared, retrieved his beer from the counter, looked toward the other man who was now leaning over the railing staring at who knows what, and said, "You'll never guess who that is." He tilted his head in the other man's direction.

"You're right. Why don't you tell me?"

"Raymond Whitley."

"Shelly's husband?"

"In person."

"What was he doing here with Kyle? Were they friends?"

"Friends, no. Kyle had seen him at the job site a couple of times. That's when he learned about Raymond and Shelly being hitched. Saw him here tonight and wanted to express condolences." Charles looked at Raymond. "Kyle said it was a mistake, actually said it was a 'big-ass mistake.'"

"Why?"

"As soon as he told Raymond who he was, the guy started in about life insurance he was fighting the builder about, how the builder claimed there wasn't any, how the builder was trying to screw Raymond out of what was his. Then Raymond topped it off by saying he was going to sue the builder, all the guys working on the job, and probably the company that made the shingles on the roof that he claimed made Shelly slip and fall." Charles set his beer on the counter then said, "He's leaving." He then made a beeline for Raymond.

At the same time, Bobbie, one of the servers, tapped me on the arm and said our table was ready. I followed her to the table near a seating area made from a converted VW bus. I figured Charles, being a private detective, could find me once he'd finished with Raymond.

As predicted, Charles did find me, but not as predicted, he wasn't done with Raymond.

"Chris, you'll never believe who I ran into over by the bar."

Yes, I would since Charles intentionally went to meet Raymond. This wasn't the time to correct him.

"Who?"

"Would you believe this is Raymond Whitley? He's Shelly Whitley's husband, you remember the lady who tragically fell from that new house she was working on."

I turned to Raymond. "I'm terribly sorry about your wife. You have my deepest sympathy."

He shook my hand, said, "Thank you. Your friend Charles invited me to share a table with you for supper. Hope you don't mind."

"Raymond was going to eat by himself, but I figured he may not want to be alone during such a dreadful time. I told him we'd buy his supper."

We meant yours truly.

"Glad you could join us."

"Did you know Shelly?"

Bobbie returned before I could respond. Charles and I said we were fine with our drinks; Raymond said he'd have another beer.

Charles said, "No, we didn't have the pleasure. As I said over there, the only way I knew who you were was when I saw you talking to Kyle. We'd met him here and knew he worked with Shelly. I asked him who you were. I'm so sorry about what happened. I didn't know her, but everyone who did said she was a wonderful person."

"How well do you know Kyle?" I asked, in hopes of learning what they'd been arguing about.

"Met him a couple of times when I picked Shelly up after work. Wasn't often. I'm a bartender at the Twin Rivers

Bar in downtown Charleston. Most days I'm going to work when she's getting off."

Bobbie arrived with Raymond's drink and Charles and I ordered cheeseburgers and Raymond went with a patty melt.

"Did you know the man who got electrocuted out there the other night?" Charles asked as if it was a logical question after someone ordered a patty melt.

"The damned incompetent bastard," he said and took a swig of his drink.

Charles said, "Why?"

"His fault she's dead. No wonder he killed himself. Too stupid not to step in a puddle while grabbing something electric. He doesn't know a damned thing about building a house."

I said, "Why'd you say it was his fault your wife was dead?"

"He knew she was scared of heights, but that didn't stop him from making her work on the roof, of all places. Not any roof, mind you, but a slanted one." He took another long draw on his drink.

"Did she tell you she thought Randy Lee was incompetent?"

"Said he was reckless; said she wouldn't be surprised if someone got hurt out there." He looked at his drink, shook his head, and continued, "Didn't think it would be her. Know what the damned company told me?"

Charles said, "What?"

"Said they didn't have life insurance on Shelly. Got nothing for all her work and then giving her life for them to make a ton of money on the house. Tell you one thing, they ain't getting away with it."

Bobbie delivered our food and asked if we needed anything else. Raymond said another beer, again, Charles and I said we were okay. By now, I was wondering how many beers Raymond had consumed since arriving at Loggerhead's.

I knew Charles wouldn't let the interruption disrupt his interrogation. I wasn't disappointed when he said, "What'd you mean by they wouldn't get away with it?"

"I'm getting a lawyer and suing their ass off. They ain't getting away with not paying me anything."

"Good luck," Charles said. "Were you at work when she fell?"

Raymond narrowed his gaze at my friend. "Why?"

"It had to be horrible hearing what'd happened and wondered if you were working when you got the call."

"Oh. I wasn't scheduled to go in until four that day. Most days I work from four until eleven or so."

From the look in his eyes, I could tell Charles wasn't done with his questioning. "Were you with friends when you got the word? You know, someone who could help you with whatever you needed to do."

"No, was driving around."

I had no doubt Charles was thinking no alibi. I wondered if he would risk asking Raymond where he was when Randy Lee was killed.

To keep Raymond from getting suspicious about what Charles was searching for with his questions, I asked him how long he and Shelly had been married.

"Seven years last month."

"Any children?"

"She always said she didn't need any kids, that one big one was enough." He smiled for the first time since he sat down.

"Any pets?" Charles asked, as only he could.

Raymond looked at Charles as if he'd asked if he'd seen any Martians lately, before he said, "No."

I was confident Raymond wouldn't be confessing to killing his wife or Randy Lee, so I tried to keep him talking about things he was familiar with and away from mentioning the construction site, the construction company, or lawyers. I asked a couple of questions about his job. Fortunately, he appeared to want to talk about humorous things that'd happened on the job rather than anything negative.

After about forty-five minutes he kept nodding his head, and a couple of times I worried he would fall asleep. He finally jerked his head up, stood, and said he'd better be going.

We said we enjoyed having him at the table with us. He claimed the same then thanked us—me—for buying his supper and drinks.

Chapter Eighteen

The crowd had increased from two to three deep at the bar, so I figured some of them were waiting on a table. I didn't want to take up valuable real estate longer than we had to, and besides, two musicians had begun their set at a volume that made it difficult to hear anything Charles was saying. Much of what he had to say could go without hearing, but occasionally he would impart something important.

I yelled over the music, "Ready to go?"

"What?"

That answered my question whether Charles knew it or not. I waved for Bobbie to bring the check, paid, and pointed to the stairs leading off the patio. Charles followed me down the stairs and to West Arctic Avenue.

"You ready to head home or want to walk up Center Street?"

He didn't answer until we'd walked a block and were standing in front of the Sand Dollar, Folly's iconic private bar where membership was limited to people who could afford a one-dollar membership fee. Four Harley's were parked diagonally in front of the bar and a man was seated on the bench near the entry. He was holding a leash with an aging brown and white pit bull on the other end. The dog looked as exhausted as its owner.

Of course, Charles had to squat to pet the dog and say a few words only he and the pit bull understood. One belly rub later, Charles said goodbye to the dog, stood, and said, "Well, where're we headed?"

"It's early so I thought we could walk up Center Street and enjoy the music."

On any given night in the summer, bands and solo musicians could be heard playing their brands of music from several restaurant patios and decks.

Charles said, "What're we waiting for?"

Which I translated as he'd love to walk with me. At Folly's sole traffic light at the corner of Center and Ashley, we stopped to listen to competing bands from Coconut Joe's and across the street from the rooftop bar at Snapper Jack's.

A familiar voice coming from behind us said, "You two are doing what I spend a bunch of time doing every day."

I turned and said, "Evening, Virgil."

Charles said, "What are we doing that you spend so much time doing every day?"

He looked at the traffic signal. "Watching it change from red, to green, to yellow, to red, to——"

"That's fascinating," I said not wanting to see how many color changes he was going to relive. "We were on our way up the street enjoying the music."

"Holy moly, that sounds more exciting than watching the light change. Mind if I tag along?"

Charles said, "You're always welcome."

Virgil glanced at me, probably wondering if the decision was unanimous. I nodded. A block later, we were walking side-by-side in front of the gift shop Native.

Virgil put an arm around each of our waists and said, "Who could've guessed, the crime fighting trio is back together?"

When I first met Virgil, he'd proclaimed Charles and me to being a crime fighting duo, with no encouragement from Charles or me, I should add. Since he'd been a financial analyst before he lost everything, math was one of his strengths, so, again with no encouragement, he added himself to the duo and came up with trio.

I'd learned it'd serve no purpose to try to correct his analysis, so I said, "Anyone up to a drink?"

Virgil, who now lived in perpetual poverty, said, "You buying?"

Charles, who lived as a perpetual bum, said, "Chris is."

I said, "Where?"

"Planet Follywood," Virgil said. "I like their back-in-the-old-days vibe."

We crossed the street and entered the long, narrow restaurant. I wouldn't have put it like Virgil had, but there was no doubt the restaurant had the feel of the classic beach bar. The aroma of long-eaten fries remained in the air. Colorful murals drew attention to the walls and posters promoting future events competed with posters for long-past happenings. Loud music was coming from the patio out back, so I suggested we remain inside so we could hear each other rather than compete with the rock music outside. Four seats were vacant at the bar at the back of the room. We took three of them. Two men were watching a rerun of a television show from the nineties, the sound muted. Charles and Virgil opted for beers; I stuck with white wine. It didn't take Virgil long to get to what I figured the real reason for wanting to tag along.

"Guys, where are we on catching the killer, or is that killers?"

"Funny you should ask," Charles said. "We shared a meal with the guy who killed both of them."

"Wow! You tell the cops? They arrest him? How'd you figure it out?" He hesitated. "Oh yeah, who is it?"

I deferred to Charles to figure out the questions, and the answers.

Charles looked at me, then turned to Virgil as our drinks arrived. "Umm, no. We haven't told the cops."

Virgil took a drag off his beer before saying, "Why not?"

This time I didn't wait for Charles. "Because we don't know who killed the two people. We don't know for sure they were murdered."

"Of course, we know they were," Charles said. "The police know it. Your good buddy Brad Burton knows it. And we, okay, I know it."

"Holy moly, Detective Charles, don't keep me in suspense. Who did it?"

"Raymond Whitley, slam-dunk case."

"Whitley, Whitley," Virgil said. "He kin to the lady killed?"

"Her husband."

"Ah, that explains it. Everyone knows the spouse is always the leading suspect. How'd you figure it out?"

Good question, I thought. I looked forward to Charles's slam-dunk answer.

I'd have to wait. The man seated to our right paid and slid off the stool. Two men then took the next two vacant seats. I recognized them and whispered to Charles not to say anything else about the deaths.

Of course, I received an exasperated sigh and, "Why not?"

Instead of answering, I leaned back and turned to the newcomers. "Hey, Scott, Tim."

The men glanced my direction, started to speak, but I could tell they didn't recognize me.

"I'm Chris, Chief LaMond introduced us the other day on the side of the street."

"Oh yeah," Tim said. "You're the old guy she teased about walking to the County Park."

"Whoa, Tim, Chris ain't that old."

Thank you, Scott, I thought.

Tim said, "Yeah, you said that because you're nearly as old as Chris."

Charles had enough age talk. "Tim, Scott, I'm Charles. The other guy here is Virgil. Nice meeting you."

Virgil smiled at the newcomers, and said, "Want a drink? We're buying."

"Sure," Tim said.

Virgil motioned the bartender over and told her to put Tim and Scott's drinks on "our" tab.

She left to get their drinks, and Charles said, "You two are working on the new house out West Ashley?"

Scott said, "Umm, yes. How'd you know?"

"Chris and I were out there when the lady, what's her name, Chris?"

"Shelly," I said, knowing Charles knew her name.

"Yeah, Shelly. We were there when she was killed."

Scott said, "What do you mean killed?"

"I hear someone pushed her off the roof."

"No way. Everyone working out there knows she slipped. Tragic accident, nothing more."

Charles said, "That right, Tim?"

"Makes sense. That roof has a dangerous pitch to it. Easy to slip. So sad."

Virgil must've felt left out, he pointed his drink at the newcomers, then said, "I hear her husband may've had something to do with her death."

Scott said, "Don't know about that, but I'll tell you he's a damned prick."

"I agree," Charles said. "We just had supper with him."

"Oh," Scott said. "He a friend of yours?"

"Just met him. What about the foremen. Think he was murdered?"

"Nah," Scott said. "Another unfortunate accident."

Virgil said, "What do you think, Tim?"

"Have no reason to think it wasn't an accident. It is getting to me, though."

Charles said, "What is?"

"Starting to scare me to go to work there. Two accidents in less than a week. Two dead coworkers. Not that I believe it, you know, but someone out there told me there's something wrong with the house. Cursed, he said."

Charles said, "Who said it was cursed?"

"Don't recall, for sure. There's a lot of talk going around. Guys are starting to think who's next? Damned scary."

Scott said, "Foolish talk. You're young, you'll learn some day that things happen. Don't need no reason. No such thing as cursed houses."

"Hope you're right," Tim said. "Enough house talk. You guys come here often?"

"Occasionally," Charles said. "You two live over this way?"

"Not far off-island," Scott said.

Tim said, "James island. Little farther away than Scott. How about you guys?"

We each told them versions of living on Folly. They then asked what we did. We answered and I figured they were tired of talking about the deaths and the cursed house. They finished their beers and I thought they were going to order another, but instead, Scott said they'd better be going.

After they left, Virgil returned to his question to Charles, the one about how he figured the husband was the killer. Charles outlined his weak case against Raymond. Virgil must have thought it was as weak as I did.

He said, "Sounds possible."

Charles stared at him. "He did it. Mark my words."

Virgil said, "Sure it isn't because the house is cursed?"

"Of course, it isn't, unless you count it's cursed by a murderer running around bumping off workers."

"Suppose it's up to us to find out what kind of curse," Virgil said.

Charles said, "You bet."

I changed the subject, and the deaths weren't mentioned again. At least, not tonight.

Chapter Nineteen

After having supper with Raymond Whitley, then talking with Scott Rawlins and Tim Hale at Planet Follywood, I didn't have a better idea what'd happened to Shelly Whitley and Randy Lee than I had before the evening. Charles, often quick to jump to conclusions, claimed Raymond had killed both his wife and Randy based on the financial gain he may achieve. The problem with that theory is that it may be a reason for Raymond to have killed Shelly but doesn't explain Randy's death. Money, of course, was often a motive for murder, but it seemed to me there was one significant flaw in that thinking about Shelly, and the same being true about Randy's death. There was no proof that either person had been murdered. I wasn't a judge or jury, but it seemed like that would be a hole large enough to float the aircraft carrier Yorktown through in the prosecution of anyone for murder.

With my mind focused on the lack of proof, I realized

it'd been several days since I talked to Barb Deanelli, the lady I'd been dating the last few years.

I couldn't solve whatever was going on with the deaths, but I could do something about talking with Barb. She owned Barb's Books, a used bookstore located on Center Street. The mild August weather was hanging around, so the three-block walk to the store would let me see Barb, plus would give me some exercise.

The tingling of the bell over the entry door announced my arrival at the attractive, neat, and welcoming bookstore. Barb wasn't behind the counter and it took a few seconds before she stepped out of the small office behind the sales area. Barb was four years younger than me, my height, and thinner—much thinner.

"Hello, stranger. I figured you'd run off with a young, sexy chickadee."

I smiled. "You're describing yourself. Why would I want to run off with someone else?"

She returned my smile. "You've been hanging around some of your friends too long. The ones who have trouble recognizing the truth. Anyway, what brings you in this morning? I know it's not to buy a book."

"To see you. You're right, it's been a while and I wanted to rectify that situation."

"Could I entice you with a cup of coffee?"

"Absolutely."

I followed Barb to the well-appointed, professional appearing office which could pass for an attorney's office, which made sense since she'd been a successful attorney in Pennsylvania prior to moving to Folly. She fixed each of us a cup of coffee before moving her chair close to the door so she could keep an eye on arriving customers.

She took a sip of her drink then said, "Anything exciting going on in the life of a retiree?"

"Did you hear about a construction worker falling off a roof at a construction site out West Ashley Avenue?"

"I'd be an abject failure and humiliated as a Folly resident if I hadn't heard of it. Why?"

"Charles and I were walking by the house when it happened."

She frowned. "Why does that not surprise me? Did you happen to be by the same house a few days later when another worker was electrocuted?"

"No."

"I'm shocked, no pun intended. How did that slip past you and your friend?"

I shrugged and smiled. "It happened past my bedtime."

She took another sip, looked toward the front of the store, then said, "I heard a couple of things about the deaths. Someone said they suspected foul play, but most people figure they were accidents. Let me guess. Charles thinks they were murdered?"

"Why think that?"

"Simple. Charles thinks all deaths that happen in the 29439 ZIP Code are murders."

"You can add these two to the list."

"Do you agree?"

"I'm not nearly as certain as Charles, but they appear suspicious."

"Why?"

I shared what'd been said about Shelly's husband's desire to benefit financially and how Randy was a licensed electrician and how unlikely it seemed he would make such a fatal mistake around electricity. I also said it struck me as suspicious that the deaths came so close together considering the small number of overall employees on the job.

Barb listened patiently, something I wasn't used to from my friends, took another sip, then said, "If I was still an attorney defending someone accused of killing those two people, I'd shred those arguments quicker than a wood chipper can shred a twig."

"I don't disagree. All I'm saying is it appears suspicious."

"What do the police think?"

The doorbell stepped on an answer.

"Hold that answer. I'll be back."

Three minutes later, she returned, shook her head, and said, "She wanted two books on this week's bestseller list. I didn't have either. Said she'll have to order them online."

"Sorry. What was your question again?"

"What do the police think about the deaths?"

"They're leaning toward accidental."

"And they have the resources to investigate, collect evidence, analyze items that may give them clues to what happened."

I knew where she was going with her well-constructed reasons for me to leave it to the law enforcement authorities.

"Yes."

"Do you have anything, anything remotely applicable, indicating the police are wrong?"

I started to tell her about Brad Burton's suspicions but

decided this wasn't the appropriate time to bring him up. She knew my history with the former detective.

"You're right."

She chuckled. "Of course, I am."

"You said you'd heard a couple of things about the deaths. What was the other thing?"

"You do listen. I'm impressed. There's a story going around that the job site, or the house that's being built, is jinxed or cursed."

"Who said that?"

"Heard it from three customers, but it could be that only one person is saying it and the others are simply repeating the rumor."

"Do they really believe it's cursed?"

"Two of them laughed it off. The other one said she's certain it's true."

"Based on what?"

"No idea. I didn't ask. I'm not a believer in cursed buildings." She smiled. "If I was, I never would have moved into this space your gallery failed in."

"Thanks a lot."

She leaned over and planted a kiss on my cheek, and said, "You're welcome."

The bell over the door chimed.

"I'd better get to work, unlike those of us who spend all their time slaving over retirement."

I walked her to the front of the store and told her I'd talk to her later.

She said, "Great. Try not to get yourself killed."

Chapter Twenty

On my way home from Barb's Books, a black Dodge Ram pickup truck pulled beside me. The passenger side window rolled down and the driver said, "Hey, stranger, want a ride?"

The driver wasn't a stranger. I'd met Imani Marshall, aka Noelle Ward, two Christmases ago when she'd been one of the residents in a small, decaying apartment building that'd been torched by an arsonist. She's African American, thin, with a short afro haircut. After the fire, Barb had generously invited Noelle to stay in her condo until she found somewhere to rent.

"Sure," I said and slid in the passenger seat. I hadn't seen her more than twice since she moved out of Barb's unit after staying three months.

She said, "Where're you headed?"

"Home."

She smiled and looked over at me, or I assumed I was

the subject of her gaze, although I couldn't tell since she wore oversized sunglasses. "In a hurry to get there?"

"No."

"I'm headed out to the old Coast Guard property. Want to tag along?"

The Lighthouse Inlet Heritage Preserve, commonly called the old Coast Guard property, is at the east end of the island and is one of Folly's most popular attractions. It offers visitors an unobstructed view of the Morris Island Lighthouse that was decommissioned in 1962.

"Sounds good. Seems like forever since I've seen you. How's your new apartment?"

"Perfect, it's the dump I was looking for."

I smiled. "I don't often hear that."

Noelle has a well-paying job with an advertising agency in downtown Charleston but is writing her first novel and wanted to live on Folly so she could become immersed in the environment of a small, barrier island, similar to the imaginary island in Georgia where the novel is set. To get in character, she had gone so far as to purchase a nine-year-old Dodge Ram like her protagonist and moved to an apartment that would be considered by some, meager, or in her words, a dump.

"True."

"Why're you heading to the Preserve?"

"Research. I've got Gabriel slinking around in a large coastal park like the Preserve while he's looking for the bad guys."

"Gabriel is the teenager who told your private eye that he saw bank robbers, but the police didn't believe him."

She turned and faced me again. "Wow! You remembered that after what, two years?"

"A little less than that, but yes, you're the only novelist I know, so I remembered much of what you told me. How's the book coming?"

When we first met, Noelle confided that she was in the process of writing a novel, in fact, that's why she wanted to go by Noelle rather than Imani. She'd told me potential readers were more likely to choose a book if the author was Noelle. I couldn't remember the last time I'd read a novel, so had no reason to doubt her logic.

"Well, I don't think you can call me a novelist until I write a novel. I'm two-thirds through the draft. All I need to do now is figure out how the PI Gabriel hired is going to catch the bad guys."

"That going to be a problem?"

She laughed. "Nah. I'm an ad writer; spend my workdays making up stuff about products. Surly, I can make up a good ending."

We were approaching the end of East Ashley Avenue where it dead-ended at the entrance to the Preserve and Noelle started looking for somewhere to park. In season, traffic looking for places to park outnumbered legal parking spots and was always a challenge for those wishing to visit the Preserve. We turned around at the end of the street and drove a couple of blocks back Ashley Avenue and pulled off on the sandy berm in front of two houses. The temperature had to be in the upper eighties, and I was beginning to sweat as we walked toward the Preserve. Noelle had to be hotter in her black T-shirt and black jeans, but she didn't mention it. Being in her early thirties probably helped.

We walked past the stanchions blocking unauthorized vehicles from entering the Preserve, when Noelle said, "Heard something about you and your friend, umm, Charles, right?"

"Yes, it's Charles. What'd you hear?"

"You're playing like my imaginary PI and snooping around in the death of those two folks working on a house being built."

"Where'd you hear that?"

"A friend of mine works out there. Name's Mason."

"Mason Ryle?"

"One and the same."

"How do you know him?"

"Ran into him a couple of times at the Crab Shack. We're about the same age so we started talking." She chuckled. "He was doing a little flirting. I figured I'd get some ideas on having a character like him in the book, so I played along."

"You're dating?"

She tilted her head left and then right. "He thinks so, but not really."

In the spirit of Charles, I said, "What's that mean?"

"I've met him a few more times at the Crab Shack and at Rita's. Had a couple of drinks, that's all. Never left the restaurants with him if you know what I mean. He thinks he's a lot more charming than he is. More smarm than charm. He'll be perfect as a character in my book."

That sounded like the Mason I'd heard about who'd hit on Shelly.

"What'd he say about us other than we'd been snooping around?"

She stopped, looked off to the right, and said, "Let's go that way."

I followed her down a narrow path headed toward the ocean. I was going to repeat my question, when she said, "Mason said you and Charles were at the job site when the lady fell, then you'd been talking to the foreman, don't know his name, but he was the guy who died a few days after the lady."

"Randy Lee."

"Sounds right. Mason also said you'd talked to one of his coworkers with a girlfriend named Zellner. I don't remember the guy's name but remembered hers because it's a horrible name. Guess it's the ad copy writer in me, but I wouldn't use names like it in my book."

"His name's Kyle."

"That's a better name. Mason said a couple of the others said you'd talked to them. Seems that none of them liked you butting into their business."

"Did Mason say why it bothered them?"

She nodded. "He said it looked like you were thinking the deaths weren't accidents, like the police said."

"So, why'd that bother them? Wouldn't they want to know if someone killed two of their coworkers? Wouldn't they want the murderer caught?"

We'd reached where the path opened to a wide, sandy

beach. Noelle looked each direction and stared at the ocean as if she were taking a mental picture.

"Is this what you came to see?"

"Yes. Got a perfect scene in the book for this spot."

"Good," I said, not knowing what else to say.

She removed her sunglasses and wiped sweat off her forehead then returned the glasses to her face. "Seems to me the guys don't want you looking into what happened out there because one of them, or maybe more than one of them, may've been involved in the deaths." She shook her head. "Mind you, I've got a vivid imagination, and I could be looking at it from the point of view of someone trying to create a mystery where there's not one."

"So could Charles and I." *Especially Charles*, I thought.

She tapped me on the arm. "I know from experience, if there's a killer out there, a real one, not one in my imagination, you and your buddy will figure it out."

"I don't know about that."

She chuckled, took a couple of photos of the beach with her cell phone, and said, "Yes you do. I told you so. Ready to head back to the big city?"

"Whenever you are. I'm just tagging along."

As we walked back to her truck, she said, "Seen Barb lately?"

"I was coming from her store when you kidnapped me."

"Hum, there's a plot in there somewhere. Maybe that'll be in my second novel."

"Good."

She unlocked the truck's doors, shook her head, and

said, "Suppose I have to write the first one before I start talking about the second book."

She pulled in my drive, turned to me, and said, "If I can offer a suggestion, be careful out there. My extensive research on killers says if someone kills two people, killing number three comes pretty easy."

Chapter Twenty-One

I'd managed to push the deaths to the back of my mind and was enjoying a peaceful meal at Snapper Jack's Seafood Restaurant and Bar until I noticed Scott Rawlins at a table at the far side of the room seated with someone who looked vaguely familiar. Scott looked my way, smiled, then gave a tentative wave. I returned the smile and nodded at him.

I'd refocused my attention back to my food and was gazing at the television above the backbar when Scott approached.

I smiled and said, "Scott."

"Thought that was you," he said as we shook hands. "Heard anything more about the deaths at our construction site?"

"No," I said thinking it was a strange question to ask someone he barely knew. "Why, did something else happen?"

"No, nothing like that. Mason and I were talking about it, so it was on my mind."

I looked at Scott's dinner companion, and it dawned on me where I'd seen him. "Is that Mason Ryle?"

"Yeah. We were putting in overtime and finished after everyone else, so thought we'd grab a bite before heading home." He looked over his shoulder at Mason before turning back to me. "You sure you haven't heard anything new about the deaths?"

Even if I had, it wouldn't have been a good idea to share it with Scott or any of the other workers who might've had something to do with the deaths.

"No," I said for the second time. "Why do you ask?"

"Nothing really. We were talking about how weird it was that two of the crew died so close together. Mason thinks there's some sort of curse on the house. He's not the only one. One of the other guys don't think it's the house but something about the old house that was on the property."

The curse on the house had been mentioned but this was the first time I'd heard about the previous house.

"Who mentioned the old house?"

"Don't recall. Could've been Lucius Walker."

"Why Lucius?"

Scott chuckled. "He's shared ghost stories with some of us. Think he believes in that kind of crap. I don't." He again looked back at his table. "Don't want to interrupt your meal. Better get back to my food. Good talking to you."

We shared a couple more pleasantries before he returned to his meal with Mason. My peaceful meal of not thinking about the deaths had ended. This was what, the second or third time someone had brought up the house being cursed? I didn't believe in curses, but at this point, it made as much sense as two fatal accidents at the house under construction. What was I missing?

I finished my meal as Scott and Mason headed to the exit where they went opposite directions. I wasn't far behind and nearly collided with Mason.

"Sorry," I said. "Wasn't paying attention to where I was going."

"No biggie, happens all the time at work."

"You're Mason Ryle?"

"Yeah, and you're Chris Landry. Scott and me were talking about you in there." He pointed his thumb to the restaurant we just left.

"Chris Landrum," I corrected. "Something good, I hope."

He shrugged. Not a good sign about what they were saying about me.

His shrug appeared to be the end of his comments, so I said, "I remember seeing you at your worksite the day Shelly Whitley fell."

"Bad day."

I waited for more, but he stopped and stared at me. Foot traffic was heavy on Center Street, so I inched around the corner to the side of the restaurant to get out of the way of a group of vacationers waiting for the traffic light to change so they could cross Ashley Avenue. Mason didn't say anything but did come with me.

I said, "Noelle Ward, a friend of mine, told me she knows you."

He came close to smiling but failed. "Yeah, we're dating. How do you know her?"

Not her version of their relationship, but I wasn't about to challenge him. "We met a couple of years ago. I met her after her apartment building burned."

His gaze narrowed. "So, it's true what they say about you."

I smiled hoping to receive a similar response from him. "Depends on what they say."

"You're a busybody, nosing in other people's business." His gaze turned to a stare.

How do I respond?

"I don't know what you're referring to."

"Word around the job is you're butting in, trying to talk to all us guys. Throwing accusations around that instead of accidents causing Shelly and Randy's deaths, you're stirring up rumors they were murdered." His hands balled into fists. "Then you're saying they were not only murdered, but one of the crew, one of us, did it."

"I don't know who's saying that, but I'm doing no such thing. I do know some people, even a police officer or two, who are thinking the deaths look like too big a coincidence to be accidents."

"You saying you don't have a reputation around town as being the busybody who caught the guy who left a body in a boat a few months back?"

"I'm not denying that. All I'm saying is I have no reason to think the deaths on your job site are anything other than accidents. If they weren't accidents, I have faith the police will figure out what happened. If it turns out the workers were murdered, the person or persons responsible will be caught."

He pointed a finger in my face, took a deep breath, and said, "I'm telling you one thing, it's none of your damn business what happened and I'm not the only person thinking that. You can call it whatever you want, but don't be nosing around any of us." He stomped his foot on the pavement, turned, and left me staring at his back as he headed west on Ashley Avenue.

Chapter Twenty-Two

What brought that on? I was clueless, but if nothing else, it piqued my interest in learning more about what was going on with the guys working on the new house. If Mason's goal was to get me too, as he said, stop nosing around the construction workers, he'd failed—failed badly. If anything, I was more determined than ever to find out what was going on.

It was still early, so I decided walking up Center Street would either help me get my mind off the strange conversation with Mason or change my focus enough to allow some incredible insight into the deaths to reach my consciousness. I also smiled to myself when I realized the true reason was to enjoy the walk.

Charles wasn't with me, so I didn't have to stop and converse with each canine I encountered. Three blocks later, I'd crossed Center Street and was in front of Woody's Pizza and surprised to see Brad Burton on the restaurant's deck leaning against the railing separating it from the sidewalk. Brad was by far the oldest of the dozen or so patrons huddled on the deck and looked as out of place as a Chihuahua in a horse show. He was drinking a Palmetto Amber Ale while staring at the street like he was watching a movie.

"Hey, Brad," I said as I stepped on the deck and moved beside him.

"Oh, hi. Have a slice."

One slice of what appeared to be a pepperoni pizza and remnants of two other slices were on a plate in front of him and a glob of tomato sauce on the front of his 1988 Cooper River Bridge Run T-shirt that was stretched to the limit around his midsection. I'd wager my house he'd not participated in the 1988 or any other 10-kilometer bridge run.

"Thanks, but I had supper at Snapper Jack's. Did Hazel throw you out?"

He laughed. "Not this time. She's gone to Charleston with a friend. They're having supper at Peninsula Grille, and I'm having an exquisite meal at Woody's. Sure you don't want this slice? I need it like I need an IRS audit."

I again declined but was glad to see he was in a relaxed, talkative mood, something I'd seldom, if ever seen from him.

"Know what I was thinking about when you walked up?"

The small area was getting more crowded the longer we talked. It'd be nice to move somewhere where we could hear each other better, but Brad appeared glued to the stool he was perched on.

"No, but I noticed you were staring off into space like something was on your mind."

"Was thinking about what Hazel's said about me needing a hobby. I think I told you the hobby wasn't for me, but to get me out of the house."

"Yes, you shared that. Decided on one?"

"Chris, I spent more years being a cop than I'd like to admit. Never got into golf, or playing cards, or bowling, or, hell, anything else that'd be considered a hobby." He took a sip, looked at the uneaten slice of pizza, then back at me. "All I know is police work."

The crowd noise made it difficult hearing everything he said, but I didn't detect him mentioning a hobby he wanted to pursue.

"I can understand that. So, what—"

He pointed the beer bottle at me and said, "I've been thinking that since all I know is being a cop, why not use some of those skills looking at the deaths out at that new house?"

That was the last thing I'd expected him to say, and it left me momentarily without a response. After all, I couldn't count the times Brad had berated me for sticking my nose in police work, rudely reminding me police business is for the police, not some busybody civilian.

"When you were a detective, you accused me of meddling in police business, pointed out it was not my business, and more. Isn't that what you're talking about doing?"

He gave me what I call a police stare, or in this case, a former police stare. I was afraid he would erupt and revert to the old cop he'd been. I rationalized that he probably wouldn't yell at me on the crowded patio. On the other hand, with the sound level as high as it was, I doubt anyone would notice if he did.

Instead of yelling, he looked around, finished his drink, and said, "Up for a walk? If I sit here longer, I'll eat this slice and regret it in the morning."

"Sure."

I followed him off the deck and another block up Center Street to the Folly Beach branch of the Charleston County Public Library where he pointed to a bench by the front door. The library was closed so this would be a quiet a spot for us to talk.

"Chris," he said, as I joined him on the bench, "I'm not talking about going Rambo and trying to catch the bad guys. I don't even know if there are bad guys. But after decades on the job, I've learned enough to tell when someone is trying to pull something over on me, or to see patterns where most civilians wouldn't. Some of that could possibly assist the police." He stared across the street at Our Lady of Good Counsel Catholic Church.

I didn't want to point out that wasn't much different than what I'd been berated for, so I said, "There's no doubt you were an outstanding detective, and could provide valuable assistance, but is that what you really want to do as a hobby?"

He smiled. "I haven't forgotten how I almost arrested you the first time we met, or how I accused you of doing exactly what I'm suggesting on more than one occasion. I also know you think I was slovenly in performing my duties during that time."

"That's not—"

He no longer had a beer bottle to point at me; instead, he held his hand in front of my face, palm facing me. "In hindsight, you were right. Those last years, I was going through the motions, nothing more. If I'd been my boss, I would've fired me." He again looked at the church. "When we were in your kitchen, I said it seemed strange that there were two deaths at that house mere days apart. I think I shared that if I'd investigated what'd happened when I was working, it'd keep me awake at night." He again hesitated.

"Is it bothering you now?"

"A bunch. Remember when we saw Randy Lee at Cal's?"

I nodded.

"He said something about how one of the other guys had been acting strange after the woman's death."

"Mason Ryle," I said, since he was fresh on my mind after my confrontation with him earlier tonight.

"Yeah, Ryle."

"Randy also said the woman's husband came around threatening to sue over her death."

"Yes."

"I also remember saying that night that it didn't appear to be unusual enough to classify the death anything other than an accident."

"Yes, but—"

"That's what I would've said my last few years on the job. I was stuck with several murders, pressured to wrap them up as fast as possible. Her death would've been easy to close as an accident. One less case to worry about."

"That's what the police are saying now."

"I understand where they're coming from, but now we have Randy's electrocution. Chris, it doesn't compute."

"I mentioned earlier that I had supper at Snapper Jack's. Two of the guys from the construction site, Mason Ryle and Scott Rawlins, were there. I'd never met Mason, Scott came to my table to say hi and told me who he was with, so I introduced myself after we'd finished eating and were out on the street. Scott had already gone, so I was standing with Mason. I didn't ask him anything about what'd happened at the house, but he suddenly turned borderline hostile. He accused me of butting into the business of some of the construction workers and claiming the two deaths weren't accidents. I'm not certain why, but he was angry."

Brad smiled. "Sounds familiar."

I returned his smile. "True, but he then came close to threatening me to stay away from them. The point is, even if I were butting in, why would Mason have reacted so strongly?"

"I'm no expert on the topic but have faced countless hostile suspects. I'm no shrink, but my antenna told me the ones who get the most hostile are often guilty. Is there any reason you know of to accuse Mason of the deaths?"

"Nothing you'd call evidence. We've heard he'd hit on Shelly only to be rejected. Plus, Randy said Mason was acting strange after Shelly's death. Finally, Mason was one of the two guys who found Randy's body, although that could've been a coincidence."

"That's all pretty sketchy; nothing I could hang an arrest on."

"True."

"It's a start," he said and looked at his watch. "I'd better head home. Wouldn't want Hazel thinking my new hobby was barhopping."

"That'd definitely get you out of the house."

He smiled and said, "Out of the house and into the doghouse." He stood to leave, turned to me, and added, "Tell you what. Why don't you let me know if you hear anything that could get us off sketchy and closer to an arrest?"

I said I would and watched him amble down Center Street.

A while back, I'd gotten to know a Wiccan family that'd moved to Folly. Their sixteen-year-old son Desmond and his dog had saved Charles's and my life. After that, Desmond told me he'd bet I never thought I'd be friends with a witch. That paled in comparison to having Brad Burton as a friend.

Chapter Twenty-Three

My day began with the sun gazing through the slats in my bedroom shades and Charles on the phone saying, "Guess who I ran into last night?"

"The President of Botswana," I said, suspecting I was wrong.

"You're a sucky guesser."

"Who?"

"You."

"You ran into me?"

"No, you're the sucky guesser."

I wiped sleep out of my eyes, sighed louder than I should have, and said, "Who did you run into last night?'

"Thought you'd never ask. Tim Hale."

It took me a few seconds to remember who that was. I blamed it on still being asleep. "And you're calling before seven a.m. to tell me because?"

"Splash water on your face, wake up, before you head to the Dog, and I'll answer your question."

I hung up on him.

Twenty minutes later, I was sitting at a table in the Dog and staring at Charles stuffing a half-slice of toast in his mouth while shaking his head in disgust at me for taking, in his words, *two hours* to get there. Amber had wisely handed me a mug of coffee before I reached the table and asked if I wanted my normal breakfast. I told her of course. She sighed, but not as loud as I had on the phone with Charles and went to place my order.

"Where did you run into Tim Hale?" I asked to move our conversation past me being Charles-late.

"I was minding my own business sitting at an outside table at the Crab Shack enjoying the music. I saw Tim, remember, we talked to him and Scott at Planet Follywood?"

"Yes."

"Well, I went over to say howdy."

I had trouble getting past Charles claiming he was minding his own business, but it wouldn't do any good saying anything about it, so I said, "Was he by himself?"

"Was until I said howdy. He didn't argue when I invited myself to join him. He was a little standoffish at first. Normal, I suppose since he'd only seen me once. Anyway, I told him again how sorry I was for the loss of his coworkers."

"What'd he say?"

"He'd miss Shelly."

"Did you mention you thought she was murdered?"

"Nah, I didn't want him to think I was accusing him. Think I said she slipped."

"Were they close?"

"Don't think so. Didn't ask, but when he was talking about her, umm, accident, he didn't tear up. He did say her husband was a jerk, but we already knew that."

Amber slipped my French toast in front of me and refilled my mug. She asked if we needed anything else. Charles said he was okay.

I said I was fine and after she headed to the next table, I said, "What'd he say about Randy Lee's death?"

"He was more emotional about that than what happened to Shelly. Guess Randy hired Tim when they started building the house."

"Did he think anything was suspicious about the deaths being close together?"

Charles smiled. "Yep, thinks the house is cursed. Think he told us that at Follywood. Think he's afraid to work there."

"Did he say he was afraid?"

"Said he'd quit the job if he didn't need the money."

That's two or three workers who've said the house was cursed.

"Why does he think it's cursed?"

"Told me he grew up in the Lowcountry, not far from here, he said. Told me he wasn't sure but had heard Charleston and the surrounding area has the most hauntings anywhere in the country. Don't know about that, but he believes it." Charles chuckled. "Think I could've said boo and he would've jumped out of his britches."

"I know Charleston is saturated with ghost tours, but why would a house under construction have ghosts or a curse on it?"

"There's still hope for you as a private detective. I asked him the same question."

"What'd he say?"

"He didn't know."

I took a sip of coffee then smiled. "Takes a mighty good private detective to get that much information out of him."

"Smartass."

"Yep."

I felt someone pat me on the shoulder.

"You talking about me?"

"Hey, Virgil," Charles said. "Why would we be talking about you?"

"Heard you say smartass, so I came to mind."

I laughed. "Not this time. Care to join us?"

"Hoped you'd ask." He took a seat and waved for Amber.

"Morning, Virgil," she said. "Coffee?"

"Miss Amber, you bringing me a cup of your fabulous elixir would make my day."

Maybe Charles's smartass comment referred to Virgil after all.

She left to conjure up his elixir and Virgil said, "Still think Shelly's evil husband killed her now that the other guy bit the dust?"

Charles said, "What do you think?"

"Course I'm not as good a detective as you two but did

until what's his name got himself killed. Now, don't know. Either of you know Mitchell Baldwin?"

"Carpenter on the house," I said.

Virgil said, "That's the one."

Charles said, "I already forgot about him. You're the one with the bad memory. How'd you remember him?"

"I wouldn't have if Dude hadn't called him Mitchell Piano."

Virgil took off his sunglasses, a rare event, rubbed his eyes, returned the glasses to their rightful place, then said, "What are you two talking about?"

I said, "It's not important. What about Mitchell?"

"I was at Loggerhead's last night, enjoying a brewski. Abel bought it for me, generous guy."

Charles, of course, couldn't let that bit of trivia go. "Who's Abel?"

"That's not the important part of my story. Abel had to get home to his wife and his Pekinese pup, so I was—"

Charles interrupted, "What's the pup's name?"

Virgil pointed his mug at Charles. "Still not the important part of my story."

Charles said, "Continue."

"Thanks. Anyway, Mitchell plopped down on the stool Abel vacated to go home to his pup, the one I don't know the name of." He turned and looked at Charles.

"Did Mitchell have anything to say about the deaths?" I said, hoping to drag the conversation back to something more interesting than the name of a dog none of us had seen.

"Mitchell's not a big talker. Charles, he's in his early

twenties so he might not have enough accumulated in all his years to have much to say. I had to use all my interrogation skills you taught me to get anything out of him."

Charles smiled like Virgil had awarded him a gold medal for private detecting, and said, "Got an answer to Chris's question?"

"I'm getting there."

His arrival would have to wait a few minutes longer. Amber returned with Virgil's elixir, aka coffee, and asked if he wanted anything to eat. He looked over at me and shrugged, his way of asking if I was buying. I nodded, he told her a breakfast burrito, and she left to seat a couple who were waiting by the door.

Charles said, "Virgil—"

"I know, I know," Virgil interrupted. "Mitchell said the crew was getting antsy. None of them could come up with a story from another job they worked on where someone got killed at work, much less, two people. Said the owner of the construction company has been on the job site nearly every day since Randy was killed. He's trying to hold everything together; can't lose more workers."

"Does Mitchell think the deaths were accidents?"

"Said he wants to but wondered what the odds were on that happening. Heck, there were only a couple of handfuls of workers on the job. That's, umm, let's see, two out of, anyway, a good percentage of the entire work force out there."

Charles said, "If they weren't accidents, does he have an idea who may be responsible?"

"Nothing I'd call a big clue. He can't see any reason one

person would've killed both workers. Said they weren't close, didn't wave any red flags. But he couldn't figure out why two people would've killed them, especially on the same job."

Charles said, "He say anything about the crew thinking the house was cursed?"

"Said some of them believed it, but he doesn't believe in cursed houses, so he thinks the guys who do are full of crap."

Virgil's burrito arrived which ended any significant discussion about the deaths, assuming anything he'd said before was significant. I wouldn't wager much on it.

Chapter Twenty-Four

After our less-than-informative breakfast with Virgil, Charles and I walked to the end of the Folly Pier. I said it was to get exercise to work-off the needless calories I stuffed in my mouth at breakfast; Charles said it was to ponder what we'd learned and to figure out what was going on at the house under construction.

We'd commandeered one of the blue tables near the Atlantic end of the structure, when Charles said, "Did Virgil tell us anything about the deaths we didn't already know other than he couldn't calculate the percent of workers on the job that'd been killed?"

"The guys are getting antsy and more appear to think the house is cursed."

"All but Mitchell, the skeptic."

"Let's try this again. Did we learn anything other than the far-fetched idea that the house is cursed?"

"The owner of the construction company has been

there more than he was before the deaths. Think it means anything?"

I said, "I don't know what. My understanding is he has more than the West Ashley house under construction, so he'd be at the other job sites at different times."

"Yeah, but—"

The distinct siren of one of Folly's fire engines interrupted Charles. We couldn't see where it was going from our vantage point, but it sounded like it turned west on either Ashley or Arctic Avenue.

Charles laughed then said, "Guess they're heading to another death at the construction site." He then air quoted. "Accidental death."

I didn't see humor in his comment. A police patrol car followed the fire engine.

"Charles, that's nothing to joke about."

"You're right. Want to check it out?"

"If they're on Ashley, they could be going two miles to the end of the road. You ready to walk that far?"

"Putting it that way, no way. Stop avoiding my question, what'd we learn from Virgil that'll help us figure out who killed the workers?"

I thought we'd covered it already but knew he had something on his mind, or he wouldn't have brought it up again.

"Charles, what do you think Virgil said that'd help?"

"Heck if I know."

Okay, maybe he didn't have anything on his mind, something he'd been accused of more times than I can count.

Other than three seagulls on the top of the structure's

roof arguing about something, the next sound I heard was the approaching siren of an ambulance coming toward us on Center Street. It then turned west on one of the perpendicular streets.

Charles looked in the direction the ambulance had gone, turned to me, and said, "Now, ready to see what's going on?"

"It could be going miles."

"Okay, here's a plan. Let's walk up the beach, let's say, umm, to where Shelly fell off the roof. If all the commotion isn't happening there, we can head back."

That I could manage. "What're we waiting for?"

We worked our way from the Pier to the beach and traipsed west. There was no sign of emergency vehicles, smoke, or any other indication anything was wrong, that was until the construction site came into view.

Two guys wearing hardhats were being escorted to the edge of the property by one of Folly's Public Safety Officers, while at the side of the house, three firefighters were standing beside a red forklift. The object of their attention appeared between the forklift and the house.

Charles stopped and said, "You're right, I shouldn't have teased about another death out here."

"We don't know anyone is dead. Construction accidents happen all the time. The forklift could've run over someone's foot."

Two more construction workers appeared and were escorted to where the first two were standing. I recognized the latest arrivals as Kyle Manger and Tim Hale. The other two were facing the house so I couldn't tell who they were.

Charles said, "Are you going to stand here all day or go see whose foot got run over, or worse?"

He didn't wait for my answer. He started up the steps leading from the beach to the patio when Officer Rodney New intercepted him. He waited for me to catch up with Charles.

"Guys, please don't tell me you were walking on the beach, minding your own business, and got to this spot for the second time when something happened at this house."

"Rodney," I said, "we were on the Pier when we heard the sirens."

Charles interrupted, "I wanted to make sure nothing bad happened out here. We know a few of the workers and were concerned about them."

"Un, huh, sure, Charles," muttered the leery police officer.

I stepped between Rodney and Charles, if for no other reason, so he wouldn't kick us off the property before we found out what'd happened.

"Rodney, another accident?"

He shook his head, looked back at the forklift, and said, "Only if you think the forklift started on its own, put itself in reverse, and pinned a man between it and the wall."

Charles said, "Is he dead?"

Rodney again looked back toward the forklift, where two paramedics were lifting a stretcher and sliding it in the back of their ambulance, then turned to us. "No, but he's in bad shape. I'll be surprised if he makes it."

I said, "Do you know who it is?"

"Not sure. Heard one of the workers say Mason."

Charles said, "Mason Ryle?"

"Don't know, just heard Mason."

"Anyone see it happen?" I asked.

"You mean other than the person on the forklift?"

I nodded.

"I haven't talked to any of the workers over there with our guys. My understanding is they were off-site having lunch and when they got back, they found Mason behind the forklift."

Out of the corner of my eye, I saw Chief Cindy LaMond beside the forklift looking our direction. She said something to one of her firefighters and headed our way. Her expression was far from *glad to see you.*

"Officer New," Chief LaMond said, "go help the guys with the workers. I'll take care of these two."

Rodney headed to the gathered workers and Cindy focused on Charles and me.

"Mr. Landrum, Mr. Fowler, what in hell are you doing here?"

The only time she refers to us by our last names is when she's irritated or angry.

"Chief," Charles said, "we know some of the workers and when we heard your emergency vehicles headed this way, we wandered over to see if there was anything we could do to help."

"Touching," she said, "although I know that's a load of crap."

I said, "What happened?"

"Don't know for certain. One thing I do know, it wasn't an accident like the other deaths on this property."

Charles said, "You mean three non-accidents. Like as in murders."

Cindy glared at him, took one step closer to the two of us, and said, "Gentlemen, as I see it, I have two choices. I could arrest you for trespassing and pissing off a police chief, or I could politely ask you to shuffle down those stairs, savor the ocean breeze, and get your butts back to the center of town. Which choice do you think I should make?"

Charles said, "Chief LaMond, we'd love to stay and continue this cheery conversation, but Chris and I have to get, umm, somewhere. Don't want to be late."

"Wise choice, Mr. Fowler."

After we *shuffled* down the stairs, Charles looked at the house and said, "What time you think we ought to meet at Loggerhead's?"

"Silly me. I didn't even know we were meeting there."

"Who's there most every night?"

I could name several regulars, then the "correct" answer came to me. "Kyle Manger."

Charles smiled. "Gold star for aspiring detective Chris."

"Seven."

"Seven what?"

"Pay attention to your questions. That's when we're meeting at Loggers."

Chapter Twenty-Five

I arrived at Loggerhead's at six-thirty knowing Charles would already be there or arriving any second. The temperature was in the low eighties with a cloudless sky; the patio packed. While I didn't see always-early Charles, I found Kyle Manger leaning against the patio's railing staring at the beer in his hand. I maneuvered around a large group of young people I assumed to be college students since several were wearing University of Georgia T-shirts.

Kyle was still staring at his beer like it was the most fascinating thing he'd ever seen as I inched closer. He was still wearing his Donnelly Plumbing shirt and the dirt on his jeans made me think he'd been working under the house.

"Hey, Kyle."

That jarred him out of his trance. "Oh, hi, umm, hi."

"Chris."

"Sorry, I knew that. This has been one hell of a day."

"You okay?"

"Will be. I'm a lot better than Mason."

"My friend and I were out by the construction site today when all the commotion was going on. All we heard was a worker was injured. Was that Mason?"

"Thought it was you out there. Yeah, Mason Ryle was the—"

"Hi, Kyle," Charles said as he barged between us interrupting whatever Kyle was going to tell me.

"Kyle," I said, "you remember Charles?"

"Sure. Weren't you with Chris at the job site today?"

"Yeah," Charles said. "What happened?"

Kendra, one of the servers I'd known for a couple of years, patted me on the arm. "Chris, can I get you something to drink?"

Charles interrupted before I answered. "Kyle, you had supper?"

"No."

"Want to more genjoin Chris and me? Chris is buying."

"Sure, why not."

After Charles's generous invitation, I ordered a glass of white wine, Charles, a beer, and an even more generous Charles ordered another beer for Kyle. Kendra said she'd get our names on the list for a table and headed to the bar to get our drinks.

Charles said, "Kyle, you were telling us what happened."

"Like I told Chris, Mason Ryle was hurt, hurt bad, when the forklift backed up pinning him between the machine and the wall."

"That's horrible," Charles said like he hadn't already heard the same thing from Officer New. "How'd it happen? Don't those machines start beeping when they're backing up so anyone behind them can get out of the way?"

"Don't know what happened. The rest of the guys and I were off having lunch. And yes, they're not required, but the forklift out there has one of those irritating alarms beeping whenever it backs up."

I said, "Did anyone see the accident?"

"Someone must've."

"Who?" Charles said.

"Whoever was driving the forklift. It didn't back up on its own."

"Who was driving it?"

"Don't know."

Charles said, "You don't think it was an accident?"

"Don't see how it could've been."

Faux detective Charles said, "Did someone out there have a beef with Mason?"

"I wasn't close to him since we worked for different companies. He didn't strike me as the most likable fellow, but I don't know anyone who." He hesitated, snapped his fingers, and continued, "Shelly's husband was pissed with him."

"Because he'd been harassing or flirting with her?"

"Yeah."

Charles said, "Did you see Shelly's husband today?"

"No, but I wasn't near the house over lunch, so he could've been. I usually eat my energy bar with Joshua in his truck, but he wasn't there today. He's the other plumber on the job. This morning was frustrating because of a couple of plumbing issues, so I took a long walk on the beach during lunchtime."

I said, "Have you heard how Mason is?"

He shook his head. "All I know is he was unconscious when they loaded him in the ambulance."

Charles said, "That's too bad. Where was Joshua today?"

"Called in sick. That's why I was having such a hard time with the plumbing. Doing a job needing two guys by myself sucks." He shook his head. "It ain't as bad as getting squashed by a forklift."

Kendra arrived with our drinks, apologized for taking so long saying the bar was backed up, then added that our names were on the list for a table. We thanked her and Charles continued his interrogation.

"How come Mason didn't leave the job site for lunch?"

"He usually eats there. Has one of those big silver lunchboxes, you know, like you see old pictures of coal miners carrying to work. Don't know for sure but guess that's what he did today."

"What about the other guys?"

"Charles, you ask more questions than that damned detective."

"What detective?" Charles said, adding one more question.

"Young guy. Think his name was Fisher. He kept us from getting any work done for two hours, and even then, we couldn't go anywhere near the forklift. Some lab guys combed over the site like they were looking for gold."

Charles repeated, "What about the other guys?"

"What about them."

"What did they do during lunch hour?"

"How would I know. Like I said, I was walking on the beach and didn't see any of the others out there."

I could tell he was getting agitated with Charles, so I said, "Kyle, I know you didn't see where the others were, but we were wondering what they usually did during lunch." I smiled. "Most of us are creatures of habit and do the same thing most days."

Kyle glanced at Charles before turning to me. "Sorry guys, this has been a day for the freakin' record book. It's got me shook."

Charles put his arm on Kyle's shoulder. "I know what you mean. I've had more than one of those days lately. Chris is right about us doing the same stuff every day. What do the other guys normally do during lunch?"

Kyle took a long draw on his new beer, looked over the railing at the parking lot, then turned his attention back to Charles. "Lucius, he's the black guy, doesn't seem to be with any of us more than he has to be. Every couple of weeks, Joe, the company owner, takes a few of us to one of the restaurants for lunch. Lucius always declines to go. That's probably more than you wanted to know. The answer is I don't know where Lucius was."

I said, "Was Joe on-site this morning?"

"I was trying to get the plumbing connected under the house most of the morning, so I don't know if he was there all morning but saw him once when I went to the truck to get PVC couplings. He was talking to Tim and Scott."

Charles said, "What do Tim and Scott usually do for lunch?"

"Umm, let's see, know he doesn't do it every day, but Tim often sits out on the beach. Told me once it reminded him of growing up out that way."

"How about today?"

"He was there when I walked away. Was back at work when I came back since our lunchtime was over and I was running late getting back. Now Scott's another story."

"Why?" Charles said instead of letting Kyle tell it on his own.

"Ever since Randy Lee got himself electrocuted; Scott's been sucking up to Joe. I haven't heard Scott say it but would put money on him trying to get Joe to make him foreman."

Charles said, "How do you know?"

Kendra returned to tell us our table was ready, so we followed her to a table near the center of the patio. She said it wasn't her table and Ellie would be with us shortly.

Kyle said something about how great the weather was and how much he enjoyed eating outside. I smiled to myself knowing Charles wouldn't let him get distracted that easily.

Charles being Charles, said, "Eating outside is great. So, how do you know Scott wants the job?"

"I like watching people; watching how they interact with each other. Scott follows Joe around like a lonely puppy nearly every time Joe's there. I'd be embarrassed if it were me acting like that. He's always out of money, so the promotion could help. That, plus I overheard him once say something to Joe about how he thought he'd be good at the job."

That's it?" Charles asked.

A server I hadn't seen before approached our table and asked if we were ready to order. Charles said we were and to put it all on one check. Mine, of course. Charles and I went with chicken fingers and fries. Kyle selected the flounder platter after Charles told him to order anything he wanted before reminding him I was paying.

"Anything else about Scott?" Charles asked after our server headed to the kitchen.

Kyle smiled. "Anyone ever tell you that you ask a lot of questions?"

Anyone ever not tell him that, I wondered.

"Sorry, I'm a curious guy," Charles said, then proved it by repeating, "Anything else about Scott?"

"No."

I said, "Anyone else there this morning?"

Kyle rubbed his chin then said, "Umm, Mitchell was the only other regular there. Luis Ortez was at another job for Argyle and I already told you Joshua was sick."

Charles said, "What does Mitchell usually do at lunchtime?"

"Don't rightly know about every day. I remember one day he grabbed his surfboard off his truck and went surfin'. Said there were boss waves; couldn't pass them up." He chuckled. "Don't know how he works the rest of the day all soggy and salty. Other times, I don't know." He hesitated before continuing, "How come you two are asking about all of us? Seems weird."

"You probably don't know this, but Chris and I have helped the police a time or two solve crimes."

"So, you're playing cop?"

"Not really, simply curious," Charles said. "That's three incidents in what, the last couple of weeks? Don't you think that's strange?"

Kyle sighed. "Yeah, two accidents and someone hurting Mason on purpose."

Charles said, "Ever think if Mason doesn't live it could've been three murders?"

"Not really. Who would've wanted to kill three of us? That doesn't make sense."

"That's what we're trying to figure out," Charles said. "If the first two deaths weren't accidents, do you know anyone who would've wanted two and almost three dead?"

"Know what some of the guys think about it?"

I said, "What?"

"The damned house is cursed."

We'd heard that, but it didn't answer Charles's question. I waited to see how long it took for Charles to repeat it.

In less time than it'd take an egg to break while being run over by a semi, Charles said, "Who would've wanted all three dead?"

"No idea."

Our food arrived and remained our focus for a few minutes until Charles said, "Sure you don't know anyone who—"

Kyle pointed his fork at Charles. "Guys, I honestly appreciate this meal and our conversation, but it's been a damned horrible day at work. How about no more talk about it?"

Charles said, "Just a couple more—"
"You're right, Kyle. No more questions."
"Thanks."

Chapter Twenty-Six

Cindy LaMond called the next morning interrupting my peaceful first cup of coffee with something I'm certain I'd never heard her say.

"Good morning, Sunshine."

I recognized her voice, but not the sentiment. "You on drugs or hallucinating?"

"That's none of your business. Want to meet me for breakfast? I'm buying."

Now I knew I must be talking to a Cindy impersonator. "Sure, whoever you are. When and where?"

"Now. Blu," she said, and the phone went dead.

Hanging up on me was more like the Cindy LaMond I'd come to love.

Blu was the upscale restaurant in the Tides Hotel. Fifteen minutes later, I was greeted at the hotel by Jay, a friend who works as the hotel's unofficial greeter, bellhop, fount of knowledge about everything Folly that hotel guests might ask about.

"Good morning, Chris," Jay said as he looked at his watch. "Chief LaMond told me to escort you to her table."

"Thanks. I think I can find her on my own."

"She said it wasn't so you don't get lost, it was so you wouldn't scare any of our guests."

Further proof Cindy was back to being Cindy.

"Lead the way."

The Chief was at a small table against the window overlooking the ocean. She greeted me with a smile and slight wave. Jay said he'd leave me in her hands and headed back to the lobby.

"Good morning, Cindy."

"It's not nearly as bad as most of them. Want to know why?"

"Of course."

"Because I'm hiding here rather than my regular breakfast spot at the Dog. Few people would think to look for me in this classy joint."

A middle-aged server arrived with coffee before asking if I was ready to order. I told him Cindy's pancakes looked good and I'd have the same with a side order of bacon.

He went to put in my order and Cindy said, "Sure that's all you want? Remember, I'm buying."

"That's kind of you. What'd I do to deserve such a treat?"

"Not a speck of anything."

Again, that's the Cindy I know. "Thank you anyway."

"Suppose you're wondering why I invited you."

I smiled. "It'd crossed my mind."

"I wanted to apologize for being so cranky with you yesterday at the construction site."

She apologized nearly as often as she bought me a meal.

"That's okay. You know some of my friends, so you know I'm used to being around cranky people."

"I'll pretend you're not comparing me to Bob Howard."

"Never, Cindy. Never."

"Good. That'd really make me cranky."

"Me, too."

"Know why I was so pissed yesterday?"

"Stumbling on Charles and me?"

"That should be it, but it isn't. Hell, I'm used to seeing you two at crime scenes. No, it was the third time I'd been to that house. Not because someone wanted to give it to me, but because the first two times there was a dead body. Each looked like an accident. Yesterday's wasn't. Add to that, you and your buddy tried to tell me the first two were murders rather than accidents."

"I don't think we were saying that. All I know is they appeared suspicious."

"I'm thinking you're right, but know who doesn't?"

"Detective Fisher?"

"Bingo."

"Why are you leaning that way?"

The server interrupted Cindy's answer when he slid my plate of pancakes in front of me along with a side order of bacon. He asked if Cindy wanted anything else. She said she didn't, and the server left us so we could eat in peace.

She watched me take a bite of pancake and said, "What was your question again?"

"Why do you think the first two, umm, deaths weren't accidents?"

"Nothing beyond a gut reaction based on what the law of averages would attribute three deaths in nine days at one small construction job?"

"Three deaths?"

She frowned. "That's the other thing I wanted to tell you. Mason Ryle died before the ambulance got to the hospital."

"I hate to hear that. Did he say anything before he died?"

"Like who killed him?"

I nodded.

"That'd be too easy. He never regained consciousness."

"I assume getting caught between the forklift and the wall caused his death."

"Massive internal injuries, the docs said, but he's being autopsied to make sure."

"Did any of the guys working out there say anything that could help find whoever was driving the forklift?"

She shook her head. "Detective Babyface Fisher interviewed everyone working there yesterday. He called me later to report that he learned nothing, *nada*, bupkis. Most claimed they were at lunch and nowhere near where it happened."

"Do you think the detective was thorough enough to learn anything significant?"

"He's been a detective six months. He wants to do a

good job, I get that, but from what he said, I wouldn't bet my worn-out tennis shoes on him succeeding in identifying Ryle's killer. Add to that, he still doesn't believe the first two deaths were anything but tragic accidents. Therein lies most of my frustration."

"Fisher might be right about where the others were at the time of the, umm, murder."

"Why?"

I told her about Charles and I having dinner with Kyle Manger at Loggerhead's. I ignored her cold police stare and went on telling her what Kyle said about where everyone was or claimed to have been when Mason was killed.

"What's it going to take to get you and your witless buddy to stay out of police business?"

"All we did—"

She waved her fork in my face and said, "Never mind. Don't waste your vocabulary. I know as well as I'm sitting here that you were going to say you were simply having a meal with one of the workers and talking about what happened yesterday. No butting in police business, no interfering in an investigation, blah blah blah."

I smiled. "Cindy, you're a mind reader. No wonder you're the top chief in South Carolina."

"Don't press your luck. I already said I was buying breakfast." She looked out at the ocean, shook her head, then turned to me. "Besides, from what you told me, you learned more about what happened than Detective Baby-face came close to learning. With that said, can I ask two favors?"

"Of course."

She held up her forefinger. "First, will you share anything significant you learn while you and Charles are not butting into police business?" She held up her middle finger. "Second, will you try, try really hard, not to get yourselves killed while you're not butting in?"

"Yes, ma'am."

The rest of our breakfast conversation revolved around how busy her husband Larry's business was at Folly's small hardware store and how hard she was working on losing a few pounds she'd gained over the winter from spending too much time in her office writing reports the council had requested. Trying to keep from breaking the second promise I'd made her, I didn't ask how her pancake breakfast was helping her lose weight.

Chapter Twenty-Seven

On the walk home, I saw Charles heading my way. He would've been hard to miss in his bright red Maryland Terrapins long-sleeve T-shirt and navy-blue shorts. I waited for him in front of Dude's surf shop.

"Ready to go?" he said instead of an appropriate greeting.

"Where?"

"It's Saturday so I thought a pleasant walk out Ashley Avenue would get us, especially you, some much-needed exercise."

I ignored the exercise cut and said, "What's Saturday have to do with anything?"

"We could stop on our walk at the cursed house. Being the weekend, there probably aren't workers there and we could, umm, check out where Mason was injured."

"Aren't you curious about where I've been?"

"Yes, but thought you'd tell me while we walked," he

said before crossing the street on his—our—exercise walk.

Charles was right about it being a great day for a walk. The temperature was in the low eighties with a cloudless sky. It was still early, so traffic was much lighter than it would be later.

"Where?"

"Where what?"

"Where you have been without me. Must've been important or you wouldn't have mentioned it."

Charles is more perceptive than most give him credit.

"Having breakfast with Cindy."

"Why?"

"We were hungry," I said knowing it would irritate him. One must take pleasure whenever possible.

"And?"

"She told me Mason died on the way to the hospital."

"Crap. Did he say anything on the way; anything like who tried to kill him?"

I shook my head and said, "He never regained consciousness."

"What else did you learn?"

"Fisher, the detective who caught the case, will investigate Mason's death, but still believes the first two were accidents. Cindy says he's been a detective only six months and she doesn't have much faith in his ability to catch whoever is responsible for Mason's death."

"It's coming clearer, she wants us to solve the murders."

"I didn't say that."

"You didn't have to. It's as clear as today's sky."

Charles was righter than he thought, but I wasn't about

to tell him what Cindy had said about us getting involved.

We'd reached the Ashley Avenue side of Loggerhead's when Charles pointed to the restaurant. "Did we learn anything last night when we were with Kyle?"

"Nothing useful. No one saw the forklift strike Mason. Kyle wasn't certain but told us where he thought everyone was when it happened."

"Don't forget him saying several of the guys are beginning to believe the house is cursed."

"You believe that?"

"It's as good a theory as any but even if it's cursed, someone, like a real, live person, hopped on that forklift and rammed Mason."

We were within sight of the house under construction. The lack of vehicles parked in the lot or on the street near the house told me Charles was right about no workers being there.

"See, no one here," Charles said as if I wouldn't have figured that out on my own.

"So, what's your plan?"

"Follow me and ye shall see."

We were near the spot where we'd seen the forklift surrounded by first responders, when Charles stopped, bent down, and rubbed his hand in the sandy soil.

"Charles, you think the killer dropped a confession?"

"That'd be great, but I doubt it. I was looking for anything that'd give us a hint of who was here."

"You know the ground around here was trampled by the first responders, and, most likely, some of the construction workers. I can't imagine anything useful still being here."

Charles stood, wiped his hands on his shorts, walked to the back yard, then looked at the roof. "Do you think Shelly could've slipped and fell on her own?"

"That's a steep pitch, so it's possible."

"But we've heard from a couple of people that she was afraid of heights. I know if it'd been me and I was afraid of being up there, I'd be more than careful. It'd take a push to get me to fall."

"I agree, but that still doesn't eliminate it being a freak accident."

"Yes, but—"

A black Mercedes E 450 backed into the drive and a distinguished-looking gentleman slowly exited. He was in his mid to late sixties, six-foot two with styled gray hair and wearing a white polo shirt and gray dress slacks. He clearly wasn't here to work. He glanced at the house before heading our way.

"Who might you two be?" he said in a northern accent.

"Hi, I'm Chris Landrum and this is my friend Charles Fowler. And you are?"

"Chris, Charles, this happens to be my property, so please tell me why you're trespassing?"

"You're Oliver Trescott," I said. "One of the city council members told me your name." I hoped that'd give some, although slight, idea that we weren't simply thieves getting ready to steal equipment.

"That's correct. Again, why are you here?"

"Charles and I were here when the young lady fell from the roof. We were also nearby yesterday when the man was killed by a forklift. We're good friends with Folly's police chief and had been talking with her about what'd happened, so we wanted to come by to look more closely at the scene of the, umm, unfortunate deaths. We apologize if you don't want us here."

"I'm confused. Are you working with the police or simply damned nosy nellies snooping around?"

Charles responded before I could say anything. "Mr. Trescott, I'm a private detective. Chris and I have helped the police bring more than one murderer to justice."

He glared at Charles then said, "What's your friend's number? I'd like to confirm what you've said."

I gave him Cindy's cell number knowing nothing good would come from his call to her. He put the phone of speaker and dialed. Four rings later, Cindy's voicemail kicked in. To my surprise, Trescott hit *end call*.

He put the phone in his pocket, smiled, and said, "I suppose you wouldn't have given me the chief's number if you were getting ready to break in. Sorry for giving you such a hard time. I'm pretty upset about what's been happening."

"I understand, Mr. Trescott."

"Please call me Oliver. Let's stand over there in the shade."

We followed him to the shady side of the house where he said, "You know more about what's going on than I do. All I was told when Joe Argyle the owner of the construction company called me last night was someone had been killed."

I said, "Were you aware of the other two deaths in the last few days?"

"I knew about the guy who got electrocuted but not

about someone falling."

We filled him in on the facts as we knew them but avoided speculating that all three victims were murdered.

"That's awful. Joe's going to hear from me for not telling me about the other death."

"The councilmember who told me about you building said you were from Maryland."

He nodded. "Just outside D.C."

Charles said, "How long have you been over here?"

"Got here a few months ago. Been back and forth several times. Took me longer than I anticipated to get my businesses where I could leave them. I'm staying in a condo at the Oceanfront Villas until the house is finished."

"What kind of businesses do you have?"

"Had," he said followed by a smile. "I finally managed to retire. I had a couple of holding companies, owned a seven-story office building, and a couple of retail buildings."

Charles said, "That's a lot to keep up with."

"That's why I was happy to retire. What do you two do besides trespass?"

"We didn't mean to—"

Oliver laughed. "Kidding."

Charles smiled. "Good, Chris is retired; worked at a big insurance company in Kentucky; then had a photo gallery on Center Street. I worked for him before retiring."

I chose not to correct Charles's stretching of what he'd done, and said, "Someone told me you'd owned this property for years before starting this house."

"Bought it nearly a decade ago. Got a deal I couldn't pass up." He chuckled. "Some called it a steal. There was a small old concrete block house here. The owner came into hard times and had to unload the house. I was lucky to hear about it and grabbed it fast. I had the old house torn down right away and planned to start this one then."

Charles said, "Why didn't you?"

"My businesses were growing faster then I could keep up with. Had to hire a passel of others and as you may know, when you have a bunch of employees you need to stay tethered to your work."

"I know what you mean," Charles, the person who never owned anything, said.

Oliver added, "Didn't even get a building permit until this year."

Charles said, "You married?"

He smiled. "Yeah, my wife is a retired schoolteacher. She's the reason this is such a large house, and expensive, I might add." He looked at his watch. "Guys, speaking of my wife, I promised to take her shopping on King Street. I'd better go, or I might be moving in by myself."

"We enjoyed talking with you," I said.

"Maybe I'll see you around."

We watched him climb in his Mercedes and pull out on West Ashley Avenue.

"Interesting fellow," Charles said. "I forgot to ask him about the house being cursed."

"It was wise not to mention it."

"Not that wise. As Woodrow Wilson said, 'Wisdom doesn't necessarily come with age. Sometimes age just shows up all by itself.'"

Whatever, I thought.

Chapter Twenty-Eight

Brad Burton was standing in my yard when I returned from the encounter with Oliver Trescott. I'd talked with the retired detective more in the last two weeks than I had during the entire time he'd lived next door. I was still surprised to see him.

"Hi, Brad. You going to or coming from Bert's?"

"Neither. I was coming to see if you were home then I saw you heading this way."

Sweat was running down the side of his face.

"Want to come in where it's cool?"

"Affirmative."

He followed me to the kitchen. "Want something to drink? I've got beer, wine, Pepsi, Diet Pepsi, coffee, and a faucet full of water."

"I'll go with Diet Pepsi." He patted the front of his Patriots Point Naval and Maritime Museum T-shirt. "Hazel says I'm getting fat."

Hazel was right, but I had enough sense not to agree with anyone about getting fat. Okay, I probably should say not agree with anyone in front of the person being accused of getting fat. Instead of commenting, I busied myself getting Brad's drink out of the refrigerator and grabbing one for myself.

I nodded toward the kitchen table then set his drink on it. He took the hint and sat.

"Brad, I suspect you weren't waiting for me so you could share Hazel's thoughts on your weight."

He took a sip, leaned forward, and said, "I heard last night Mason Ryle had been killed."

I nodded. "Charles and I were near the construction site after it happened."

"Dare I ask why?"

"We'd been on the Pier and heard sirens heading out West Ashley, so we took a chance on them going to the house. Sadly, we were right."

He took another sip, stared at me long enough to make me worry about what he might say next.

"Know who I concluded had been the person responsible for the first two deaths out there?" He held up his hand to stop me from answering. "The person I thought was responsible until yesterday afternoon?"

"Mason Ryle?"

"Yes. If I was still on the job, I wouldn't have had enough evidence to arrest him, but from everything you'd said, and stories going around, he would've been my prime suspect."

"For what it's worth, he was mine as well. Let me throw out an idea and get your take."

"Let's hear it."

"You still could be right about Mason."

"He killed the first two victims and someone else killed him?"

"Yes."

"Good point although it strikes me as unlikely. When you were out there, did anyone or anything appear suspicious?"

"We didn't get to talk with any of the workers who'd gathered around the body." I smiled. "You'll appreciate this. The police escorted us off the property before we could speak with anyone."

Brad returned my smile. "Wise cops."

"We talked to one of the construction crew that evening. Ran into Kyle Manger at Loggerhead's."

Brad stared at me. "Accidentally ran into him?"

"Sort of. We were looking for any of the workers and knew a couple hung out at Loggerhead's."

Brad shook his head. "Butting into police business."

I repeated, "Sort of."

"Don't keep me in suspense, did you learn anything helpful?"

I was beginning to like Brad's new hobby.

"The incident happened during their lunch break. Kyle gave us his best thoughts about where everyone was when it happened. It didn't help much since he said none of the guys stayed at the site, other than Mason, that is."

"Did he strike you as being candid or evasive?"

"I didn't get the impression he was hiding anything."

"Did Kyle think the other employees stayed together during lunch or did any of them spend the break apart from the others? In other words, could one of them have returned without the others knowing?"

"It sounded like they go their separate ways during lunch."

"Little help."

I agreed.

"He did say he talked with a detective and had the impression the guy didn't think the first two deaths were anything but accidents."

"Did he identify the detective?"

"Some young guy, thought his name was Fisher."

Brad looked at the ceiling then at me. "Len Fisher. I talked to a buddy of mine in the Sheriff's Office. He said Fisher was recently promoted to his vaulted status. Also said Fisher will be good someday, but he said he wouldn't bet on him solving whatever happened over here."

I had difficulty grasping that Brad still had a *buddy* in the department. A couple of years ago, another detective in the Sheriff's Office shared that Brad had the reputation as being a COF, or for those who aren't conversant in acronyms, a Cranky Old Fart. And that wasn't the worst thing he was called.

I shook that image out of my head and said, "That's not encouraging."

"Add to his lack of experience, Fisher is on the team investigating the murder case of that former politician who's been in the headlines the last couple of weeks. The Mayor is getting pressure from all sides to get that one solved. As you can guess, when the Mayor gets pressure, he passes it along to the local cops. The guy was killed in the county, so the Sheriff's Office is getting all the pressure."

"Fisher is focusing on that case?"

"The Sheriff will deny it, but I've been there and know what's happening."

"Not good news."

"While I still have a friend in the Sheriff's Office, do you have a list of guys who are working out there? I can see if my friend can run background checks on them."

"Isn't that something Fisher would've already done?"

Brad grinned. "Should've and would've are two different things. And don't forget, he's only looking for the person who killed Mason. There could be some connection with one or both other victims."

I grabbed a legal pad from my office, returned to the table, and wrote down the names of as many workers on the job site as I could remember. I tore the sheet out and handed it to Brad and warned him that I may not have the spelling correct.

"I understand. This is a long shot at best. Also write down the approximate age of each guy."

I did but shared I was worse at guessing ages than I was at spelling names.

He thanked me for the drink and list of names.

He smiled as I walked him to the door. "Chris, I know murder is a horrible thing and shouldn't be taken lightly, but this hobby is a hell of a lot more fun than golf."

Chapter Twenty-Nine

By the time the sun finished its long day illuminating Folly Beach, I was also finished, more accurately, exhausted. Breakfast with Cindy, followed by meeting Oliver Trescott, then the session with Brad Burton had depleted my daily ration of energy. I'm in my recliner in the living room staring at a mind-numbing documentary on Abraham Lincoln. If I had the energy to follow the history presented on the screen, I'd learn some interesting facts about the sixteenth president, possibly even a quote I could throw at Charles. But when I realized the show had ended and I was staring at a drug commercial I knew no more about Lincoln than I did when I plopped down in the chair three hours ago.

I also realized after talking with many of the construction workers at the ill-fated house, the house's owner, Chief LaMond, Brad Burton, and several others, I was no closer to learning the identity of the person who killed the three workers than I was to accumulating Lincoln trivia. If I was honest with myself, I wasn't even certain the first two workers were killed. Sure, Charles and I thought their deaths weren't the result of accidents, Brad Burton was on the same page, and even Chief LaMond had her doubts, but to my knowledge there was no evidence.

If there were three murders, shouldn't there be something tying the victims together? If they weren't connected, is it conceivable that there's a serial killer out there who chose the three victims, because—because what? Could it simply be they worked on the house? If that's the case, wouldn't the remaining workers be in danger? Taking that logic one step further, not only would the remaining workers be in danger, but wasn't it likely the killer is one of them? Otherwise, how would he have gotten away with killing three people at the job site without being seen? Someone who didn't belong at the house would've drawn the attention of one or more of the workers. Whoever pushed Shelly had to know when and where she'd be so he could shove her and get away with it without anyone seeing him. The same is true with Mason's death. How would the killer have known where each of the other employees would be during lunch so he could get away with getting on the forklift, backing it into Mason, then escaping? Electrocuting Randy Lee would've been easier to do without witnesses, but how would the killer have known Randy would be at the house at midnight? Unless the culprit is the luckiest serial killer who ever lived, I'd wager he's one of the workers. The only outlier to that theory is Shelly's husband Raymond. He could've known where she was scheduled to work the day of her death. He could've learned from her the lunchtime habits of the others including where each normally chose to spend that time. Finally, she could've told him about Randy's habit of returning to the job site some evenings to make sure everything was in order.

Yes, the killer could be one or more of the workers or Raymond Whitley, but other than not knowing who, I keep coming back to why kill the three people? The optimist in me said the answer to that question was within my reach and all it'd take was one more piece of information before it's revealed. My realistic side laughs at my optimistic tendencies. For good reason, I conclude.

I know little about the victims. I'd never met Shelly and only had limited encounters with Randy and Mason, so how could I possibly know the reasons for their deaths? In addition to knowing little about the victims, I know near nothing about the possible suspects.

The last question I had before falling into bed was, is it possible the house is cursed?

No way.

Or was there?

I WAS AWAKENED, not by a eureka moment realizing I knew the identity of the killer, but by the ringing phone. The first thought I had before reaching for it on the bedside table was *not another murder*, followed by the realization of how sad it is for a retired bureaucrat to have the thought of murder bubble to the surface.

"Good morning, Christopher," said the voice on the other end of the call.

Virgil is the only person who uses my given name. He knows I prefer the shorter version, but with Virgil being Virgil, I've learned to accept his quirks.

"Morning, Virgil."

"Didn't wake you, did I?"

I lied and said no.

"Good. Got something interesting for you. Was talking to Mitchell, you know the carpenter at the death house."

"I know him."

"Well anyway, was talking to him last night at Loggerhead's. He told me a couple of things I knew you and Charles would find interesting."

"What?"

"Umm, are you getting hungry? I know I am."

"Want to meet for breakfast?" I asked knowing the answer as well as I knew my name, short or long version.

"Great idea. Tell you what, why don't you head to the Dog?"

"Are you there?"

"Yep, see you."

I may not know the identity of the killer but was certain I'd be buying Virgil Debonnet breakfast.

He was seated at a table on the side patio. He stood and waved for me as I approached as if I wouldn't have seen him otherwise. Heather, one of the restaurant's friendly servers, met me with a mug of coffee before I had time to get seated.

"Virgil told me to keep an eye out for you. Said you were

buying his breakfast so I should treat you well. French toast?"

I said yes, thanked her, said hi to Virgil, then took the seat opposite him.

"Glad you could make it," Virgil said. "I called Charles first, but he didn't answer, so I called you."

There's nothing like being second, especially if it's second behind Charles. I didn't share that with Virgil.

"Anyway," Virgil continued, "Mitchell doesn't usually say much, but was in a talkative mood last night. Think it corresponded to the number of beers he had. Anyway, I knew you'd be interested in what he said."

I motioned for him to continue.

He took a bite of his breakfast burrito, a sip of water, then said, "Remember the last time I told you what he said when I saw him at Loggerhead's?"

No. "Remind me?"

"Some of the guys on the construction site were getting antsy. Some were even saying the house was cursed."

"That I remembered."

"Anyway, Mitchell said five or six of them are ready to walk off the job."

"Because they think the project is cursed?"

"Yes."

"Do they really believe that's possible?"

"Just reporting what Mitchell said. Don't you find it strange that three out of what, ten, workers are now dead?"

"No doubt it's unusual."

"Three people out of ten having the same first name

would be unusual. Three people getting themselves killed out of ten is beyond unusual."

"Did Mitchell say why the house is cursed?"

"He didn't know."

"Is he one of the guys who're talking about walking off the job?"

"He wasn't certain but is leaning that way. Said the only reason he wouldn't was because the company had been good to him. He figures the job would shut down if many of the guys quit. He didn't want to leave Custom Builders Group in a bad way."

"Did he say who else was considering quitting?"

Virgil smiled. "Think so, but I'd been at Loggerhead's awhile before I saw Mitchell. A couple of guys have been nice enough to buy me drinks. Who was I not to show them how appreciative I was for their offer? It's possible I may've had a beer, umm, or two, too many. Life experiences tell me that made it sort of hard remembering names Mitchell had thrown out, if you know what I mean."

I was afraid I did.

"Remember any of them?"

Heather arrived with my breakfast. Virgil waited for her to leave then said, "Let's see. Think he mentioned Kyle and Tim. Give me a sec, there were more."

I took a sip of coffee and gave him a second which turned into a minute, possibly longer.

Virgil snapped his fingers. "Got it. He said the Puerto Rican guy, what's his name?"

"Luis Ortez."

"That's it, Luis."

"Anyone else?"

"Yes, but their names escape me." He smiled. "Probably forever."

"Did he really think some of them would walk off the job because they thought the house was cursed?"

"Don't know if they would or not, but the way he was talking, I wouldn't be surprised. Any of that helpful in figuring out who did the three folks in?"

Not really, I thought but said, "You never know. Every piece of information can be critical in figuring it out."

He smiled and said, "That's what I thought, Christopher."

If only if it was that simple.

Chapter Thirty

The next three days, I focused on getting my mind off the deaths. I took long walks on the beach, intentionally staying west of the Folly Pier to avoid seeing the "death house" as some were calling it. I even cooked myself two suppers in my kitchen. Okay, my definition of cooking meant sticking Stouffer's TV dinners in the microwave, but hey, that's still cooking, isn't it?

During this same period, Charles found himself busier than he had been at any point during the last thirty-something years. A builder he occasionally provided manual labor for had asked him to help with a room addition on a house on East Erie Avenue. In addition to making deliveries for Dude's surf shop, these off-the-books, aka cash, jobs helped my friend earn enough money to live.

I was close to putting the deaths out of my mind when Brad Burton appeared at the door. I invited him in, offered him something to drink, then grabbed two Diet Pepsis from the refrigerator while he was making himself at home at the kitchen table. Sweat rolled down his cheeks.

"Been jogging?" I asked as I set his drink in front of him.

"That's a joke. It's hot out there in case you didn't notice."

I smiled. "That's why I'm in here."

I waited to hear what I'd done to get another rare visit from the retired detective. I didn't have long to wait.

"My buddy in the Sheriff's office got back with me first thing this morning. Figured you'd want to know what he learned."

Apparently, my avoiding what'd happened at the construction site was coming to an end.

"Sure."

Brad took a small notebook out of his pocket. The book looked old enough to have been used by Columbus to document his trip to the new world.

"Roman, that's my friend, didn't find much. He didn't have access to all the databases available to his office, something about being afraid the sheriff would know if he'd been snooping without it being tied to a case. Something about signing in and passwords. I was never big on using the office technology but assumed Roman knew what he was doing." Brad turned a few pages then set the book on the table and said, "Rawlins, Scott, sixty-one. He has one DUI from three years ago. Also, his wife accused him of abuse a couple of years ago. They divorced and she never pursued the charges. That's all he found on Rawlins."

"Interesting," I said, then grabbed a notebook from the

kitchen counter. "With my memory being what it is, I'd better take notes."

Brad smiled. "I know the feeling. Now we have Walker, Lucius, fifty-three. Roman found nothing on him. That doesn't mean much. The databases he had access to only covered South Carolina. Walker could be a mass murderer from Georgia and Roman wouldn't find anything about it."

"I understand. Anything about the others?"

"Be patient. Manger, Kyle, thirty-seven, has a juvenile record but it's sealed and Roman had no way of gaining access. Ortiz, Luis, fifty-three. Nothing to show about him, again, that doesn't mean anything for the same reasons I gave for Walker."

"Okay."

"Same was true for Bennett, Joshua. Nothing there. That brings me to Hale, Timothy, twenty-two. A speeding ticket last year."

"That's all?"

"All for Hale, now Baldwin, Michael, that's another story. He's twenty-seven. Three years ago, he was convicted of firearm possession. Served a year."

"Isn't that severe for having an unlicensed firearm?"

"Yeah. I suspect there was more, and he pled guilty to the possession to get off lighter than he would for whatever the other charges were."

"Your friend couldn't find out what the other charges involved?"

"Nope."

"Anything else?"

"You didn't mention him, but I had Roman check on

the owner of the construction company. It got a little interesting there. Argyle, Joseph, fifty-seven. He'd been sued
three times for not fulfilling promises he'd made to people
he built houses for. All three were settled out of court. That
doesn't necessarily mean he did anything wrong. Everybody
is suing everybody nowadays."

"Did your friend find out anything about the house's
owner, Oliver Trescott?"

"Nothing, not even a speeding ticket, but he hasn't lived
here long, so that doesn't mean squat."

I looked down at my notes then said, "Is that it?"

Brad smiled. "Saved the best for last. Whitley, Raymond,
thirty-five. The boy got one DUI a year ago, add public
intoxication two years ago, then here's the kicker. He was
convicted eleven years ago for spousal abuse, gave the state
two years of his life."

"Do you think he killed his wife?"

"He'd be at the top of my list."

"Who else would be on your list?"

He tapped his finger on the notebook. "Everybody I
talked about since I came in your front door."

"If you were still on the job, what would you do next?"

Brad looked at his watch. "Go to lunch."

Chapter Thirty-One

Brad headed home, and I headed to the living room to review my notes to see if anything he learned about the others provided a clue to what was going on. I'd love to say I found some hidden nugget that pointed to one of the names as being the killer. If it was there, it evaded my search, so I was relieved when I heard another knock on the door and didn't have to find something in my notes where nothing existed.

I opened the door and stood face to face with a stranger. He wore a navy blazer, a white dress shirt, and a red and blue rep tie, so I figured he wasn't here to rob me. The five-foot-seven, stocky gentleman with wavy black hair looked no older than a teenager, which should've given me a clue as to his identity.

"You Chris Landrum?"

"Yes."

He flashed a badge and said, "I'm Detective Fisher, have a few minutes?"

I nodded and said, "Come in."

I pointed to the couch and he detected the hint and sat. Before moving to the recliner, I asked if he wanted something to drink. He declined and I sat opposite him.

"Mr. Landrum, I'm investigating the death of Mason Ryle. I believe you know who that is."

"Sure, he was the worker killed at a construction site on West Ashley Avenue."

"How well did you know him?"

"I'd seen him a couple of times at the site, but only talked to him once, and that was on the sidewalk outside a restaurant."

His right foot tapped the floor like a nervous tic. "What reason did you have for being at the new house? You're not a contractor or anyone required to be there, are you?"

I explained how a friend and I had been walking on the beach and heard the commotion at the site.

"Twice?"

Umm, twice not counting the day we saw Oliver Trescott there. "Yes."

"That strikes me as beyond coincidences, especially knowing how far that is from your house."

Was he accusing me of something? I didn't know how to respond, so I kept my mouth closed and looked at the detective.

He pointed his finger at me and said, "You have nothing to say to that?"

"No. If I may ask, why are you here?"

"Do you know Scott Rawlins or Kyle Manger?"

"I've met them, but don't know them well. Why?"

He jotted something in a notebook he took out of his coat pocket then stared at me. Instead of answering my question, he said, "Did you know Shelly Whitley or Randy Lee?"

"Never met Ms. Whitley. I talked to Randy Lee once. Why?"

He again wrote in the notebook. I don't know what, but it took him as long as it would to write the Gettysburg Address.

He finally turned his attention back to me. "How about Pat Zellner?"

It took me a few seconds to recall who that was. "She's Kyle Manger's girlfriend. I met her once when she and Kyle were at Loggerhead's." I watched him as he jotted that down in his notebook. "Detective, I've answered all your questions, so don't you think it's time you told me why you're here?"

"Mr. Landrum," he said as his foot continued to tap the floor, "your name's come up a couple of times at the office. I believe you know my colleagues Detectives Adair and Callahan."

They were detectives with the Sheriff's Office whom I'd dealt with on murders that I got involved in solving over the years.

"Yes."

"They've shared stories how you and a few of your

friends had interfered in investigations they'd been involved with."

"Yes, and with my help they—"

He interrupted, "Mr. Landrum, those days are over, do you understand?"

"I'm not certain what you're getting at."

"You know why I asked about Pat Zellner?" he said as his voice got louder.

"Not really. Like I said, I only saw her once."

He pointed his notebook at me. "She said you and some other guy, a friend of yours, I suppose, cornered her and her boyfriend at the restaurant and started interrogating them like they were public enemy number one and two."

"Detective, all we did was ask—"

His face started getting red as he leaned toward me. "I'm not done, sir. Who gave you the right, the audacity to stick your nose in police business? Who said you could play cop and harass law-abiding citizens who were having a peaceful meal?"

"Did either Detective Adair or Detective Callahan tell you how I, and to be honest, a few of my friends, helped take murderers off the street? Did they tell you how they weren't making any headway on those cases until I got involved?" I leaned forward and matched his glare.

"They mentioned how you butted in, how you kept valuable information about the cases from them." He took a deep breath, his shoulders relaxed, and he leaned back on the couch. "Mr. Landrum, all of that is ancient history. In addition to Ms. Zellner telling me how you harassed her and her boyfriend, she added she felt intimidated by how you pounced on them. Furthermore, do you deny talking with Scott, umm," he glanced down at his notes, "Scott Rawlins?"

"No. We had a pleasant conversation about what was happening at his job site."

"That's not the way he saw it. He wasn't as upset as Kyle, and especially Pat, but said he felt uncomfortable when you were interrogating him."

No sense in having him interrupt whatever I would say, so I shrugged and remained silent.

He leaned forward one more time and said, "I don't give a rat's patootie about what you did regarding investigations last year, or for that matter a dozen years ago, but consider yourself warned. If I hear anything else about you nosing in the murder investigation of Mason Ryle, I'll stick you in jail quicker than you can say crap. Do you understand?"

"Loud and clear."

"I'm serious."

"I don't doubt it."

He started to push up off the couch.

"Detective, I'm not butting in, but could you answer one question?"

I imagined feeling handcuffs on my wrists as I said, "You didn't mention the other two deaths. Are you investigating Shelly Whitley and Randy Lee's deaths?"

He sat back down on the couch. "Why would I? They were accidents, nothing more."

"Just curious."

He glared at me for what seemed like an eternity before saying, "I sincerely hope this is the last conversation you and

I have." He gave me a faux smile and added, "If it isn't, you have a lot more to lose than I have. No need to walk me to the door. I can find my way out."

I remained in the recliner and watched him leave, ending with a slamming door.

Chapter Thirty-Two

The rest of the day, much of the evening, and part of the next morning was spent trying to figure out why Detective Fisher was so upset with me. If I were stereotyping him, I'd say he was overcompensating because of his youth and short stature. What else could it be? If he'd talked with the other two detectives in his office like he said he had, they would have told him my efforts had helped them catch killers. Sure, they'd say I did butt into police business, but didn't the ends justify the means? Regardless, I didn't doubt Fisher would honor his threats if he caught me nosing in the case.

The rest of the morning, I tried to figure out why Kyle and his girlfriend had been so down on me. She was irritated that Kyle and I had been talking so much about Shelly, but me harassing her, never. Had Scott Rawlins shared anything negative about me? If he had, I don't recall Fisher mentioning it. Other than Kyle having an obnoxious girlfriend, I hadn't given much thought to him being the killer.

Maybe I should. If nothing else, he appeared to want me to stop looking at what might have happened.

The thing Fisher said that worried me the most was his denying that the other two deaths could be anything other than accidents. Did he honestly believe three deaths in such a short period of time weren't related? Or was I doing what I've been accused of by more than one person, that being looking at every death on Folly Beach as being a murder.

After concluding absolutely nothing, a walk up Center Street and lunch at one of the restaurants sounded much more productive than pacing the living room, achieving nothing.

I was in front of the Crab Shack when I saw Noelle Ward on the corner, looking across the street at the mural painted on the side of Planet Follywood. I assumed that's what she was staring at because I couldn't tell for sure since she was wearing sunglasses. She was in her typical garb of black jeans and a dark gray T-shirt.

I tapped her on the shoulder and said, "Researching?"

She'd told me once she liked watching people so she could get ideas on how they could act in her novel.

She smiled. "Caught me. I was watching people staring at the mural. You can tell a vacationer visiting the island for the first time by how long they gaze at the thing. Who knows, I might add a mural to one of the buildings in my fictional town. Are you walking around catching random researchers?"

"Was on my way to get lunch. Have you eaten?"

"Yes, but it was yesterday. Where are we going?" she asked, placing the emphasis on we.

"You're standing beside it."

She smiled and said, "The Crab Shack it is."

We were greeted at the door by Britany, one of the Shack's longer tenured servers. She asked if we wanted inside or outside. I glanced at Noelle who said outside. I figured it was so she could observe the foot traffic along Center Street. Britany escorted us to a large table on the corner of the deck and said a server would be with us shortly.

"Are you off today?" I said after our server delivered water to each of us.

"I had a presentation to a group of bigwigs last night. It ran until eleven and my boss said I could have the day off." She chuckled. "He didn't have to say it twice."

"Did you get the account?"

"Yes. If we hadn't, my boss wouldn't have been so generous about me taking off."

"Yours is a tough business."

"You can say that again. But know what's tougher?"

I said I didn't as the server returned and asked what we wanted to eat. We each ordered a flounder crunch sandwich and iced tea then the server headed to the kitchen with our orders.

"What's tougher?"

"Writing a danged novel. Wouldn't you think making stuff up would be easy?"

"Noelle, I can't imagine anything about writing a novel being easy, except maybe giving up and deciding not to do it."

She laughed. "You're not far off. My granny used to tell

me I was the most stubborn person she knew. I suppose that stubborn streak is what's keeping me going on the book."

I was going to brag on her making the effort when someone from the sidewalk said, "Hey, Chris. Having lunch?"

I turned and saw Brad Burton leaning on the railing separating the sidewalk from the restaurant's deck. I resisted offering him a smart aleck remark about what else would I be doing at lunchtime sitting at a table in a restaurant. Instead, I said, "Yeah, want to join us?"

He looked around and said, "Don't want to interrupt anything."

Noelle said, "You're not, come join us."

Brad smiled and headed to the entrance.

I said, "You know Brad?"

"Not yet," my lunch companion said. "He looks interesting, sort of street person chic."

I laughed. "You may not want to share that observation with him."

"Why?"

Brad reached the table before I could answer.

"Thanks for the invite," he said and turned to Noelle. "I'm Brad Burton, live next door to Chris."

Noelle shook his hand and told him who she was.

Britany brought our tea, said our server was slammed so she'd be taking care of us, then asked what Brad wanted to drink and if he was ready to order. He looked at me and I told him what we'd already ordered. He told Britany he'd have the same and she left to get his started.

"Noelle," Brad said, "what do you do for a living other

than hanging around with old guys like Chris, and I guess me?"

"I work at an ad agency in Charleston."

I waited for Brad to ask her why she wasn't working today, but he didn't.

I said, "Brad, Noelle's writing a novel."

"Really? What about?"

"It's a murder mystery set on an imaginary island in Georgia."

I said, "Noelle moved here since her imaginary island is similar to Folly."

Brad's brow scrunched up as he said, "What do you know about writing about murder?"

I said, "Brad's a retired detective from the County Sheriff's Office."

"Cool."

"Young lady, there's nothing cool about it," Brad said.

"Sorry, I didn't mean murder was cool. I think you had a fascinating job, a tough job, a job not many people could handle."

Brad nodded. "True. So, what makes you think you know enough to write that kind of book? Were you ever a cop, ever study police science?"

"No, but in my book the protagonist is a private detective and doesn't have to follow all the procedures police must follow."

Brad turned to me. "Sort of like your buddy Charles?"

I smiled. "I suspect Noelle's private detective will do the job much better than Charles."

Brad said, "I hope so."

Our food arrived and hopefully would distract Brad enough so we could get on a more positive topic. We each took a couple of bites, before Brad said, "Chris, hear any more about what's going on at the construction site?"

"Not really," I said then wondered if I should share the visit I had from Detective Fisher.

I didn't have to decide, Noelle said, "You mean where Mason Ryle was killed?"

"Yeah," Brad said. "Did you know him?"

"Yes, we shared a few drinks and a couple of meals together."

"You were dating?"

"No, nothing like that, although I heard he told a couple of his friends we were."

Brad said, "You don't know anyone who had anything against him, do you?"

"No, but I don't think he was the most liked guy out there."

"Did you know either of the others who were killed?"

"No. Mason never said much about the others. If I was writing this story in a novel, I'd start having my private detective look at the rumors about the house being cursed."

I said, "Why?"

She nodded slowly, then said, "Cursed is another way of saying evil. You've had three deaths there. Sure, two are supposed to be accidents, but regardless, three deaths at one place strikes me as evil. After all, doesn't a mystery story have to have some mystery? Adding a curse gives more depth to the plot."

Brad pointed a fry at Noelle. "Young lady, that's bullshit."

Her head jerked back then she said, "Could be. I'm simply saying that'd add to the intrigue of the mystery. Besides, if I were writing this story, I wouldn't have a new house cursed. Most cursed places are old, have squeaky floors, spiderwebs, a rat or two scampering about, and dust flying around."

"That's my point," Brad said. "There's nothing real in a novel. It's all made up so the writer can wrap everything in a nice package with a red bow tied around it at the end of the story. Real life murders don't fit in that box."

Noelle leaned toward Brad. "I'm not telling you what happened out there. Truth is I have no idea, but what I do know is most good novels have enough truth in them to be believable. Otherwise, they're no good."

"Noelle," I said, "did Mason say anything to you about believing or others out there believing the house was cursed?"

"Yes, otherwise I wouldn't have brought it up."

I said, "Two or three of the other guys have told me the same thing. Some of them are considering quitting the job because they're afraid they might die next."

"That's crap," Brad said. "I was a cop longer than Noelle here has been alive. Before I became a detective, I saw countless ways man inflicts harm on others. After being promoted to detective, it was my job to catch the ones who inflicted the harm. Chris, Noelle, in all those years, not a single person was killed because of a curse, or voodoo, or any other supernatural force. People kill people, period."

I didn't see much hope for a pleasant lunch if the deaths at the construction site remained the focus of our conversation.

"Noelle, Brad's probably right. He's also right about you and I not having the information and skills needed to solve whatever happened out there. It's in the capable hands of the Sheriff's Office, and I'm certain they will get it sorted out. Before Brad joined us, you mentioned that you had landed a big account at work. That sounds exciting and interesting. Do you mind sharing what it is?"

She spent the next few minutes sharing the details of her presentation and how much the new account meant to her agency. Watching her come alive while talking about it told me she not only was good at her job but loved the work as well. Even Brad got into it and asked a couple of pertinent questions. Best of all, nothing else was said about the three deaths and a battle between my lunch mates was averted.

Chapter Thirty-Three

To prevent another battle, I wanted to share with Charles Detective Fisher's visit and what Brad had learned about the construction workers. The weather was perfect, so instead of calling, the five-block walk to Charles's Sandbar Lane apartment would do me good. He'd anticipated being done with the room addition he was helping with, so there was a better than average chance he'd be home.

Charles's classic, 1961 Schwinn bicycle was leaned against his apartment building and his Toyota was in the gravel parking lot, so the odds were now more than better than average that he was here.

"To quote Virgil, *holy moly*! What'd I do to deserve a visit to my humble abode." Charles said after seeing me on his front step.

"I thought you could only quote Presidents."

"I'm multitasking. Do I have to guess why you're here, or are you going to enlighten me?"

He often had me guess things I had no way of knowing the answer, but to prove I have better manners, I said, "No need to guess. I thought I'd stop by to tell you who I've talked to since we talked."

"Then why are you standing out there?" He waved me into the tiny apartment.

The apartment felt even tinier since it contained more books than are in the Library of Congress, or so it appeared. He has floor-to-ceiling bookshelves on three of the living room walls holding the quantity of books that'd be more comfortable on more bookshelves than he owned. In addition, there were foot-high stacks of books in two of the corners. He motioned to a wicker rocking chair in another corner, I assumed for me to have a seat. I moved another stack of books from the chair while he plopped down on his navy-blue velour recliner.

"I didn't know you were coming, so I didn't fix hors d'oeuvres and my wine cellar is empty."

No surprise there since in all the times he knew I was coming, he'd never had hors d'oeuvres.

"That's fine. I just ate. I wanted to let you know I had a visit from Detective Fisher. He came—"

"The detective on our murder cases?"

Yes about the detective; wrong about it being our murder cases. Rather than parse words, I nodded then continued telling him what I'd wanted to before he interrupted. I made it through Fisher's visit with a minimal number of questions. That ended when I ended my story with Fisher slamming the door on his way out.

"What's Kyle talking about? Each time we talked with

him we were polite, never accusing him of anything. He never said anything about us bothering him, much less, harassing him.”

“I agree.”

“Then what’s got him riled?”

“The detective didn’t say, but I had the impression the main complaints came from Kyle’s girlfriend.”

“Obnoxious Pat?”

I nodded. “Remember how upset she was at Loggerhead’s?”

“Yeah, but she was pissed at Kyle more than at us.”

“I agree. She’s the one who said Shelly was a looker and irritated that Kyle was taking up for her.”

Charles stared at the front door, nodded, then said, “What if Kyle’s the killer?”

“Why say that?”

“He knows you and I are closing in on him. He wants the cops to force us to step aside.”

“Why do we think Kyle is the killer?”

“Don’t you remember, he hinted that Mason was the killer? Then, I remembered this, he told us there had been a sixth carpenter on the job and he got fired. See, a fired guy would want to kill the guys who were left working on the job. Kyle wanted us to suspect the fired guy.”

“But—”

“Finally,” he interrupted, “he’s trying to get us off the case. Sec, he’s *numero uno* on my list.”

“Before we make a citizen’s arrest, let me tell you what Brad learned about the other guys working there?”

He shook his head. “First, Virgil attaches himself to my

private detective agency, now Brad? Am I going to have to put him on the payroll?"

If Brad were put on the payroll, he'd be the only one, and that's including Charles. Instead of adding to the rapidly deteriorating discussion of Charles's imaginary agency, I said, "Let's start with Scott Rawlins."

I quickly listed what Brad's friend in the Sheriff's Office learned about each worker. I made it though the names with few questions, few for Charles.

"Are you sure Brad said the person who got this for him is a friend?"

I smiled. "I know. I was as surprised as you are that Brad has friends, especially friends working in the Sheriff's Office."

"Anyway, it still looks like Kyle's the killer for the reasons I said earlier."

"He might be, but why not see what we can learn about some of the others?"

"Like who?"

"Scott Rawlins. We know he'd been accused of abuse, so he probably has a temper. When Shelly was killed, he claimed to be alone in the owner's suite. That's on the top floor of the house. No one would have seen him if he pushed her."

"Yes, but—"

"He's sucking up to the construction company's owner trying to get promoted to foremen, the vacancy that became available with Randy Lee's death. Finally, he said he thought Shelly's husband could have killed her."

"Trying to blame the husband. That doesn't mean anything."

"That's the same argument you used when accusing Kyle of killing them."

"Moving right along. What about Michael Baldwin and the talk about the house being cursed?"

"Add to that, Brad learned that he'd spent time in jail for firearm possession."

Charles said, "That'd be a good reason for him killing without using a gun. Oh yeah, isn't he the guy spreading gossip about the house being cursed? Them dying from a curse would let him off the hook."

"He's not the only guy there who mentioned a curse."

"True, but he's only one pushing that rumor who's spent time in the hoosegow. Think it is?"

"Cursed?"

"Yeah."

"I don't believe in curses or cursed houses, but it doesn't matter what I think. Some of the guys are scared, and I suspect only staying because they need the job."

"What about Tim Hale?"

"Brad didn't find anything about him, and from what we've heard, he wasn't close to Shelly."

"What about when Mason was squashed?"

"Kyle said Tim was sitting at the beach staring at the ocean when Kyle took his walk on the beach. When he returned, Tim had gone back to work."

Charles held both hands out to his side and said, "See, more proof that Kyle did it."

"Because he was walking on the beach?"

"Yep. No one saw him and he could've easily come back and fired up the forklift."

"That's possible."

"You don't believe it, do you?"

"Kyle is still a good suspect, but again, we need to look at the others as well."

"Whatever. Who's next?"

"Joshua Bennett," I said. "We were told he had some run-ins with Randy so he could have had a reason to kill him. Killing the others, I don't know. And remember, he wasn't at work the day Mason was killed."

"That doesn't mean he couldn't have snuck back and did Mason in."

"Unlikely, but yes, that's possible," I said. "I think we can eliminate Luis, umm, Ortez. He was working at another project the day Mason was killed. That brings me to Lucius Walker. I think he was the first person who told me he thought Randy's death wasn't an accident."

"Because Randy was an electrician and wouldn't have grabbed a hot wire while he was standing in water."

"Yes."

"So, he could be using backward psychology on us. Thinking we wouldn't suspect the person who killed Randy if he said Randy had been murdered."

"Reverse psychology," I said.

"Whatever."

"That's possible."

Charles shook his head, walked to the kitchen, returned with two cans of Coke, handed me one, then said, "I'm seriously confused."

It would've been way too easy to say he was way beyond confused, so instead, I said, "What's bothering you?"

"Okay, let's agree that there were three deaths."

"No question."

"The first two have been called accidents by the police."

I nodded.

"So, look at the possibilities. One could be an accident; two murders. Two could be accidents; one murder. I'm certain all three were murders. Follow, so far?"

A second nod.

"Add to that, there could be one, or two, or three murderers."

"Yes."

"So, how in holy hell are we supposed to catch one, or two, or three killers?"

"That's a great question."

He chuckled. "In all the years we've known each other, that's the first time you gave one of my questions that much credit."

Most likely because it was the first great question he'd asked, I thought, but said, "You always have good questions, but let me throw one more person in the mix, Shelly's husband Raymond. Brad learned he was married before he and Shelly got married. He was convicted of spousal abuse eleven years ago and served time for it. Brad thinks he's the most-likely killer."

"Okay, he killed his wife and I suppose could've killed Randy because he saw something or heard something that's implicate Raymond."

"Possibly."

"Then why kill Mason? Besides we haven't heard anyone saying that Raymond was on the property when Mason was killed."

"True, but if we assume one person killed all three, no one appears to have a motive for killing the three. The only thing we know they had in common was each worked on the house."

Charles took a sip of Coke, leaned back in his chair, and said, "So, Mr. Logical Thinker, what's our next step?"

"Try to learn more about our most-likely suspects."

"Who would be?"

"Kyle, umm—"

"See, I told you he was the killer."

"Tell you what, for now why don't we say he's the top suspect. In the unlikely event he's not guilty, we should see who else may be."

"Okay, for now. So, who else should we add to the list?"

"The most logical candidate would be Raymond Whitley, then I'd add Scott Rawlins."

"Because he appears to have the most to gain by Randy's death?"

"Yes," I said.

"Anyone else?"

"Nobody jumps out at me, but we shouldn't eliminate any of the others. We don't know any of them well enough to make a guess if they're involved. How about you?"

Charles's phone rang interrupting whatever he'd planned to say. He answered, said okay twice, then ended the call.

He shook his head. "I thought I was done with the room

addition. Now he wants me to meet him out there and clean up."

Our meeting had officially ended.

On the walk home, I thought it'd be wise for me to tell Cindy about Detective Fisher's visit before she heard it from the Detective.

She answered the phone with, "What are you pestering me about this time?"

"Chief LaMond, I was calling to see if I could buy you breakfast in the morning?"

"I'd prefer supper at Halls Chophouse but since you're so tight, I suspect breakfast is the best offer I'll get."

Halls Chophouse is one of Charleston's finest restaurants.

I swallowed back a chuckle and said, "Is that a yes?"

"Absolutely. Seven-thirty at the Dog."

The phone went dead.

Chapter Thirty-Four

Cindy's pickup was in the small parking area in front of the Dog when I arrived. Amber met me at the door, leaned close, and whispered, "I've already told your breakfast date we don't have filet mignon and caviar on the menu, but she'll probably tell you that's what she wants. Said you're picking up her check."

I thanked Amber for the warning and headed to the booth in the back of the room where Cindy was reading what looked like a police report. I slid in the booth and waited for her to finish whatever she was doing before speaking. Amber set a mug of coffee in front of me.

Cindy slipped the paperwork in a manila folder, sighed, and said, "Remember when Brian became mayor and appointed me chief?"

Brian Newman was the long-time chief before running for mayor after the previous occupant slinked out of town under a cloud of controversy.

"Of course."

"Why in all that's holy didn't you tell me to say no? Why?"

I smiled. "Because I knew you would be a fantastic leader and the city needed you. So did Brian."

"It'll take way more sweet talk than that to make me believe you."

This is where I would ask most people I know what the problem was. It wouldn't work on Cindy. She'd tell me when and if she chose to.

Amber returned and asked if we were ready to order.

I said, "Do you have filet mignon this morning?"

Cindy slapped me with her napkin and gave Amber a dirty look. "You told him, didn't you?"

Amber laughed. "Who me?"

Cindy said, "Get this old geezer French toast and I'll have whatever costs the most on your breakfast menu that doesn't even have caviar on it."

"Yes, ma'am," Amber said and laughed again as she left to put in our orders.

"Okay Mr. Tightwad who invited me to the cheapest meal you could find, why the invite?"

I took a sip of coffee, then said, "I had a visitor at the house the other morning."

"Do you want me to guess or are you going to tell me who?"

"Detective Fisher."

She rolled her eyes. "Don't suppose he arrested you, or you wouldn't be buying me breakfast."

"Some of the people who work on the new house on

West Ashley, plus the girlfriend of one of them, claimed Charles and I were harassing them about what happened at the job site."

"You were, weren't you?"

"No. Charles and I ran into Kyle Manger, he's one of the plumbers on the job, and his girlfriend Pat Zellner on the patio at Loggerhead's. We had a pleasant conversation, and everybody left happy, or so I thought."

"Was that the only time you saw the girlfriend?"

"Yes."

"Did she seem okay or pissed about anything?"

"She got irritated when Kyle kept talking about Shelly and her death, but I didn't detect any problem with Charles or me."

"Did you talk with Kyle any other times?"

"Yeah, a couple more times at Loggerhead's."

"So what, that's three times in a week or so. Don't you think he could feel you were, umm, harassing him?"

"I suppose so."

"Did Fisher mention anyone other than Kyle and Pat?"

"Yeah, he said Scott Rawlins told him we were also pestering him, or something like that."

"Were you?"

Breakfast arrived before I could respond. Cindy told Amber she could use more coffee, since she didn't serve bourbon at breakfast. She also told Amber she'd need something strong if she had to put up with me much longer. Amber said she knew what Cindy meant, chuckled, and headed for the coffee pot.

Cindy watched her go, and said, "Well, were you?"

"Pestering Scott?"

Cindy said, "Yes."

"No."

"Okay."

"Okay what?"

"I believe you. I had two phone calls after I got home last night."

Do I ask from whom? Why ask knowing she'll tell me? I waited.

"Well, aren't you going to ask who they were from? Larry certainly did. I told him they were from my boyfriend. Don't know if I should feel good about his reaction or not. He laughed." She took a sip of her refreshed coffee, then added, "Well, aren't you going to ask?"

"Cindy, who called you last night?"

"The first call was from someone you know, Detective Fisher."

"What'd he want?"

"Wanted to share a fascinating conversation he had with one of my city's residents. I think you know him. He's the geezer sitting across the table from me."

I sighed. "Why didn't you tell me that before I went through the conversation with him?"

"It's too much fun watching you squirm. Besides, I wanted to hear your version of what happened."

"How'd it compare with his version?"

"You used fewer profanities and didn't sound nearly as angry as he did. Two things you need to know. First, I've known you a long time. I trust you're telling me the truth, even if it can get you in trouble. If you say you and

Charles didn't harass Pat what's-her-name, you didn't harass her."

"Thanks. We didn't harass her and our conversations with Kyle were always pleasant even though we were talking about death, not a pleasant topic. To be honest, it strikes me as strange that he's trying to make us be the problem. Charles thinks he's saying bad things about us, so we stop asking questions about what happened."

"Do you think he had something to do with it?"

"Wouldn't rule him out, but it's only a gut reaction. What did Fisher want you to do?"

"I think he wanted me to cuff you to Charles then ship you off to Provo, Utah, or some other far-away place."

"What'd you tell him?"

"Said I'd keep my ears open and if I heard anything negative about you two, I'd, umm, didn't tell him what I'd do."

"Thank you."

She pointed her mug at me. "You're welcome." She set her mug down and tapped the manila folder beside her. "Know what I was reading when you got here?"

"Whatever's in that folder."

"Wow, maybe you are a detective like hallucinating Charles thinks you are."

"You know—"

"Was reading a report about something that happened out by the County Park last night a little after midnight. That was call number two. I still don't know why Officer Bishop thought I needed to know, but she did."

"What happened?"

"A pickup truck driven by one Scott Rawlins drifted off the road and had an encounter with a palmetto tree. Officer Bishop caught the call and found Rawlins in an alcohol-infused state. He wasn't falling down drunk but blew enough to get him a night behind bars as opposed to standing in front of a bar which got him in trouble to begin with. His passenger, umm," Cindy looked at the paper in the folder. "Timothy Hale was more sober, so Bishop let him call someone to come get him. There wasn't much damage to the truck, but enough to where it wasn't drivable."

"Isn't it unusual for one of your guys to call you for something that minor?"

"Yes, that's what I mumbled to Bishop after she dragged me out of my sleep. She said she knew both guys worked at the house where three had died. She said it was pure luck that Rawlins didn't run into a house killing its residents and both guys in the truck."

"You see anything connecting the three deaths with the wreck?"

"Not really. I think Bishop was making a CYA call in case some connection is found."

"Speaking of the three deaths, does Detective Fisher still think the first two were accidents?"

"Yes."

"I think he's wrong."

"For what it's worth, so do I."

Chapter Thirty-Five

On the walk home, my mind kept wandering back to why Kyle felt the need to complain to Detective Fisher about Charles and me. Could it be as simple as he believed the talks we had had about the deaths were inappropriate? Could it be because his girlfriend raised a stink about it since she was there when Charles and I were talking with him about Shelly's death? Clearly, it irritated her when her boyfriend expressed sympathy for his dead coworker. Or could it be because he was the killer and thought Charles and I were getting close to figuring it out and wanted to have the detective warn us off? The fact was, we were nowhere near figuring it out and because of his efforts to deter us, I was more intent on getting to the bottom of what had happened.

I stopped in Bert's to grab one of their deli sandwiches for lunch when I saw Lucius Walker with a box of donuts.

I said, "Feeding the crew again?"

"Oh, hi, umm—"

"Chris."

He smiled. "One of these times, I'm going to remember your name. Yeah, I'm trying to stay on everyone's good side with a bribe. You'd be surprised how well crews from different companies work together if they like each other. Even if the like is from a box of donuts."

"You're a wise man."

He smiled again. "Wise, not a bit. Just been around the block more than a time or two."

"Speaking of work, how's the project going?"

"Lot of bitchin' going on this morning. Couple of the guys didn't show up leaving those there in a pickle. That's another reason I got these." He glanced at the donuts.

"Who didn't show?" I asked, figuring I knew who one of them was.

"Mitchell and Scott. Funny thing about it is neither called in sick, or anything although Tim told the company owner that Scott wasn't feeling well when he left work yesterday."

I doubt Scott would've used his one call from jail to call work but didn't share that with Lucius. Tim knew what'd happened, so he was covering for Scott saying he was sick.

"That's too bad."

"That's one more thing slowing progress. I can't imagine what would happen if some of the guys walk off the job."

"Because of the rumor that the house's cursed?"

"Not a rumor, it's a fact."

"You believe it's cursed?"

"Yes sir, I sure do."

There wasn't much I could say to that, so I said, "How many of the guys do you think would walk?"

"Six are talking about it, but when it comes to losing money for food, housing, and car payments, I'm not sure how many would actually do it."

"Are you one of the six?"

"Afraid so, except there's one thing that's holding me back."

"What's that?"

"I believe in things being cursed, truly do, but from everything I heard from my relatives when I was a youngster, ghosts, goblins, and things that curse buildings do it in old places. My grandpa was the community expert on that kind of stuff. Not saying it can't happen, but it seems unlikely that a new house like what we're building would've had time to get itself cursed." He smiled. "Guess I'm sounding like one of those kooks who go around spreading ghost stories." He looked at his watch. "Chris, umm, see I got your name right this time. Anyway, I need to get back. Don't want any of those guys to starve."

I told him I enjoyed talking with him then he headed to the register. I grabbed a Southwest wrap from the deli and followed Lucius to pay.

Sean Aker called as soon as I stepped in the house.

"Did I catch you at a bad time?"

A socially acceptable way to begin a conversation. I was surprised I recognized it since they came so seldom.

"It's a good time. What's up?"

"Think you could stop by the office in the morning?"

"Sure. I could come sooner if you want me to."

"No, I'm heading out in a few minutes to meet a potential client in Charleston. It could take the rest of the afternoon."

I chuckled. "You mean you might actually get a client? Won't that screw up your life of leisure?"

"Marlene has this archaic idea that I should pay her for sitting on her hands in the reception area every day. The sacrifices I make for my staff."

"You're all heart."

"Aren't I though? Gotta go. See you in the morning. Get here around eleven, that'll give me time for my morning nap."

"Okay. I wouldn't want to have Marlene wake you up."

"Smart ass," he said and ended the call.

Okay, at least he began the call with a civil opening.

Chapter Thirty-Six

On the walk to Sean's office, I found Virgil leaning against City Hall. He was in his typical garb of a frayed-cuff long-sleeve dress shirt, navy slacks, his beloved resoled Guccis, and, of course, sunglasses.

"Morning, Virgil. What are you doing?"

He grinned. "Supporting local government."

I smiled. "I think City Hall can stand on its own."

"Don't put money on it. What're you doing out this early?"

I didn't think ten-thirty was early, but told him I was on my way to see Sean Aker.

"You been arrested again?"

"Not this time. He called and wanted me to stop by this morning. Want to come with me?"

"I know Sean's an okay guy, but going through my divorce, the forced sale of my mansion, my boat, hell, my everything, I've had my fill of lawyers. You're on your own. Besides I'm working."

"Supporting city government?"

"In addition to that, I'm heading to the hardware store to get some plumbing stuff for an apartment I'm working on."

Virgil lived in a tiny apartment in a run-down apartment building and did odd jobs for the landlord in lieu of paying rent, something that otherwise would be difficult to do since he was unemployed.

I smiled. "That sounds exciting."

"Yeah, right. I am glad I saw you this morning. Last night I was at the bar at Rita's enjoying a cold beverage, or two. Guess who I ran into?"

"Pope Francis."

Virgil rolled his eyes. "No, he was at Planet Follywood. Mitchell Baldwin was at Rita's, and believe it or not, he recognized me."

"You're glad you ran into me so you could tell me you saw Mitchell?"

"I doubt that's newsworthy. What he told me might be in the breaking news category."

"What did Mitchell tell you?"

"Thought you'd never ask. He said Scott, umm, Rawlins, I think that's right."

"There's a Scott Rawlins on the crew with Mitchell."

"You're right and wrong."

"Care to explain?"

"Scott quit yesterday, no notice, didn't show up to quit.

He called Joe, the owner of the construction company and said he was history."

"He give a reason?"

"No, but Mitchell said it had to be because he thought the house was cursed and he was afraid he'd be next to turn up dead."

"Why was Mitchell so sure that was Scott's reason?"

"He and Scott talked about, as he put it, 'the curse problem' the day before yesterday and Scott apparently was convinced the house was a disaster waiting to happen. That's all he shared with me. Now here's something that isn't news yet but could be soon. Mitchell said he may do the same thing the next day or so."

"The same reason?"

"I don't know what kind of bee they have in their construction bonnets but yes, Mitchell and some of the others are scared. Scared enough to quit their jobs."

"He say anything else?"

"Only 'you're welcome' after I thanked him for buying my beers."

"I should have asked the question better. Did he say anything that could help catch the killer?"

"Nope. I'd better get to the hardware store. You'd be amazed how royally pissed a tenant gets if he can't flush his toilet."

I wouldn't, I thought, but instead said, "Thanks for letting me know about Scott. Good luck with the toilet repairs."

He saluted, headed in the direction of Pewter Hardware, and I headed to Sean Aker's office.

The office was on the second floor above one of Folly's gift shops.

"Good morning, Marlene. Is Sean Aker, Esquire in?" I asked as I petted the Shih Tzu sitting in her lap.

"Don't you mean is he awake?"

"Yes," came the voice of the attorney who was standing in the doorway to his office.

"Thank you, Marlene," I said with a tinge of sarcasm.

She laughed and said, "I believe Mr. Aker, Esquire is available to see you."

I followed Sean into his office. A scuba dive tank was propped against a wall in the corner of the room, a surfboard in another corner, and a packed parachute on one of the two side chairs in front of his desk, all tools required for some of his hobbies. I sat in the unoccupied chair.

Sean pushed aside a manila folder, leaned back in the chair, and said, "Thanks for stopping by."

"I always jump when my attorney summons me."

"I wish you could teach Marlene that trick. She's convinced I work for her, and don't do enough of it."

"We all need someone to keep us on the straight and narrow."

"Whatever. I suppose you're wondering why the invitation."

"I am."

He leaned forward in his chair. "In the last three days, I've received two calls from attorney friends who work in law offices in downtown Charleston. Someone you may be familiar with has been attorney shopping in some of the hoity-toity firms over there." He tapped his pen on a legal pad in front of him.

"Care to share who?"

"I told the attorneys I wouldn't divulge their names, and that doesn't matter anyway, since neither of them took the case. The shopper was Raymond Whitley."

"The late Shelly Whitley's husband."

"Correct."

"Why did the attorneys contact you?"

"They knew my office was a mile from where Shelly took her last breath and figured I may know something about the situation out there."

"Why didn't they take the case?"

"First, they said Raymond was a sleaze." Sean hesitated, smiled, and held his hand in front of me. "I know, I know, we attorneys represent people of the sleaze persuasion all the time, but they said in addition to that, they didn't see where he had much of a case. They said they could've taken it on but saw years of battles with the contractor's insurance company, and even if they won, it wouldn't have been worthwhile, especially if they had to deal with Raymond."

"You think Raymond will find an attorney to take the case?"

"Absolutely, he just didn't talk to two who were hungry enough."

"Is his case good enough to win?"

"Possibly, especially if you and your buddies can't prove her death was murder and not negligence on the part of the construction company."

"You mean if the police can't prove it was murder."

"I said what I meant," Sean said as he tapped his fingers on the desk. "You're not going to try to convince me otherwise, are you? Anyway, I thought you'd want to know what's going on."

"Thanks. While I'm here could you do me a favor?"

"Is it going to cost me a ton of money, or worse, incur Marlene's wrath?"

"No to the cost, but I'm not sure about Marlene."

"Let's hear it."

"I was told Oliver Trescott bought the property the house is being built on about a decade ago. There was an old concrete block house on the property at the time. After Trescott bought it, he tore the structure down and didn't do anything with the property until he got a building permit for the current house seven months ago."

Sean took notes on the legal pad then looked at me. "Okay, so what's the favor?"

"Could you see what you could find on the transfer from whomever to Trescott when he bought it and if there's anything else that's happened with the property since then?"

"Hmm, it'll be easy for me to check the registry of deeds to see what they have on the transfer. Beyond that, I doubt I could find much. Why is this important?"

"I don't know that it is. It strikes me a little strange that Trescott bought it that long ago and didn't do anything with it until recently."

"That's not unusual, happens all the time. Someone inherits a property and doesn't touch it for years. Someone gets a good deal on a vacant lot and waits until they have enough money to do something with it. Someone buys a property, and something changes in his or her personal life to where nothing can be done with the property."

"I understand. I know it's a long shot, but at this point, I don't know what else to do."

What I didn't tell him was the stories about the house being cursed made me wonder about the history of the property. Hadn't Lucius' grandfather said things that're cursed are old and not new? I didn't believe houses were cursed, but Virgil just told me Scott Rawlins had quit because of the rumors, and Mitchell Baldwin may not be far behind. I also know Lucius Walker believes the rumor. I have no idea how those stories may be related to the deaths, if at all, but I was honest when I told Sean I didn't know what else to do.

Chapter Thirty-Seven

"Know where I am?" Charles asked as the phone interrupted me sipping my morning coffee on the front porch.

"Madrid, Spain."

He sighed into the mouthpiece. "Why do I keep asking you anything?"

"If you continue asking questions I couldn't know the answer to, I'd assume you're a glutton for punishment. So, where are you?"

"That's better. On the walking pier at the Folly River Park."

The Folly River Park is a small community park at the corner of Center Street and East Indian Avenue.

"You called to tell me that because?"

"It's a beautiful August day. The temperature is tolerable, and there's a group of kayakers going in circles in the river in front of me. Figured you'd want to be here."

I hated to admit it, but he had good points. "I'll be there in a few minutes."

"On your way, why don't you grab me a cup of coffee from Bert's. While you're there, how about picking up a couple of sweet things, things that'll go good with coffee?"

Clearly, he wanted more than my company. Instead of answering, I hung up on him and realized it felt better than the other way around.

Twenty minutes later, I'd reached the walking pier while carrying two cups of coffee and a bag containing two cinnamon rolls. Charles was standing on the far end of the pier, leaning against the railing, and watching a small fishing boat pass in front of the structure. He was wearing a long-sleeve, Kelly green Notre Dame T-shirt, his Tilley, and tan shorts.

He looked back at me and said, "You're late. You done missed some vacationers taking kayak lessons going around in circles; now they're somewhere out in the marsh."

I didn't share any sorrow for missing that exciting spectacle. I sat on the wooden bench and took his roll out of the bag.

He looked at the roll, took a sip of coffee, and said, "You're forgiven."

"You're so kind."

"Smartass."

I smiled and said, "You bet."

"Where've you been the last few days? Thought we'd be spending time catching the killer."

"Do you know who it is?"

"No."

"Then how're we going to catch him?"

"Guess our plan has a couple of holes in it."

"Couple of big ones. I did learn more about the house and its crew." I proceeded to tell him about Scott and Tim's wreck." After he berated me for not telling him sooner, I shared what Virgil had said about talking with Mitchell and that Scott had quit without giving notice.

"That's because he's the killer. He knows we're getting close and took off. By now, he's probably in California, or Canada, or in, well, you get my point."

If we were getting close to revealing him as the murderer, he knew way more than we did. "He told Mitchell it had something to do with the rumor that the house is cursed. Mitchell told Virgil he may be quitting sooner rather than later."

"Why?"

"Same reason."

"They're grown men. Don't they know there's no such thing as a cursed house?"

"Apparently not."

"Well, they should. That brings me to why I invited you here."

"You mean other than me bringing you food and drink."

"Of course. That was a bonus."

"For you. Okay, why invite me?"

"Aloysius called last night."

"Aloysius?"

"The remodeler I helped with the sunroom."

"Okay, he called, and?"

"He got a call yesterday from Joe Argyle, you know, the guy who owns the company building the death house."

I nodded.

"Joe asked him if he knew any carpenters who'd be available to work immediately."

"Aloysius called you?"

"He knows my skill set, the one that lacks, umm, skill in carpentry. He thought since I help contractors, I might know someone. I didn't. That's not my point."

"What's your point?"

"Joe told Aloysius he was in a tight spot with the death house. Of course, he didn't say death house. Anyway, he said he'd lost three employees, and unless he found replacements soon, he may have to shut down the job until more workers are found. Said there are only two carpenters left and according to rumors, one is considering bailing. Something about if he didn't have carpenters, the plumbers and electricians wouldn't be able to work since some of their work couldn't be done until the carpenters finished doing stuff."

"What'd you tell Aloysius?"

"I only know a couple of carpenters and they're happily employed."

"Doesn't Argyle's company have other jobs in the area? Couldn't he free up workers to help over here?"

"He must have at least one other job," Charles said. "Remember one of the other guys was at another job the day Mason was killed?"

"Yes, Luis Ortez. Besides, Argyle must've explored all his options before he called Aloysius."

Charles took the final bite of his roll and mumbled, "What do we do now?"

"Sit back and wait for the kayakers to come back from the marsh."

"I meant about catching the killer."

"I know."

Charles said, "Well?"

"No idea."

This is our time together catching the killer.

It'd been several days since I'd seen Barb, so I called her on my way home to see if she wanted to meet me for supper. She did and we agreed on a time and location.

Chapter Thirty-Eight

I'd agreed to meet Barb at Pier 101 Restaurant & Bar located at the Folly Beach Fishing Pier with outstanding views of the ocean and the beach. Pier 101 is the second iteration of the restaurant since I'd moved to Folly. Many folks hated to see Locklear's, its predecessor, go, but many had returned to the new restaurant because of its menu and location. I was one of those returnees. It was often crowded this time of year, so I arrived a half-hour early so I could get our name on the waiting list.

I was waiting for Barb at the outside bar when she reached the top step to the Pier's deck and looked around. She joined me, asked how long I'd been waiting, then ordered a beer. I told her I'd been here a half hour and there should be a table for us relatively soon. As if I coordinated it with the management, the receptionist approached to tell me the table was ready. Barb acted impressed although we both knew it was luck.

We took our drinks as we headed to the table along the side of the patio overlooking the ocean. Lauren, one of the restaurant's college-age servers, was quick to the table and asked if we needed anything else to drink. We declined and she said she'd give us a few minutes to decide on our dinner selections.

Barb took a sip of beer, leaned back in her chair, and said, "This has been one busy day. You can tell it's the middle of the season."

I would've been thrilled to have had one busy day during the time Landrum Gallery was housed in the bookstore's current space, but instead of sharing that, I said, "Then take a deep breath, enjoy the late afternoon sun, the view, and me."

She smiled. "You were doing fine until you got to the last part of that."

"The *me* part?"

"You got it." Her smile turned to a laugh. "Sorry, teasing. You're almost as good to look at as the view."

I didn't ask why almost. At my age, I'll take any compliment or near compliment I can get.

"I was talking to Noelle the other day. She told me again how much she appreciated you offering her your condo's spare bedroom after her building burned."

"She was a delight to have around. I haven't seen her for a few weeks. How's her book coming?"

I told her Noelle's novel is nearly finished, at least the draft. I also told her how I was with her when she met Brad Burton and how they clashed on her lack of law enforcement experience or training when she offered her thoughts on the deaths at the house on West Ashley.

"He's right, you know. He has what, forty plus years working in law enforcement and she, along with a couple of guys I know, managed to get involved in one real-life criminal investigation."

I would've felt better if she hadn't interjected Charles and me into the conversation.

I limited my response to, "True."

Lauren returned to see if we were ready to order. Barb said she'd like a big, juicy hamburger then asked if the fries were the "big, chubby ones; not those skinny ones some restaurants serve." Lauren assured her they were, so Barb said she'd have an order of them with her burger. I said I'd have the same.

Lauren headed inside and Barb said, "I'm not going to ask if you're getting involved in the deaths out there. Wouldn't want you to lie to me, so, has anything new happened to help you get a better idea who might've committed the crimes?"

"Did you hear about the guy getting pinned between a forklift and the house?"

"I'd have to be deaf, dumb, and in Mozambique to not have heard about it. Nobody thinks it was an accident like the other deaths, do they?"

"No, but the Sheriff's Office detective thinks it's the only murder out there."

"And you and, I suppose, Charles think the other two deaths weren't accidents."

"Correct, and neither does Cindy."

"Then let me ask this, do you think they were killed by the same person?"

"That appears the most likely scenario."

"Okay, so let's go with that assumption. What did the three have in common?"

"Great question."

"Of course it was. Did you expect anything less?" She then laughed.

"Never. But, to your question, I keep coming up with nothing in common other than working on the house. From everything I've heard, they didn't know each other outside work. Their ages ranged from thirty to sixty-two. They didn't live near each other; didn't have the same friends. One was married. I've talked with several others who worked with them and none of them said there were conflicts among the victims." I shrugged.

Lauren delivered our food, asked if we needed anything else to drink, we each declined, and she went to the next table to ask the same question.

"Then why they were killed must be answered before the police, yes, the police and not you and Charles, can focus on who did it."

"That's much more difficult since the police aren't looking for anyone other the person who killed Mason Ryle."

"The guy between the forklift and the building?"

"Yes."

She slathered a fry in ketchup then stuck it in her mouth. She put her hand in front of her face and mumbled, "I love chubby fries."

I envied her metabolism. I could eat far less than she did and gain weight. She could out eat most people I know and never gain an ounce.

She took a sip and said, "Unless there's a serious nutcase out there killing people for no reason, there has to be something in it for him or her other than the perverted thrill of killing people."

"I agree, and since the first two deaths were made to look like accidents and the third murder committed while others working on the project were nearby with nobody seeing anything unusual, I would tend to eliminate the *serious nutcase* explanation."

"Back in my days practicing law, I defended a couple of guys who would qualify as nutcases. Don't confuse that with them being dumb. Some are, of course, but they can also be smart, wily, cunning, and able to plan near-perfect crimes. With that said, those are few and far between. What would the killer gain by these three alleged murders?"

"I don't know."

"Okay, let me throw out a couple of possibilities. Three deaths on such a small project would bring a heap of negativity on the construction company. I'm sure OSHA is investigating. Seldom does anything good come out of their involvement. Companies get shut down, fines get levied, and negative publicity often results." She took another bite then continued, "What do you know about the company?"

"Custom Builders Group is owned by Joe Argyle. I've heard good things about it. They've built several houses over here and more in Charleston, Mt. Pleasant, and Kiawah.

I've not heard anything negative about him or his company. But there is one thing." I hesitated and took a sip of wine.

"But what?" Barb said doing a no-patience Charles imitation.

"This may sound silly, but several of the workers think the house is cursed. Charles told me about one of the carpenters quitting out of fear."

"Why do they think it's cursed?"

"I think they attribute the high number of, umm, deaths in such a short period of time to a curse. I've not heard anyone saying why they think the house is cursed, but it may directly affect the builder."

"Meaning?"

"Charles was contacted by a builder he occasionally does work for. Aloysius, he's the builder, asked Charles if he knew any carpenters who could use work. Apparently, Joe Argyle contacted him to ask the same thing. Argyle told Charles's acquaintance that unless he could replace a couple who've quit and one he fired, he might have to temporarily shut down the project."

"So," Barb said, "Custom Builders Group would be hurt by the deaths, more than possibly getting a bad reputation for safety standards, or anything OSHA does."

"True."

"Okay, what about the person they're building the house for?"

"His name's Oliver Trescott. Bought the property a decade ago. Moved here earlier this year from the D.C. area. I've met him once; seems like an okay guy."

"You don't know any reason a killer would want to cause harm to the homeowner?"

"None I know of."

"Unless you can learn what's in it for the killer, there's little, if any chance you'll be able to find him, or her." She gave a slight nod. "Need I remind you, doing any of this is the job for the police, and not two gentlemen I'm familiar with."

"I know."

True, I knew that, but it wasn't going to stop me from trying. Barb also knew that, so there was no reason to revisit what I should do, and what I will do. A change of subject was in order, and Lauren returning to see if we were ready for another drink provided that change.

"Yes," I said and ordered a second glass of wine for me, another beer for Barb.

The deaths weren't mentioned the rest of the evening; not here, not on the brief walk to her condo, and not during the next two hours there.

Chapter Thirty-Nine

"Did I catch you at a bad time?" Sean said as I answered the phone while taking a box to the trash container by the back door.

"No, you're fine."

"Good, if you're out and about this morning, think you could stop by the office?"

"Sure, but what are you doing there on Saturday?"

He laughed. "Marlene's off and I didn't want her to catch me doing legal work."

"That'd ruin your reputation with the rest of your staff. I can be there anytime, so what's good for you?"

"Around eleven."

"See you then."

"Call when you're downstairs. I keep the door locked on the weekend."

I was surprised he called, but not as surprised as I was knowing he was working on a Saturday. At a few minutes before eleven, I called and was told he'd be down shortly. Good to his word, two minutes later he opened the door and motioned for me to follow him upstairs. Instead of going in his office, he pointed at one of the chairs in the reception area and asked if I wanted something to drink. I said no, and he sat in Marlene's chair.

"I hate getting cooped up in my office all the time. That's one of the reasons I spend so much time at the Dog or walking around. Of course, Marlene assumes I'm goofing off when I'm away from the office."

"Aren't you?"

He smiled. "Most of the time. Marlene's a wise lady. Anyway, I didn't ask to take up your time to discuss my claustrophobia. Hang on." He walked into his office and returned with a legal pad and returned to Marlene's chair.

"I had to be in Charleston yesterday afternoon, so I went by the ROD office to see—"

I interrupted, "The what?"

"Sorry, the Register of Deeds office, it's in the County Office Building on Meeting Street. It's where land titles, liens, and other documents related to property transactions in Charleston County are maintained."

"The property on West Ashley Avenue?"

"You're catching on."

"What'd you learn?"

"Not much." He looked at the legal pad then said, "Ten years ago, this month in fact, David and Sarah Halloran sold the property to IH Financial Group, a holding company out of Connecticut."

"Oliver Trescott, the current owner told me he owned a

couple of holding companies in addition to several properties."

"Then you know more than I learned from the ROD office."

"Do you know the Hallorans?"

"Don't think so, or if I did, I've forgotten about it. Do you?"

I shook my head. "This is the first I'm hearing about them. Was there anything else related to the sale in the records?"

"There was a handwritten note on the paperwork that said, *Reginald Salyer, Realtor.*"

"The buyer or the seller's realtor?"

"No idea."

"Was anything else included?"

"Nothing other than the lot's description."

"I appreciate you looking into it."

"Don't suppose that helps much. I looked to see if there was any mention of the property being cursed."

"Didn't figure there was. With that out of the way, why are you working on a Saturday, other than not to confuse Marlene?"

"Got a client who's going to make an offer on an office building on James Island. He got all antsy about it early this morning, so I told him I'd research something for him before his meeting with the owner Monday."

"Thanks for the help."

"Sorry I couldn't find out more. Any hot leads on who killed from one to three people out there?"

"If there are, I don't know about them."

"Try not to get yourself killed looking."

"Excellent advice, Counselor."

It was another perfect August morning. Puffy white clouds dotted the sky, and the temperature was in the upper seventies, so instead of heading home I walked three blocks to Loggerhead's then up the ramp to the patio. Ed asked if I wanted a table. His twisting my arm worked. It was still before noon so there were a couple of vacant tables. He pointed to a small one by the railing overlooking the parking area and said a server will be with me as soon as he found one.

He succeeded because Shelia, a server who'd waited on me a few times over the last couple of years, was at the table before I'd settled.

She said, "White wine?"

"Not today. A diet Coke."

She said she thought she could handle that and headed to the bar.

As I was waiting for my drink, I called Bob Howard. Instead of the phone's cranky owner, I got his cranky voicemail "greeting" that said, "You know who you've not reached, so if you insist on talking to me, leave a message at the sound of the tone, and I might return your call. Have a nice day."

"Bob, this is Chris, your sweet voicemail message warmed my heart. Got a question. Do you know a realtor named Reginald Salyer? If you do, give me a call. I may answer."

Shelia set the drink in front of me while I was having the warm and fuzzy conversation with Bob's voicemail. I took a sip and replayed the conversation with Sean Aker to see what, if anything, I'd learned new. Other than the name of a realtor, the only thing I didn't know was the name of the holding company listed as the purchaser. I assumed it was one of Oliver Trescott's.

Shelia returned to ask if I was ready to order. I said yes and she left with my order for a cheeseburger, and as my effort to cut back on calories, I didn't order fries. Okay, I agree, that wasn't much of an effort considering I ordered a cheeseburger. It's the thought that counts, or so I told myself.

Forty-five minutes later, all I'd achieved was consuming a cheeseburger. I was no closer to learning who killed the workers out West Ashley Avenue. The deck was now crowded with several groups waiting on a table, so I paid and headed home.

As soon as I opened the door, I knew something was wrong. Two magazines I'd left on the small table by my recliner were on the floor. The wise thing for me to do would be to step outside, call 911, and wait in the yard until an emergency responder arrived. So, of course, I didn't follow my wise counsel.

I slowly walked though the living room and looked in my second bedroom, aka my office, and immediately wished I hadn't. A windowpane was broken, and the window was pushed up enough for someone to climb through. Two of the four drawers in my filing cabinet were open with their contents spread haphazardly on the floor. I'd left three files on the desk beside my computer. They had joined the other files and papers on the floor.

I backed out of the room and headed to my bedroom. I took a sigh of relief when nothing appeared to be disturbed. The kitchen was my next stop and it appeared undisturbed. All that was out of place was the back door, which was partially open. I glanced in the bathroom on the way back to the office. Seeing no one hanging around with a knife, gun, or hand grenade, I returned to the office and was more relieved than I'd been in the bedroom when I saw my camera bag untouched in the corner. My computer was switched off just as I'd left it. I doubted someone who'd leave the back door open would've turned the computer off when he or she was done snooping through it.

I went to the refrigerator, poured myself a glass of white wine, made sure the front and back doors were locked, moved to the recliner in the living room, and called Chief LaMond.

Chapter Forty

Ten minutes later, Cindy was pounding on the front door and yelling my name.

"Are you okay?" she asked as I opened the door and waved her in.

"Yes. Thanks for coming."

"Don't read too much into it. I'd do most anything to get out of the office and the pile of paperwork that's growing faster than Jack's beanstalk. Tell me again what happened."

"There's not much to tell. I'd been at Sean Aker's office then went to Loggerhead's for lunch, came home to find evidence someone had been here."

She nodded, then said, "Then you got out of the house as fast as your aging legs could carry you because whoever broke in could still be here. Then after you were safely outside, you called me."

"Well, that's not—"

"Hold on," she interrupted. "That's what a normal,

careful, sane person would do." She put her forefinger on the side of her head, and continued, "Using my psychic powers and outstanding chiefly skills, let me guess. You came in, saw someone had been here and instead of getting out of here faster than a roadrunner, you went through each room to see what'd been taken or disturbed, never thinking the burglar could still be here ready to put a bullet in your thick skull. How'd I do?"

I translated that to say she cares about my safety and is glad I was okay.

"Cindy, want to see what's been done?"

"I knew it. I'd ask you to pat me on the back, but as reckless as you've been, you'd probably miss." She sighed, looked around, and said, "It's your tour."

She followed me into the room I use as an office. I left everything as I'd found it, so it didn't take all her *psychic powers and outstanding chiefly skills* to see what physical damage and disruption had occurred.

She pointed to the broken windowpane. "Since I've known you, how many times has Larry had to replace glass in that window after someone broke in?"

I smiled. "Enough times I'm beginning to think you're the one breaking it so I can keep Larry in business."

"Right, three or four times replacing the glass in that small window is going to keep Pewter Hardware in the black." She laughed and continued, "Before I leave, I'll call him so he can come over and take care of it, again. He probably keeps a supply of panes that size just for your window."

She sat in the folding chair I keep in the office for my

rare guests in that room. I took the desk chair and pulled up in front of her.

"If you're done marketing for your hubby's store, want to hear what was taken?"

She took a small notebook out of her pocket and said, "Okay mister aggrieved citizen, what was taken?"

"Aggrieved?"

"The mayor's still insisting I need to increase my vocabulary, something about it helping me communicate with our diverse and highly educated vacationers and citizens. I'm going with the idea of learning a word a day to keep the mayor away. Now, am I going to have to call you yesterday's word of the day which means troublemaker, or are you going to tell me what's missing?"

One of Cindy's talents is making people feel comfortable regardless of the situation. I think it helps her communicate more effectively with people than springing new words on them. I know I'm way more relaxed since she'd arrived.

"Nothing."

"Nothing is missing?"

"Correct. To be honest, I can't say some of the papers from the filing cabinet aren't missing. It'd be almost impossible to tell what if any of them are gone. Those two drawers hold files and papers from my first couple of years here. Nothing recent."

She pointed at the filing cabinet. "Did you touch those two open drawers?"

"They're how I found them."

"How about the window?"

"I haven't touched it since I got home."

"Good. I'll have one of my guys come over and see if there're any prints on the window or the filing cabinet." She looked back at the door. "You sure nothing else has been disturbed other than those magazines in the living room."

"I can't be a hundred-percent sure, but nothing appears to have been moved."

"It looks to me like one of two things. It wasn't a burglar since your TV, computer, and camera are still here, or it was a burglar and he cut his scavenger hunt short when he or possibly she heard you coming in the house."

I smiled and said, "So your *outstanding chiefly skills* told you it was, or it wasn't a burglar?"

She nodded, then said, "When you opened the front door, did you hear anything?"

"Like someone opening the back door and running out?"

"That'd be what we highly trained, professional law enforcement officials call a clue."

"I wasn't thinking about it, but it's not that far from the front door to the back door, so I think I would've heard someone leaving."

"If that's the case, then I would assume whoever was in here was looking for something, and not something to hock."

"I agree."

"You said you were at Sean's before coming home, right?"

"Sean's and then Loggerhead's."

"What were you doing at Sean's on Saturday?"

"I'd asked him to try to find out who sold the property

on West Ashley to Oliver Trescott. He looked it up yesterday and was in the office today working up some information for a client, so he called and asked me to stop by."

Cindy leaned back in the chair and said, "So, you're still butting in business you have no business doing."

"I'm only asking questions since I'm interested in finding out more about the house to see if there is some possible connection to the three deaths. As you know, the only thing the victims have in common is they were working on the house."

"Has it entered your pea-sized brain that you might be getting too close to learning something that the person who killed Mason Ryle, and possibly killed the other two people, doesn't want you to know?"

"Chief—"

"Hang on, I'm not done."

I motioned for her to continue.

"And, that person broke in here looking for anything you may've had that could point to him or her."

"Yes."

"Yes, what?"

If Charles or a couple other of my friends asked that, I would've told them if they paid attention to what they'd asked me, they would know what I was saying yes to. Folly's top cop wasn't one of those people. Instead, I said, "Yes, I'd thought about it being the person who killed the three workers."

"Good, because if I had to guess, that'd top my list." She looked at the papers on the floor and continued, "You're not going to back off, are you?"

"No."

She sighed and shook her head.

I said, "Now that you're here, let me ask a question."

"If all you wanted to do was ask me a question, you simply could've called. You didn't have to break in your house to get me to come over."

"You know I—"

She stuck her palm in front of me and said, "That was an attempt at levity."

"Hilarious. The question is do you know the Hallorans, David and Sarah?"

"Who're they?"

"The couple who sold the house to a holding company that's probably owned by the current owner, Oliver Trescott."

"Wasn't that a decade or so ago?"

"Ten years this month."

"That's not long after I moved to Folly. Hell, at that time, I didn't know where the public restrooms were, much less who owned houses. Do you think the sale of the house is somehow related to the three deaths?"

"I'm grabbing at straws. What I know is the only thing tying the victims together appears to be the house. Do you know if Detective Fisher is looking at it that way?"

"Since he's only looking at one being murdered, I doubt it. You still think all three were killed?"

"Yes, don't you?"

She nodded and said, "But with nothing more than playing the odds on what would be the chance that the other two had fatal accidents days before Ryle was killed."

She leaned forward in the chair. "Now it's time to ask you a question."

"And it is?"

"During all your snooping, have you and Charles learned anything the police might be interested in?"

"Don't know how much it'll help, but one of the workers told Charles that Scott, he's one of the carpenters, quit and the rumor's going around that Mitchell Baldwin, may be next."

"Why?"

"The rumor about the house being cursed appears to be picking up steam. Charles also said the guy he occasionally helps on construction jobs, contacted him, and asked if he knew any carpenters looking for work. Apparently, the owner of the company building the house contacted him saying unless he finds more workers, he may have to shut down the job."

Cindy leaned back in the chair. "All because of a damned curse, excuse me, rumor of a curse?"

I nodded.

She sighed and said, "Anything else?"

"Sean told me Raymond Whitley, Shelly's husband, is shopping lawyers in Charleston so he can sue the builder for negligence causing her to fall."

"Are you saying Raymond snuck up on the roof and pushed his wife off to get a bundle of money from the contractor?"

"Unlikely, but possible."

She looked at her watch. "I'd love to sit here and talk about ghosts, or curses, or whatever, and deranged husbands pushing their wives off roofs, but I'm already late for a meeting with two of my guys. There's some matter of life-or-death they have to talk to me about."

"Life-or-death?"

"No biggie. They always talk that way. They probably want longer breaks or other such life-or-death issues." She looked around the room. "Need help picking up all this stuff?"

I told her I could handle it.

Before she left, she repeated that she'd have someone stop by and take fingerprints, she'd have Larry call me to schedule repairing the window, and for me not to get killed before I could buy her more meals.

That was further proof of her saying she cares about me and wants me to stay safe, or so I told myself.

Chapter Forty-One

The next morning, I started thinking about yesterday's *unwelcome* visitor and thought I should warn Charles since he was as involved as I was. I called him and after four rings, and an out of breath Charles answered.

"Are you working out at the gym?" I asked, knowing the odds on that being true were about the same as me winning the lottery.

"Did you call to make a joke?"

"Okay, then where are you?"

"Six-hundred block of your street making a delivery for Dude. Why?"

"What are you doing after you make the delivery?"

"Have two more to make. What's all the interest in my location?"

Instead of getting into it over the phone, I said, "Meet me for lunch at the Crab Shack."

"If you insist," he said and hung up.

The phone rang seconds later.

"Noon," I said.

"What in the hell are you talking about?" Bob Howard asked.

"Sorry, I thought it was someone else."

"Who do you know named Noon? Sounds like some kind of freakin' New Age, crystal healing, whatever name."

"It's a time, not someone's name. Now, why did you call?"

"A bit cranky this morning, aren't we—meaning you."

"I'm fine."

"Fine and cranky. Anyway, your message said you wanted to know if I knew Reginald Salyer. Yes."

I waited for more, but hearing nothing, I said, "What do you know about him?"

"Don't know him well. He was in the business nearly as long as I was. From what I could tell, he seldom handled upscale housing, in layman's terms, expensive houses. His bread and butter was hawking starter homes and fore-closures."

"Anything else?"

"Hell, Chris, you think I'm Wick-e-opedia?"

A little sucking-up is often appropriate when talking to Bob. "No, but you were one of the most successful realtors in the area, and I figured if anyone knew something about Salyer, it'd be you."

"Damn right. That was a little too syrupy, but right. Okay, you dragged it out of me. When good ole Reggie was in his prime, he had the reputation as not being reliable."

"What's that mean?"

"I think it's a quaint, nonjudgmental way of saying he couldn't be trusted. His word couldn't be taken as gospel."

"Did you have dealings with him during those years?"

"Only once. He was handling a foreclosure. My client looked at it but decided on another property. And before you ask, no, Reggie didn't do or say anything to me that I found to be inaccurate. I don't know if his reputation was based on fact, or gossip."

"Anything else?"

"Tell you what, why don't I call him and see if I can entice him into coming to Al's for lunch. He's retired now like you and since you're both worthless members of society, he probably could find time. You can happen to be here at the same time and talk with him. And best of all, I can make money off both of you. A win-win."

"That's a great idea."

"That's still too syrupy, but truthful. I'll let you know."

I ARRIVED at the Crab Shack at eleven-thirty. After telling the server all I needed to drink was water, I saw Charles pulling up to the side of the building and parking his Schwinn in the bike rack at the corner.

"Sorry I'm late," he said, although I hadn't told him what time to meet me. "Dude had me deliver one more thing. This has been a prosperous day. I made enough money to buy both of our lunches. I won't but I could."

"That's almost generous of you."

"Sarcasm, right?"

"Close enough."

The server arrived with my water and asked Charles what he wanted to drink. He told her to bring him the same as I was having. She left to try to find water for Charles then he said, "I figure you wanting to have lunch with me wasn't the only reason you called."

"True. Someone broke in my house yesterday."

"Whoa, you waited this long to tell me?"

"I called this morning, and you were making deliveries for Dude."

"Excuses, excuses. Okay, apology accepted. What happened?"

I shared what little I knew about the break-in and added, "I wanted to let you know so you could be careful. Have you seen or heard anything around your place that could be suspicious?"

"Not really. I know nobody's been in my place because everything's a mess."

Charles's apartment suits his needs, but too many would be considered a hoarder's paradise, so I knew what he meant about it not being neat. If anything was straightened up, Charles hadn't done it.

The server returned and took our orders, and Charles leaned back in his chair and said, "Sounds like someone thinks we're about ready to learn who killed those folks."

"That's what Cindy thought."

"Then who is it?"

"No idea."

"If you ask me, I think it's Kyle for all the reasons I already told you. He's tried to get us off the case from the beginning. He and Shelly had their conflicts, so he had reason to shove her off the roof."

"All of that may be true, but is it enough for him to go on a killing spree?"

"Sure it is, but, umm, what about Scott? He wanted to be foreman so killing Randy would've sped up the process. And now he's quit and probably decided we were getting close and plans to skip the country."

"Now I'm confused. Do you think it's Kyle or Scott?"

"Yes."

"Yes, what?"

"Could be either."

"There you go, you've figured it out."

"Picking on me again?"

"Yes."

"Figures, so what's our next step?"

"Eating lunch," I said as the server slid lunch baskets in front of us.

The phone rang before we'd finished. The screen said Bob.

"Hello, Mr. Howard."

"That's better than calling me a moon rock, or New Age guru. Just got off the phone with my good buddy Reggie. Guess where he's having lunch tomorrow?"

"Al's."

"You're getting to be as good a detective as your quarter-wit friend Charles."

I glanced over at Charles, and said to Bob, "Okay if he comes with me tomorrow?"

"You bet, that's more bucks in my pocket. Bring more if

you can find anyone else who'd want to eat with you," he said and hung up.

Charles looked at me like what are you getting me into. I shared what I'd learned about Reginald Salyer, aka Reggie, and about his invitation to lunch tomorrow at Al's.

Charles gave me a thumbs-up and said, "That'll put us one step closer to solving the crimes."

Chapter Forty-Two

I was in front of Bert's on the way home when the phone rang. This time I looked to see who it was before answering.

"Hello, Brad."

"Are you home?"

"I'm about fifty yards from the front door and heading that way. Why?"

"Mind company? I wanted to bounce a couple of ideas off you."

I told him to come on over, then shook my head thinking how much he detested me and my meddling when he was a detective. Has he changed that much or am I different than I was not that long ago? Or, has Hazel's pronouncement that he get a hobby the reason for his changing?

He was knocking before I had time to give his metamorphosis more thought. I invited him in and asked if he wanted something to drink. I was pleased when he declined since I wasn't sure what I had. He had a manila folder in his hand so I suggested we sit in the kitchen so he could spread whatever he had in the folder on the table if he wanted to.

"I suppose you're wondering why I invited myself over."

"Yes."

"I got a call this morning from Len Fisher, the detective on the Mason Ryle case. I take it you've met."

"He came knocking on my door a few days ago. Said he'd heard I was asking questions about the murder he was investigating and said if he heard I was continuing to butt in, he'd have me arrested." I smiled and continued, "His people skills need some work. What'd he want?"

"Today was the first time I'd talked to the guy, so I was surprised when he called. He said some of the guys in the office had told him I used to be with the Sheriff's Office, had retired, and now lived next to you."

"So?"

Brad rubbed his chin, looked at the folder on the table, and said, "He said since we lived so close, I might know something that would strengthen his case against you. For some reason he's mighty upset with you."

"Why?"

Brad chuckled. "It wasn't that many years ago that I spent a good portion of my time pissed at you. Whenever I caught a murder over here, I kept running into you. If I asked you about it, you kept saying all you were doing was asking a few questions. And how many times did those, umm, questions get you in the middle of my investigation?"

"Brad, you know—"

"Yes, your involvement helped take some bad guys off the streets. And yes, you saved my life because of your butting in. The point is, he's got a burr under his saddle about you."

"What'd he want you to do?"

"He didn't use these exact words, but from what I could tell, he wants to get evidence that you're meddling so he can come down on you like a load of bricks. He wants you in jail."

"Again, what does he want you to do?"

Brad smiled. "Said I should keep my trained detective eyes on you and let him know if you are still snooping in his case."

"What'd you tell him?"

"I figured someone in the office told him about our, umm, disagreements over the years, so I said I knew what he meant about you snooping and said I'd try to see what I could find."

"What are you going to do?"

"Seeing what I can find out about your snooping." He laughed. "I didn't tell him I'd let him know what I learned. If he assumed I would, he's got a lot to learn before he becomes a good detective." He shook his head. "Young know-it-alls. Now that brings me to why I'm here." He opened the folder and took out two sheets of lined paper with scribbling on them. They were either written in code or the quality of his writing equaled his ability to run a marathon. He then took a pen out of his pocket and set it on the paper. "I've been giving a lot of thought to the murders. What's making it so difficult to get a handle on, it's not known how many of the deaths were murder, right?"

"Yes. Your new detective buddy Fisher is stuck on the

idea that only Mason Ryle was murdered and the other two were accidents. I'm convinced all three were killed. You still agree?"

"Yes, but what perplexes me is motive. The vics have nothing in common other than working at that house. Have you learned anything to dispute that?"

"No and that makes me think the murders have something to do with the house."

Brad pointed the pen at me. "You're not falling for that ludicrous idea your friend, umm—"

"Noelle?"

"Yeah, her idea the house is cursed and that's somehow killing the workers?"

"I don't believe in curses, but there still could be something about the house that's involved with the deaths."

Brad shook his head. "Like what?"

"I don't know, but it should be considered."

"Whatever. Remember I first thought the dead woman's husband would've been my top suspect if I was working the case?"

"Yes, Raymond Whitley."

"I changed my mind."

"Why?"

"Because I think the same person killed all three, and if that's true, I don't see how it could've been him. Sure, he could've somehow gotten in the house and pushed her off the roof without anyone seeing him. Remote, but possible. He also could've electrocuted the next guy since it was at the deserted house at midnight. But that brings me to the third death. All the workers were eating lunch. Some close to the house, some not so close. You can't tell me the husband could sneak up to the house, start a loud forklift, back into the guy, then climb off and walk away without anyone seeing him."

"Brad, if you're right, and I think I agree with you, the killer is one of the workers."

"Yes. And that brings me to this." He tapped the papers he took out of the folder. "These are the guys who are working on the house. Since we don't know the reason for the crimes, we have to approach it by seeing who couldn't have done it and take it from there."

I liked his use of *we*.

"Makes sense."

"Were any of the guys not working the day the woman was pushed or the day of the forklift incident?"

"I haven't heard about any of them not being there the day of Shelly's death."

"That didn't help, did it?"

"No. About the day Mason was killed, I heard Joshua Bennett was out sick."

"Good," Brad said and marked through his name on his list, or I assumed it was Joshua's name since I couldn't read Brad's writing. "Anyone else not there?"

"Luis Ortez was working on another job the day of Mason's death."

Brad marked through Ortez's name. "That all?"

"That's all I know about."

"See if I have this right. That leaves the following guys there when Shelly and Mason were killed: Lucius Walker, Tim Hale, Mitchell, umm."

"Mitchell Baldwin."

He wrote Mitchell's last name on his paper, then said, Kyle Manger, and Scott Rawlins. "Anyone else?"

"That covers it."

"Anything you've heard sound suspicious about any of them?"

"Scott Rawlins quit the other day."

"Why?"

"I heard he was worried he might be the next victim."

"What made him think there'd be more deaths?"

I was prepared for an outburst when I said, "He thought the house was cursed."

Brad stared at me and didn't say anything.

I continued, "Like I told you before, I don't believe in curses, but if he's a believer, that's what counts. I also heard Mitchell Baldwin was considering quitting for the same reason."

"Who started the damned rumor about the place being cursed?"

I realized I didn't know. Several of the workers had mentioned it, but I had no idea how or when it started.

"That's a good question. I don't know." I then shared Charles's call from the contractor he'd done some work for, then added, "Whether the curse rumor is true or fiction it still could endanger the project. Getting it closed down could be a motive for the killings."

Brad stared at his list of workers, then looked at me. "Good point, but why wouldn't the construction company be able to find more workers, even if he had to pay more, to complete the job?"

"That seems like his best option. He couldn't afford to permanently shut it down or even shut down for an extended period."

"None of that gets us closer to knowing the identity of the killer."

"No, but it narrows the list."

He again looked at his list. "Okay, unless we learn otherwise, that leaves: Manger, Walker, Baldwin, Hale, Rawlins." He looked at me. "Agree?"

I agreed with his list and then debated telling him about my efforts to learn more about the previous owners of the property. What would it achieve, other than him thinking I was joining the list of people thinking a curse was the reason for the deaths? What I did share was the break-in at the house. He said it was interesting but didn't elaborate.

He looked at his watch. "Think I'll take a walk out to the construction site and see if I can talk to a few of the workers."

"Want me to go with you?"

"Thanks for offering, but no. Haven't most of them seen or had contact with you?"

"Yes."

"I'll approach it from the angle that I haven't heard anything about what's going on and see if I can learn something that way."

"Good luck."

"I'll let you know if I succeed."

He left the house with a bounce in his step. His new hobby apparently was giving him a purpose in life.

Chapter Forty-Three

The twenty-minute drive from Charles's apartment to Al's Bar, a block off Calhoun Street near downtown Charleston, consisted of my friend asking me no fewer than five times what I thought we were going to learn from Reginald Salyer, and me responding no fewer than five times that I didn't know. I told him if I knew what we would learn, we wouldn't be making the trip. Traffic was always heavy around the Medical University of South Carolina, a couple of blocks from Al's, so Charles decided silence was the best way for me to safely finish the trip. Occasionally, he exhibits a glimmer of wisdom. Al's doesn't have a parking lot, so the closest vacant on-street parking spot was a block past the bar.

Al's shared a concrete block building with a Laundromat in a pre-gentrified, aka rundown, section of town. At one point, the building had been white but that was a long-gone memory.

It took our eyes a minute to adjust from the sunny day into a near pitch-black bar. The only illumination came from Budweiser and Budweiser Light neon signs behind the bar and a few rays of sun sneaking in the large plate-glass window that had its lower half painted black to give diners privacy. Roy Acuff's version of "Blue Eyes Crying in the Rain" was playing on the jukebox near the front door. When Al owned the bar, he'd salted the jukebox with country classics in deference to Bob, a huge country music fan. To put it mildly, the country tunes weren't well received by the primarily African American clientele, but Al's friendship with Bob was stronger than the objections and the songs remained.

We were warmly greeted by Al Washington, the bar's former owner, who'd agreed to stay on after Bob bought the struggling business to serve a role like a Walmart greeter. The unpaid position gave the eighty-three-year-old something to do plus it helped bridge a divide the width of the Atlantic Ocean between the bar's diners and the pasty-white new owner.

"Chris, Charles, it's great seeing you," Al said as he gave each of us a hug. "Blubber Bob," an endearing term, I assumed, "has been pestering me every five minutes about if you were here yet." Al chuckled. "It's like he couldn't see everyone entering since he's sitting forty feet from the door."

"It's good to see you too, Al. How're you feeling?"

"I'm still here."

"Al, you're looking good," Charles said, probably feeling left out of the conversation.

Al laughed. "That's why we keep the lights off."

"Al, damnit," boomed Bob Howard's voice from the back of the room, "earn your astronomical salary and let those skinny honkies get over here and spend money."

Al turned to me and said, "What's not to love about that guy?"

I said, "We'd better get back there. Wouldn't want you to get fired and lose your astronomical salary."

"Good idea. I'd hate to lose the nothing he's paying me."

We each gave Al another hug and headed to Bob's table; the table everyone knows is Bob's because he'd installed a plaque on the top of it telling anyone who could read that it was his. Only two other diners were in the room plus Bob with his stomach pinned between the chair and the table. He wore a green T-shirt, tan shorts, and a four-day old beard. With the lack of illumination in the room he resembled an out-of-season Santa, although his demeanor was anything but Santa-like.

Bob looked at his watch then said, "Reginald said he'd be here in about ten minutes. Want something expensive to drink while you wait? Lawrence, get over here and wait on these two."

Lawrence was Al's part-time cook and ever since Al's arthritis kept him from getting around the room like he used to, the cook doubled as server.

"Morning, Mr. Chris, Mr. Charles, what can I get you?"

"It's good to see you, Lawrence. I'll have a glass of white wine. Charles, want a beer?"

Charles said yes and Lawrence headed to the front of the bar to get our drinks.

Bob watched him go and said, "Reggie might act surprised when he sees you. I didn't tell him anyone else would be joining us. I figured he might not have accepted my generous offer if he knew you'd be pestering him for information. I did tell him I was interested in a deal he'd been involved in around a decade ago and gave him the name of the holding company that bought the property."

Lawrence returned with our drinks and Bob glanced at the entry. "He's early."

I turned to see someone headed our way. The man was roughly my age, thin, and dressed like a used car salesman in a light-blue suit, white shirt, and a red tie. Bob had said he was retired, but you wouldn't know it from his appearance. He carried a file folder that matched the color of his tie.

"Reggie," Bob said, "good to see you." Bob leaned toward the newcomer without getting out of his seat and they shook hands. "Meet my friends Chris Landrum and Charles Fowler."

We all shook hands and Reginald, aka Reggie, took the seat beside Bob and across from Charles and me.

Lawrence delivered our drinks and asked Reggie what he wanted. He looked at the beer bottles in front of Bob and Charles and said he'd have the same.

Reggie glanced around the room and said, "You own this place?"

"Yes, it's a goldmine," Bob said.

Reggie hesitated like he couldn't tell if Bob was serious then said, "Quite different than when you were a successful realtor."

Lawrence was quick to the table with Reggie's beer then asked if we were ready to order.

Bob said, "We've got the best cheeseburgers in the state, and possibly the country. I'd go with that if I were you. That's what Chris and Charles are having."

It was the first time I was hearing about my menu choice, but he was right since they're good, although I couldn't vouch for them compared to everywhere else in the state.

Reggie said, "Sounds good."

"And fries, too," Bob added.

"Sure."

Lawrence headed to the kitchen to start on our order, and Bob started on Reggie.

"Thought you'd retired?"

"I have," Reggie said.

"Then what's with the sartorial splendor?"

I suspected anyone wearing long pants and a shirt with a collar would meet Bob's definition of sartorial splendor.

"It's a hard habit to break. After dressing like this for forty-three years, I'm more comfortable this way than how, hmm, you're dressed."

"Did you find out what I called about?" Bob said, apparently tired of the conversation about clothing.

Johnny and June Carter Cash were singing "Jackson" as Reggie tapped on the red folder. "Everything I know about it is here."

"Good," Bob said. "Chris and Charles are investigating some deaths over on Folly and were asking about the property that was sold a while back. I told them you were the expert and if anything could be found, you'd find it."

I'd never seen Bob's sucking-up skills in action. It wasn't bad for someone who spews insults most of the time.

Reggie looked at me then at Charles. "You law enforcement?"

Before I could say no, Charles said, "Private detectives."

Bob nearly choked on his beer.

Reggie said, "Oh."

Bob pointed at the folder and said, "Let's hear what you've got."

"This goes back a few years, so I'll have to refer to the paperwork to refresh my memory," Reggie said then opened the folder. "I was the seller's agent. The property on Folly Beach was oceanfront as I recall. I didn't know the seller until I got a call from a friend of mine at the Folly police department. Anyway, he called and said there was a family that needed a realtor and needed one fast."

Charles said, "Why the rush?"

"A sad story. The owner's wife had died a year earlier after a protracted battle with cancer. They had two kids. The husband was unemployed at the time. I don't recall what he did for a living when he was working. Couldn't find anything in the file about that. Anyway, he spent all his savings and borrowed past his limit to pay for healthcare for his wife." Reggie looked toward the front window like he was remembering something from the past. "Don't know if I have all this right, but it seems like the medical expenses, hospital and docs cost, plus medicine put him a couple hundred thousand in debt, a massive amount back then."

Lawrence returned with our lunch and set a plate in front of us, and a smaller plate piled high with fries in front of Bob. The cook/server knew how to keep his boss happy.

We each took a bite and Bob said, "Well, Reggie, isn't it the best you've ever had?"

"It's good."

"Good, hell," Bob said, "it's the best."

Reggie had taken another bite and put his hand in front of his face before saying, "I think you're right."

Reggie might not know Bob well but knew him enough not to argue over something that couldn't be proven.

Charles, who has the patience of a starving chipmunk said, "So what happened with the guy and his house?"

Reggie turned to Charles, "The world was closing in on the poor guy. The bank was hours from foreclosing on the house. Credit card companies were calling almost hourly. The utility company had shut off his electric. He was in a world of hurt." He shook his head. "That's why my buddy on the police department wanted me to get involved. He wanted to see if the guy could get out of any of it." He hesitated and took another bite of maybe the best cheeseburger Reggie had ever eaten.

"What happened?" Charles asked after waiting as long as he could for Reggie to continue.

The smooth sounds of Sammi Smith singing "Help Me Make It Through the Night" filled the air combined with the aroma of the burgers. I hadn't heard anything yet that'd help learn who killed the workers.

"Charles," Reggie said in a raised voice, "by the time I met with the homeowner on a Monday afternoon, he already had a court order to be out of the house by midnight Thursday or the police would forcefully remove him along with his belongings. He was in a panic when we met. He was bouncing off the walls screaming about being left with nothing and two kids. What'd he think I could do with only three days until he was kicked out?"

"Hell, Reggie," Bob said, "stop turning this into a soap opera and tell us what happened."

Reggie glared at Bob then turned to Charles. "I knew a guy down in Savannah who handled some distressed properties and brokered some deals with out-of-state holding companies. He owed me a favor or two. He gave me the name of an outfit out of Connecticut that invested in under-valued properties. I called them and with luck got the right person on the phone; somebody who could wheel and deal. The guy had a cousin living in Columbia. My contact had his cousin come see the property. The house didn't look like more than a teardown, but it was beachfront. Property values over there weren't escalating like they are today, but he still saw it had potential."

Bob leaned toward Reggie. "Unless you speed up this story, you'll be buying supper here."

Reggie straightened his tie and turned back to Charles. "The out-of-state company offered nearly what the owner owed but said they would make sure the bank didn't come down on him for the rest. I don't know what they did, but it worked. To make a long story shorter, for Bob's sake, the family was out on Thursday like they had to be." He looked at his cell phone, and added, "It'll be ten years in a couple of days."

Bob said, "Reggie, you've given us a blow-by-blow description of everything that happened except the important parts. What's the name of the family, the company that bought the property, and, well, that's enough for now."

Reggie flipped through the papers in the folder and said, "Family's the Hallorans. Like I already said, the father is David. Sara's the mother and the kids are named Austin, age thirteen, and Hannah, sixteen."

Bob sighed before saying, "The company that bought it?"

"The property was purchased by IH Financial Group."

Sean had already told me about the sellers, the Hallorans, and the buyers but hadn't mentioned the children's names.

"That is sad," I said.

Charlie Rich was singing "Behind Closed Doors," Bob was stuffing his mouth with fries, and Charles said, "What happened to them?"

"I'm afraid it gets sadder," Reggie said as he closed the folder. "I heard most of this from my friend on the police force. He left Folly's force and hired on in North Charleston. Died last year in a truck versus car accident. Anyway, I don't know where my friend got the information, but I have no reason to doubt it. He said the family moved to a tiny apartment in a bad section of North Charleston. The dad took to heavy drinking and blamed all his bad fortune on the holding company that bought the property. I didn't see where he had a case since he had no choice but to be out. At least the company kept him out of bankruptcy. Anyway, he died less than two years after moving. Alcohol got him."

Charles said, "What happened to the kids?"

"No idea," he said and took the last bite of cheeseburger.

Lawrence returned to see if we needed anything else. Reggie said no and asked for his check, saying he had a doctor's appointment. He didn't offer to buy lunch for Charles and me, and, of course, neither did Bob. We said our appropriate goodbyes and Bob told him to come by anytime and bring his friends with him. Reggie said he would in a tone that screamed *no way*.

Charles and I stood to shake his hand and Bob leaned his direction to gracelessly stick out his hand to shake.

"Well, what'd we learn?" Charles asked as soon as we returned to the car.

"Not much. That's a sad story about the family who sold the house to the holding company, but I don't see how it's connected to anything going on now."

"We learned the name of the family and the company that bought it."

"Sean had already told me that much. All I heard new were the kids' names."

I felt Charles's eyes beaming at me before he said, "When did Sean tell you their names?"

"Couple of days ago."

"And I didn't learn about it until now?"

"I didn't see where it was important. The family name wasn't familiar."

"That's still no reason to keep it from me. I could've known them."

"Did you?"

"No."

"You're still right. It still seems irrelevant since I don't see any connection between what happened a decade ago and now. Do you?"

"Not really."

Nothing else was said until I crossed the bridge to Folly, when Charles broke the silence with, "Why don't we meet at Loggers at, umm, let's see, how about four-thirty? Maybe one or more of the workers from the house will be there and we can, umm, do something."

I doubted anything productive could come from that, but it was a nice day and sitting outside would beat being holed up at the house, so I told him I'd see him there.

Chapter Forty-Four

The problem going to a restaurant with outdoor seating in good weather is good weather makes everyone want to be outside, or so it seems. Today was no exception. When I arrived at Loggerhead's, every patio table was occupied, and the bar was packed. Today was one time I was glad Charles arrived thirty minutes early for everything. He was seated at the far side of the bar talking to someone I didn't recognize.

"Chris," he said as I moved beside him, "meet Lonnie. He works at Crosby's."

Crosby's Fish & Shrimp Company is the go-to spot for most people on Folly who seek fresh food from the sea.

"Nice to meet you, Lonnie."

"Likewise," he said and looked at his watch. He took the last sip from his beer and turned to Charles. "Gotta head out. Nice meeting you, Charles, you too, Chris."

Charles watched him go, turned to me, and said, "Good timing. You show up late and get a stool beside me."

I ignored his comment as the bartender asked what I was having. I told him white wine before turning to Charles. "Okay, here we are. Seen any of the construction workers?"

"No, but they're probably getting off about now. You need to be patient like me."

I didn't laugh but should have. Charles claiming to be patient was by far the funniest thing I'd heard all day, possibly all week.

I said, "Have you thought about what Bob's friend said today? Any new ideas?"

"Not really, but it doesn't matter. I still think the killer is Scott, possibly Kyle, or could be Mitchell."

"You think it's Scott because he quit?"

"That and he was itching to become foreman which would've given him a reason to kill Randy."

"Why Kyle?"

"That's an easy one. He's the one who sicced the cops on us, well, mainly on you to try to get you, us, off the case. Besides, I don't like his girlfriend. Don't know what he sees in her."

That wasn't much, but I couldn't disagree. Couldn't prove it either.

"Then, what about Mitchell?"

"Virgil said he's pushing the *house is cursed* stories. If people think a curse killed those folks, it'd get Mitchell off the hook. Deflection, my friend."

"Okay, let's say it's one of those three. If you had to choose one, who would it be?"

"Kyle."

"Why?"

"He's worked the hardest to keep us off his trail. Who would you choose?"

"I'm not certain it's one of those three, but if I had to choose one of them, I'd agree with you."

Charles took a sip of his beer, then said, "How do we prove it?" He hesitated, looked over my shoulder, and added, "Hold that thought and my seat."

He hopped off the stool and weaved his way around the crowd gathered in front of the bar. He stopped but I couldn't see who he was talking to until he was on his way back with his arm around Kyle Manger's shoulder.

"Hey, Chris, look who I found."

"Hi, Kyle," I said and slid my stool a few inches farther away from Charles's.

Kyle shook my hand, moved between Charles and me, then said, "Charles said you were buying drinks. I appreciate it."

I would too if someone else was buying the drinks, although that seldom happens.

He leaned over the bar and told the bartender he'd have a beer.

Charles said, "Kyle was telling me he just got off work."

No surprise, since that was the reason Charles suggested we meet here.

Kyle said, "Chris, this has been a bear of a day. Every time I turn around, I'm forced to stop working on what I need to do until one of the carpenters gets his work done."

I said, "I understand they're having a hard time getting carpenters."

"Yeah, they're down to two. One got fired a couple of

weeks ago, Scott quit, and, well, you know what happened to Mason."

"That's rough," Charles said. "How come Scott quit?"

Charles was beginning his fishing expedition.

"Don't know for certain," he said before taking a long draw on the beer that'd been set in front of him. "Heard it had to do with the rumor about the house being cursed. Damned stupid reason for giving up a good paying job if you ask me."

Since he brought it up, I thought it was a good time to add something to the cursed rumor.

"I hear Mitchell is thinking about quitting for the same reason."

"Yeah, I heard that, but I wouldn't put too much stock in it. He told me he didn't believe in silly curses." He took another sip before saying, "I'm glad I ran into you two. I want to apologize."

Charles said, "What for?"

"Sort of what my girlfriend did."

I waited for him to continue, but he didn't.

Charles didn't wait. "What'd she do?"

"I'm sort of embarrassed about it. After the deaths out at the house, that detective, believe Fishell's his name, he—"

"Detective Fisher," Charles corrected.

"Yeah, that's it. He came to talk to me about the deaths. Where I was when it happened, what I saw, stuff like that. Pat was with me, so he included her in the discussion. Pat's a wonderful gal but can get riled up. When you first met her, here, in fact, we were talking about the death of Shelly and Pat got all pissy. Think she was jealous, stupid since Shelly was dead. Anyway, she went off on you two with the detective."

"What do you mean?"

"She started ranting about how you'd harassed us, wouldn't let us eat in peace, claimed she felt intimidated by your questioning when all you were doing was talking." He slowly shook his head. "I barely got a word in edgewise. I apologize."

I said, "That's okay. I hope she doesn't really feel that way."

"I don't think she does. I know she's calmed a lot since then." He smiled. "Calm as long as I don't mention Shelly."

Charles said, "I understand. But while I'm thinking about it, where did the rumor start about the house being cursed?"

"I don't know who started it. It was going around with some of the guys as soon as Shelly fell, then after Randy got himself electrocuted, nearly everyone was talking about a curse. Why?"

"Just curious. Being that it's new, I was wondering how the idea of a curse got started. Aren't they usually in old houses?"

"You're asking the wrong guy about that. Curses ain't something I think much about. Now I don't know about it being a curse, but something sure must be wrong out there. Three dead people in such a short period of time and all of them working on one job. That's hard to believe." He took another drink then added, "Speaking of Pat getting pissed, I'm supposed to meet her for supper near her apartment. If I don't leave now, I'll be the one getting her wrath."

Charles reminded him I would pick up his tab. Kyle thanked me, patted Charles on the back, and headed to the stairs.

Charles watched him go, took another sip of the beer I was buying, and said, "Well, now what do you think of our number one suspect?"

"He seemed sincere with his apology, and I can see how Pat clouded Detective Fisher's impression of what happened when we met them here."

"That mean you no longer have him at the top of your list?"

"I'm leaning that way. How about you?"

"Yep."

Chapter Forty-Five

The next morning, I awoke to the sound of rain bouncing off my metal roof. With nowhere I had to be, this would be a good day to stay in the house and get caught up reading photo magazines that'd come in the last few weeks. I fired up my Mr. Coffee machine, found some three-day-old donuts on the counter, and parked myself at the kitchen table to wait for Mr. Coffee to do its thing. The coffee maker was acting like I was feeling: slow and aging.

It finished perking a carafe of coffee, I poured a cup, grabbed one of the magazines and the donuts, and moved to the front porch to watch people who still had jobs drive past the house. While I was glad I didn't have to go to work, I suspected few, if any, of them felt slow and aging.

Neither the articles about how to take great landscape photos or the commuters driving past held my attention, so I began revisiting yesterday's meeting with Charles and Kyle. I mainly focused on something Charles asked the plumber.

That was where did the rumor start about the house being cursed? There's one way to find out.

I grabbed my phone and tapped in Charles's number.

"Are you calling to invite me to breakfast?"

"No."

"Good, it's too yucky to go anywhere. Now that I talked you out of going to breakfast, why'd you call?"

"Yesterday, when we were talking to Kyle, you asked him how the rumor started about the house being cursed."

"Yeah, so?"

"Why'd you ask him that?"

"I've been thinking about the rumor. Didn't it have to start somewhere?"

"Yes," I said then took a sip.

"You thought Scott was trying to push blame onto Shelly's husband. Why? To deflect blame away from himself. Then early on, Kyle talked about a carpenter getting himself fired. Why? To deflect blame away from himself."

"Your point?"

"Okay, let's say the killer starts getting everyone blaming the deaths on a curse, wouldn't that deflect the blame away from him?"

"I guess so, but while the first two deaths could've been accidents and, I suppose, attributable to a curse, someone got on that forklift and pinned Mason between it and the house. A curse didn't drive it."

Charles said, "Did I say my theory was foolproof?"

"No."

"It doesn't appear more farfetched than yours about

something related to the sale of the house, or whatever that was about."

"I'll give you that," I said. "Okay, let's say the person killing the workers started the rumor that the house was cursed. How do we find out who it was?"

"Ask each worker out there. We've already talked to Kyle. That leaves, umm, several more. I've got us this far, now it's up to you to figure out how to ask each of them. That's something to do on a rainy day. Call when you get it figured out."

I assured him I would and ended the call.

Charles's logic made sense but trying to ask everybody who works there the question appeared to be a daunting task. And, by asking each of them, we would be asking the person who started it. If my theory is correct, asking a murderer who'd already killed three people sounded dangerous.

The phone rang before I could figure out a good way to interrogate the group without turning a murderer loose on us.

"This is your good buddy Bob. Hungry for a cheeseburger?"

"I was there yesterday. Why would I want to go out in this weather for a cheeseburger?"

"Figured you wouldn't, but thought I'd ask."

"So, you called to not invite me to Al's for a cheeseburger?"

"That sounds like a trick question, so I'll ignore it. I called to tell you I got a call last night around ten-thirty from my friend, overdressed Reggie Salyer. After I got him off the phone, I would've called you, but knew it was past your bedtime. Being the kind, gentle, and considerate person I am, I waited until now."

I waited for him to continue, but he didn't, so I said, "You waiting for applause?"

"Smartass."

Kind, gentle, and considerate?

"Yep."

"Well, aren't you going to ask why he called?"

"I figured you called to tell me."

"You'd be more fun to talk to in the middle of the night. Reggie remembered something else he'd heard about the Halloran family. He said it was only a rumor, so not to take it as gospel."

I sighed. "What did he tell you?"

"That's better. Remember he said the father died?"

"Yes, a couple of years after being forced out of their house. Died caused by his drinking."

"Yes. What Reggie didn't remember to tell us was that the son, believe his name's Austin, had a nervous breakdown or two after his dad died. Reggie didn't know any of the details, but heard the kid was in and out of mental hospitals for three or four years."

"Is that it?"

"Yes. Reggie said he didn't know if that'd mean anything but wanted to let me know so I could share it with you and your quarter-wit private detective friend."

"I don't know if it will help or not, but I appreciate you letting me know."

"Good. Now you owe me another meal at my upscale and wildly popular bar."

"Of course," I said to a dial tone.

There was one thing I did agree with Bob on. I had no idea if that additional bit of information about the Halloran family helped.

Chapter Forty-Six

By late afternoon, the rain had stopped and steam from the evaporating water was giving the road in front of my house an eerie appearance as the sun peeked out from behind clouds. All in all, it looked like a pleasant evening in the making. After being stuck in the house all day, I needed to stretch my legs and decided a walk out West Ashley Avenue should meet that need. Yes, I was also headed in the direction of the house under construction. Probably not a coincidence, I thought, as I left my cottage.

A red pickup truck with a Bolt Electric logo on the door was the only vehicle at the job site. I started to cross the street and see if Lucius Walker was the Bolt employee still at work when I heard, "Yo, Christopher" coming from the vacant lot beside me.

I turned and saw Virgil step out from behind a row of shrubs and walk my way.

"Hi, Virgil, what're you doing out here?"

"Honing my private detective skills. I've got a lot to learn to be near on par with you and Charles."

"Hiding behind shrubs is how you're, umm, sharpening your skills?"

He looked across the street at the job site, then at me. "Not standing behind any old shrubs, but the one that gives me a clear view of you-know-what. What brings you out this way?"

Probably the same thing Virgil was doing, but instead of sharing that, I said, "Been thinking a lot about the deaths and wanted to walk by to refresh my memory about the roof Shelly fell from, and where the forklift was when Mason was killed."

Virgil smiled. "See, I'm on the right track."

Lucius Walker was leaving the house carrying a small tool kit. He got in his truck, backed out, then headed toward town. Fortunately, he didn't notice us standing across the street.

"How long have you been here?"

"Got here after the rain stopped. There were four guys finishing for the day. They were loading tools and some scrap wood in their trucks, waving bye to each other, then headed out."

"Did you learn anything significant from watching?"

"Yeah, when four o'clock rolled around, they split like cockroaches when lights come on."

"How was that significant?"

"Christopher, you have to remember, I'm not as good as you and Charles. I doubt it was significant. I'm establishing a profile of the employees. For example, as you saw, that electrician guy didn't rush to leave like the others."

"And you found that significant?"

"Maybe it was; maybe it wasn't. He could've stayed later to set a trap in the house so when the others get here tomorrow, someone could fall for the trap and get himself killed. Probably something electrical since he's an electrician. That would be one more reason to think the place is cursed. On the other hand, he could've stayed late to finish up something that had to be done today."

I didn't think Virgil's observation meant anything, but since I had no idea what was going on, it was as good as anything I'd learned.

I said, "What's your plan now?"

"Head back to town, stop at Loggers, see if I can charm someone into buying me a beer."

"Why don't I go with you and buy you a beer? No charming necessary."

"That sounds like a splendid plan."

The crowd at the outside bar wasn't as busy as it had been the last time I was here. The earlier rain must've kept a few customers away. We took two vacant stools at the bar. Good to his word, Virgil ordered a beer, and I went with a soft drink.

Our drinks arrived, we each took a sip, and I said, "Are you still doing maintenance at your apartment building?"

"So far, I think I'm a better amateur plumber than private detective. I've handily defeated every clogged drain and toilet that've been thrown at me. They don't stand a chance against plumber Virgil."

"Speaking for all the tenants in your building, I'm glad to hear that."

He smiled and nodded before the smile faded. "Now in my other career as an assistant private detective in Charles's agency, I still have much to learn."

Him claiming to be an assistant private detective proves he has much to learn.

"Have you come to any conclusions about the deaths?"

He took a sip, looked around the rapidly filling bar, then said, "Calling it a conclusion may be giving it too much credit, but I've been thinking about how so many of the guys are calling the house cursed."

"What about it?"

"Most of them are smart guys. It takes a lot of knowledge to be a plumber, an electrician, even a carpenter. I could be wrong, but I don't believe places can be cursed. I'm not nearly as smart as most of them, so if I know there's no thing as a cursed house, why do they think there is? See what I mean?"

I nodded. "I don't understand it either."

"Seems to me, there's a killer on the loose. Seems to me, he works at the house. Seems to me, there must be a reason he's killing off his fellow employees. And, I don't have a clue why he's doing it."

"Me either."

He took a couple more sips, tapped the bottle on the counter, and said, "Still got the curse thing on my mind. You remember back when you, Charles, and I were at Planet Follywood talking with Tim and Scott?"

"Sure."

"One of us asked the guys who started the rumor about the house being cursed. I think it was Tim who said talk was going around about it, but he didn't know who started it."

"I vaguely remember that. What about it?"

"I was up here last night. Sitting at the far end of the bar to be more specific." He nodded his head a couple of times. "Saw Mitchell, you know, one of the carpenters, and started up a conversation. He'd had a rough day at work; something about an upstairs room needing to move a wall that they'd already built. I didn't understand what he was talking about, but he was PO'ed." He took another drink and stared across the deck.

"What about Mitchell?"

He smiled. "Sorry, got off track, didn't I? Anyway, that danged curse was on my mind last night like it is now. I asked him if he believed it. He said he guessed so. Pretty noncommittal if you ask me."

If that was all Virgil was going to share, he was off track again.

"Is that it?"

"No, I was trying to remember the sequence of the conversation. Oh, yeah, since the curse was on my mind, I asked him who started talking about it first. He said he didn't know but figured it must've been Tim Hale. After he said that, I asked why he thought that. Said he may be wrong, but Tim was the first person who mentioned it to him. See what I mean?"

I didn't see how that proved that Tim had started the rumor.

"I understand why he said that, but that doesn't prove Tim started it."

"I agree, but that's the best I could get out of him. It's something to think about though."

"Yes," I said, more to encourage Virgil than as a viable possibility.

"So, what do you and Charles know about Tim? I haven't heard his name mentioned as the possible killer."

"All I know is he was hired at the beginning of the job and the only thing that came back on his background check was a speeding ticket."

Virgil smiled. "Not quite the stuff serial killers are made of."

"True."

Virgil snapped his fingers, looked at his watch, and said, "Christopher, have to go. I was supposed to unclog a sink in unit thirty-four before Sammi's husband gets home and yells at her for not having supper ready."

I said I'd get his tab.

He thanked me and headed to Sammi's sink-clogged apartment.

Chapter Forty-Seven

I was awake before sunrise the next morning thinking about what Virgil had said about Tim Hale possibly being the first person who mentioned a curse on the West Ashley Avenue house. That didn't prove, didn't even suggest, that Tim was the person who'd started the rumor, but it reminded me of something Kyle had told me the day Mason had his deadly encounter with the forklift. I'd asked where the crew members were when the death occurred. He said he'd taken a walk on the beach, and that Tim either often or occasionally sat on the beach. Was that all he'd said? It seems there was more, but for the life of me I can't recall what.

Often, a good way for me to remember something that for whatever reason had slipped my memory was to do or think about something else. Maybe after a cup or two of coffee, Kyle's words would come back to me. I padded into the kitchen, started Mr. Coffee, and sat at the table to watch the liquid brain-starter drip into the carafe.

Had Virgil said anything else that could help me figure out who'd ended the three lives. He said Lucius Walker could've stayed late to boobytrap something in the house to add another victim to the growing list. That seemed unlikely although a possibility.

Now back to thinking about what Kyle had said. Some of it was coming back to me. Hadn't he said Tim was sitting on the beach when Kyle started his walk but wasn't there when he returned? Was that significant? Probably not, because Kyle had also said when he returned from the walk, their lunch break was over, and Tim was back at work.

Finally, it came to me. Kyle said Tim had shared that when he sat on the beach it reminded him of growing up out that way. I wonder if Tim could've said growing up there, as in where the house was being built, rather than *in the area*. Hadn't Bob's acquaintance Reggie said the Hallorans had two children, a boy and a girl, Austin and Hannah? If I remember correctly, Reggie had also mentioned the two kids and said the boy was about thirteen years old, the girl a couple of years older?

What were the chances that Timothy Hale was Austin Halloran? Tim was about the same age as Austin since it's been about ten years since his father was forced to sell the house. Even if he was the same person, what would be his motive for killing three people? If his motive was revenge, none of the victims could have known about or been part of forcing the Hallorans out of their house. Also, how easy would it have been for Austin to change his name?

On my second cup of coffee, I then remembered what Bob had said Reggie told him about the son having one or more nervous breakdowns and spending time in mental health facilities. I suppose he could still be suffering issues and in a confused state, sees logic in killing people at the site that was so traumatic for him.

Was it merely a coincidence Tim was hired at the beginning of the job or had he planned it? If killing the other workers was his plan, what better place to be than on the crew?

While there were still many unanswered questions, Tim being Austin appears to be the most logical scenario for what'd happened at the job site.

I wonder if Reggie remembered anything else about the family, especially Tim. Of course, the best way to find out was to ask. I didn't have Reggie's number, so going through Bob would be the best way to contact the retired realtor. He wouldn't be at Al's yet, but should be awake, or so I hoped.

"Bob, this is Chris, did I catch you at a bad time?"

"You always catch me at a bad time. You calling to make a luncheon reservation?"

"Not this time. Could you give me Reggie's phone number?"

"I could, but I need a lot more information than that before I give it to you."

"Like what?"

"Like why in the hell do you want his number? He can't fix you any great cheeseburgers. He can't sell you any real estate that I can't. And he ain't going to give you any gossip on me because I have too much on him and he knows it. So, why want his number?"

I told him I was looking for more information about the Halloran family.

"You're still nosing in those deaths."

No reason to deny it.

"Yes."

"Tell you what, let me call him. He's more likely to tell me things than he would be to tell you. Tell me what you want to know."

That wasn't my preferred way to approach Reggie, but Bob probably knew how to get information from him better than I did. I told him I was more interested in learning more about the son, Austin.

"Don't suppose you're going to tell me why, are you?"

"Not yet, but it could be important. Thanks for offering to make the call."

"Yeah, whatever. I'll call you after I talk to him. I'll also expect a customer for lunch as payment for my valuable information."

"If it's valuable, you can count on me for that lunch."

He apparently got what he wanted to hear since he'd hung up.

My next call was going to be more difficult.

"Brad, this is Chris. Catch you at a bad time?"

"If you called ten minutes earlier, it would've been bad. I was in the middle of a stack of hotcakes Hazel fixed. Never disturb me when I'm eating hotcakes."

"I'll keep that in mind. Got a question."

"Does it have to do with you meddling in the deaths out at that house?"

"Yes."

"Good. What is it?"

"When you were giving me the information your buddy in the Sheriff's Office found out about the guys employed at the construction site, you said Timothy Hale had a speeding ticket. Did you say how many years back that was?"

"Hang on a second. I have that information somewhere in my office."

I heard him tell Hazel who was on the phone and he'd help her clean the living room when he got off the phone.

"Here we go. Let's see, Timothy Hale, one speeding ticket a year ago."

"And that's all you got on him?"

"Yes, my buddy said he was a little surprised. Said twenty-two-year-old guys don't usually stop with one speeding ticket. He had a good point. Back in the dark ages when I was a patrol officer, I'd get the same kids two, three, or more times speeding. Of course, there were always exceptions, but they were rare. What's the deal with Timothy Hale?"

"Not sure there's anything. I'm following up on some of the things I've been told. I'll let you know if it comes to anything."

"You better. Now I have to clean the living room. Sure you don't need me to drive you somewhere?"

I dreaded the next call but knew that if I didn't make it and something happened, I'd never be able to live it down.

"Cindy, good morning."

"What's good about it? I've got three guys out sick. Another one turned in his resignation ten minutes ago, and I have a headache."

"Sorry. That sounds like a rough morning."

"Are you going to make it rougher?"

"Maybe, so let me start with a question."

"No, you're too old to replace the officer who quit."

I smiled then said, "Then let me try another question."

"Well, what is it?"

"How difficult is it to change your name?"

"Legally or illegally?"

"Either."

"Legally, there are some hoops to jump through, but it's possible."

"How about illegally?"

"Find a good forger. He can forge documents you normally have. Things like a birth certificate, driver's license, even a passport if your friendly, neighborhood forger is really, really, good."

"Would the illegal documents get by if someone gets a speeding ticket, for example?"

"Possibly, but that'd depend on the cop issuing the ticket. If he, or she, ran the information through an on-board computer, there'd be a problem. But many forces don't have access to that technology in their vehicles, so most likely, it wouldn't get flagged. You planning to change your name?"

I then told her my theory about Timothy Hale being Austin Halloran, the son of the man who had to sell the house and who later drank himself to death. I was surprised when she didn't interrupt several times, scream at me calling me a nutcase at best, and telling me to mind my own business. Her headache probably prevented her from exploding. After I finished sharing my story, she had me repeat a couple parts of it, said something about needing a dozen pain pills, and telling me she'd share my story with Detective Fisher. I thanked her and asked if she was okay.

"No, but it's early, so the day can get worse."

I managed to say I was sorry before she hung up on me.

The other call I needed to make was to Charles.

He didn't answer and his voicemail kicked in after six rings. I told him to call when he got a chance, then realized Cindy's headache had worked its way through the phone and into my skull.

Chapter Forty-Eight

I spent the rest of the day nearly as frustrated as I'd been early this morning. The phone remained so silent that I hoped for a robocall. Charles hadn't returned my call and Bob Howard hadn't gotten back to me with whatever he'd learned from Reggie. A walk next door to Bert's to get something from the deli for supper was my only venture out of the house. Nothing on television interested me and I went to bed a little before ten.

The phone jarred me out of my sleep. I focused my half-asleep eyes on the clock on the bedside table to find that it was nearly midnight. Surely, Bob or Charles wouldn't be calling this late. I grabbed the phone to discover I was wrong. The screen read *Charles*.

I mumbled, "What were you thinking calling me this late?"

"Get to the house on West Ashley," he said, barely above a whisper. "Don't park close."

I couldn't believe I heard him correctly. "Now?"

"Hurry."

I heard what sounded like a door opening in the background, then the phone went dead.

It took me a couple of minutes to shake my head awake and get my bearings. I glanced at the phone like I couldn't believe the call. It read *11:47*.

I dressed and slowly walked to the car. My legs were a little wobbly but stepping outside in the cool air awakened me more.

Mine was the only car on the road as I drove out West Ashley Avenue. Once the construction site came into view, I pulled off the road and parked. The house appeared deserted. No lights were visible, nor were lights on in the house on either side of the one under construction. An old red pickup truck was parked in front of the house on the far side of my destination.

I slowly approached the house regretting I hadn't brought a flashlight. The light on my phone would have to do. Illumination from a full moon helped some as I walked slowly around the house. Charles was nowhere in sight.

On my second time around the house, I noticed the sliding glass patio door was open about a foot. Surely, the workers would've done a better job of closing the house up after they left for the day. I stuck my head into the house and listened.

Nothing.

I took a deep breath, and opened the door another foot, stepped in, and said, "Charles?"

No answer, so I tried again, this time louder. Still no answer.

Do I venture further into the dark house or back out and call the police?

If I called the police, what would I tell them? I was sneaking into a house under construction and not hearing any sounds I decided to call the police. Umm, no.

I called Charles's' name one more time. Hearing nothing, I went from room to room on the first floor. No Charles. I was approaching the stairs when I heard a sound coming from upstairs. At first, I thought it may be a mouse or a bird that managed to get in the house. Then I heard it again, and the thought entered my mind that it could be Charles and he may need help.

I walked up the steps to the sound of each stair tread squeaking as I put weight on it. At the top of the stairs, I saw what I thought was someone on the floor. My phone light wasn't bright enough for me to see who, so I took three steps closer to the person, only to find two people lying beside each other. Neither was moving.

The closer I got, I realized the person closest to me was Charles. The other person was facing the other direction so I couldn't tell who it was.

I quickened my pace then bent over Charles to see if he was alive.

I nearly tripped over my friend's body when behind me, someone said, "They're alive. For now."

I turned to see Tim Hale. He was dressed in black, had a pistol in one hand, and a gasoline can in the other."

"Tim, you startled me. What's going on?"

I was certain I knew the answer, but anything I could do to keep him talking increased my chances of leaving the house alive.

He looked at his watch, set the gas can on the floor beside a pile of six-foot-long two-by-fours, took a flashlight out of his pocket, and pointed it at me. He then said, "Eleven fifty-seven. Know what tomorrow is?"

I'm not certain why, but something popped in my head that Sean Aker had told me. He said it'll be ten years in a couple of days to when the family had to be out of their house.

"The tenth anniversary of when your family was evicted from the house that was on this site."

He sighed and said, "Knew you were figuring it out. Saw the way you looked at me whenever you saw me. That's why I broke into your house, but I didn't find anything about me." He shook his head like he was shaking thoughts out. "Who told you about the anniversary?"

I figured I knew what he had in mind for us but didn't want to say anything that'd endanger Reggie or anyone else. "A friend. Tim, or should I say Austin?"

With his voice breaking, he said, "How do you know that?"

"A lawyer told me." I hesitated then said, "The police also know."

His hand holding the pistol began to shake and he said, "It doesn't matter."

"Tim, why kill the three people? What'd they do to you? Did they know your identity?"

He pointed the flashlight at the other person on the floor. "Because of him."

I still couldn't see the person's face.

"Who is it?"

"The man who killed my Dad. The man who stole my happy place. The man who ruined our family."

"Oliver Trescott?"

He nodded.

"I understand that, but why kill three innocent people."

"I wanted him to suffer like Dad did; like my sister did; like I did."

"Let me guess. You started the rumors that the house was cursed so Trescott would watch progress on the house get slowed down and possibly stopped. You hoped he'd hear the rumors you'd started and connect them to his buying the house. Then as your final act, he would die when it burns." I nodded toward the gas can.

He looked at the can, then up at me, "I hated to sacrifice three people. I liked them, but, well, you know, it had to be done. The bastard sent me away from my happy place into a dingy, tiny apartment."

"Tim, why did it take you this long to get revenge?"

"I was a kid when it all happened getting shuffled around from foster home to foster home after Dad died. I loved the old house that was here. I'd spend hours sitting out back watching the ocean, the tide, the shrimp boats out there. Anyway, I didn't even start looking for the person who bought the house until a couple of years ago. I was, umm, indisposed, stuck in a nuthouse for a couple of years and couldn't look."

I heard Charles moan and saw his hand move. Tim also heard him and stepped back so he could see Charles and me without having to turn around.

"Why'd you change your name?"

"That wasn't easy," he said and smiled.

I waited for him to continue. When he didn't, I said, "Were you afraid Trescott might recognize your name from when he bought the property?"

He shrugged. "I've pictured this house going up in flames ever since the first day on the job here. He put me in hell, so he has to burn in hell on earth." He laughed although I didn't detect any humor. "I felt sort of silly working so hard to get the construction right knowing it would all be gone." He looked at his watch again. "All gone today." He looked in the direction of Trescott. "He killed Dad, he ruined my sister's life, and look what he did to me." He pointed his handgun at Charles. "Think I'd be grateful if you'd go over there and lie down beside your friend. If you're good, I won't have to smack you with one of those boards. I've got work to do."

"Tim, you don't have to do this. The police will understand why you've done what you did."

"I may be a mental case, or so that's what the shrinks said, but I'm not stupid. Did you know Trescott killed my Dad, ruined my sister's life, ruined mine, too?"

His gun hand was shaking more than it had been a few minutes ago. Repeating himself made me wonder if he was on the verge of losing touch with reality. If that were the case, would it make it easier for me to escape or would he shoot me sooner?

"Yes," I said in the calmest voice I could muster. "I know what he did to all of you was terrible. He—"

He interrupted, "You know I loved sitting out back watching the ocean, and those shrimp boats were something to see. All the birds flocking over them to get leftover shrimp." He jerked the pistol in my direction. "Get down there. I've work to do. Didn't you hear me the first time? Why aren't you on the floor?"

I didn't see any good options. He appeared to be bouncing between wanting us dead and reliving his time here as a child. I moved closer to Charles, bent down, and started to lie beside my friend, when I heard someone downstairs say, "Mr. Chris, you there?"

Tim took a step backwards and jerked his body around until he was facing the stairs.

I grabbed a five-foot-long piece of two-by-four lumber that was behind Tim and pushed myself off the floor.

Tim heard me and turned around. Before he pointed his gun at me, I swung the board at the side of his head. It connected with a thud, vibrated my hand holding it, knocked me off balance, to where I nearly landed on Charles.

Before I got to my feet, Tim uttered a profanity, shook his head, then managed to point the gun at me.

I kicked his leg. The blow struck hard enough that he fell sideways landing on his arm holding the weapon. This time I was able to push up enough to regain my balance. I grabbed his arm holding the gun and twisted it.

He started to get up when the voice I'd heard earlier from downstairs said, "Police. Don't move."

Tim wisely followed the order.

Officer Trula Bishop kicked the gun out of Tim's hand and told him to turn over with his hands behind his back. Again, Tim obeyed her orders. The officer quickly cuffed him and asked me if the other two people were okay.

I was surprised when I turned back to Charles. He was in a seated position and rubbing the back of his head.

He shook his head twice and said, "Where is it?"

I said, "What?"

"The train that ran over me?"

And I thought Tim was losing it.

Charles looked up at Trula, and said, "Hey, Trula. What're you doing here?"

Trula said, "Mr. Charles, stay seated. We need to have your head checked."

I'd thought that for more than a decade but remained silent while Trula radioed for an ambulance and if the dispatcher had the nerve to call her this late, Chief LaMond.

By now, Trescott began moving and Trula told him to remain still that medical assistance was on the way.

The next hour was a blur. An ambulance left with both Charles and Trescott, after Charles swore he was fine countless times. For once, he lost, and was loaded on a stretcher. Cindy arrived and castigated me for dragging her out of bed in the middle of the night, before having me tell her what was going on. Then I had to repeat it again when Detective Fisher arrived. I was relieved when he listened to my story without reminding me how he'd threaten to have me arrested if I messed in his business. Clearly, his mind wasn't operating on all cylinders. I suspected I'd hear more about it later.

Before Cindy told me I was free to leave, I asked Trula why she came in the house looking for me. She said she was on patrol when she noticed my car up the street from the job site. Trula then noticed the red pickup truck on the property that wasn't there an hour earlier when she drove by. Fortunately, she put two and two together and walked the property until she found the sliding door open, came in, and yelled my name.

I thanked her for saving three lives, especially mine.

Chapter Forty-Nine

Charles called from the hospital about ten-thirty that morning and asked when his cab, aka me, would arrive to take him home. Apparently, he was being discharged after they couldn't find anything wrong with his head. Clearly, he hadn't been seen by a psychiatrist. I told him I'd be there within an hour.

An hour and a half later, I'd learned that Oliver Trescott was in a little worse shape than Charles and had been admitted, and we were in my car and pulling out of the hospital's parking lot and headed to Folly.

"Charles, how'd you end up out there?"

"I was sipping on a beer at Logger's, minding my own business, if you can believe that, then—"

"I can't."

"Can't what?"

"Believe you were minding your own business."

"You want to know what happened or call me a liar?"

I smiled and said, "You were minding your own business, then what?"

"Looked across the street at the Oceanfront Villas, and who do you think I saw getting in a red pickup truck?"

"Tim and Trescott."

"You passed private detective quiz number one."

"Then what?"

They pulled out of the lot and crossed Arctic. I leaned over the railing to see what direction they went when they reached Ashley Avenue."

"They turned left."

"Yes, but that was so easy it doesn't count as a quiz."

"Okay," I said, "How about me saying you left Logger-head's and walked out West Ashley to see if they were going to the house?"

"Quiz two passed."

"Then what happened?"

"The truck was empty, so I headed around the house to see where they were and what they were doing. I couldn't figure any good reason for them being there. The sliding glass door in back was open. I listened and thought I heard them upstairs. I called you and learned I was wrong about where Tim was." He shook his head. "Only Trescott was up there. Know how I learned that?"

"Tim was downstairs."

"How about behind me? He stuck his gun in my back and told me to get upstairs. I did, and that's when the train ran over me, or in looking back, it could've been a piece of lumber that made contact with my head. Then the next thing I knew was you talking to Tim, or whatever his name is." He looked out the window, then turned toward me. "Now it's your turn. What happened?"

"After you called, I went to the house. Like you, I found the door open and came in. Came upstairs and met Tim with the gun and the gas can."

"How'd you know all that stuff I heard you talking to him about. Tim equals Austin, on-and-on."

"If you'd returned my call yesterday, you would've known."

"You would've told me about who you thought Tim was, but I probably wouldn't have believed you."

"You do now, don't you?"

"Every syllable."

After I delivered Charles to his apartment and got home, my next-door neighbor called.

"Chris, think I've got it figured out. Ready to hear who the killer is?"

"Before you say who, let me tell you a story." And I did.

After Brad finished saying "You're kidding," three times, he finished with, "Damn, you have all the fun."

Later that afternoon, Cindy called to ask how Charles was and to tell me that Tim, or whatever his name is, had been charged for the three murders plus a handful of other charges relating to kidnapping and assaulting Trescott and assaulting Charles. He would also be undergoing a psych evaluation.

On a cheerier note, she ended the call by giving me a message from Detective Fisher. Apparently, he told Cindy that if he ever caught me meddling in another one of his cases, he wouldn't arrest me. He'd shoot me.

I told her to tell him for me, "You're welcome."

She laughed and said, "For solving his murders. I might not forward your kind words."

About the Author

Bill Noel is the best-selling author of twenty-five novels in the popular Folly Beach Mystery series. The award-winning novelist is also a fine arts photographer and lives in Louisville, Kentucky, with his wife, Susan, and his off-kilter imagination.

Learn more about the series and the author by visiting www.billnoel.com.

Made in the USA
Middletown, DE
19 February 2024